HAROLD A. BASCOM was born in Vergenoegen, Guyana, in 1951, and began writing poetry in his teens. He made his first break as a writer of prose in 1977, when some of his short stories were read on national radio. He also began writing children's books and finished his first film script, a story based on a manhunt for the desperado Clement Cuffy which took place in British Guiana in 1959, and which gave rise to a full length novel – *Apata*.

Harold A. Bascom works as a graphic artist and book illustrator, and lives in Georgetown, Guyana.

HAROLD A. BASCOM

APATA

HEINEMANN

Heinemann Educational Books Ltd.
22 Bedford Square, London WC1B 3HH

Heinemann Educational Books (Nigeria) Ltd.
PMB 5205, Ibadan
Heinemann Educational Books (Kenya) Ltd.
Kijabe Street, PO Box 45314, Nairobi
Heinemann Educational Books Inc.
70 Court Street, Portsmouth, New Hampshire, 03801, USA
Heinemann Educational Books (Caribbean) Ltd.
175 Mountain View Avenue, Kingston 6, Jamaica

EDINBURGH   MELBOURNE   AUCKLAND   HONG KONG
SINGAPORE   KUALA LUMPUR   NEW DELHI

© Harold Bascom 1986
First published by Heinemann Educational Books
in the Caribbean Writers Series in 1986

British Library Cataloguing in Publication Data

Bascom, Harold
    Apata. ——(Caribbean writers series)
    I. Title   II. Series
    813′[F]   PR9320.9.B3

    ISBN 0–435–98828–X

    EXPORT ISBN 0–435–98829–8

Phototypeset by Wilmaset, Birkenhead, Wirral
Printed and bound in Great Britain by
Richard Clay (The Chaucer Press) Ltd,
Bungay, Suffolk

For Gweny
my big sister who helped me
in starting,
and Pat
so special
who helped me in ending.

Author's Note:
This work is purely fictitious though
inspired by an elaborate manhunt for an
armed fugitive by the British Guiana
Police Force in the year 1959.

... don't try to cold me up
on this bridge now,
I've got to reach Mount Zion,
the highest region. ...

Bob Marley

PART ONE

1939–1954

1939
PROLOGUE

Drifting back lazily below the white seaplane with red and white wings tipped with deep yellow, are square miles, square miles of turbulent rain forest. Down below, a vast clearing of felled trees is no more than a bald spot in an immeasurably vaster carpet of green. Down below pass the Essequibbean hinterlands.

Looking down, the pilot remembers the single-engined aircraft that crashed with three English geologists. Two weeks ago somewhere in the vast region below. No wreckage has yet been found.

He looks over to his co-pilot who sits with his head thrown back, eyes closed, and lips moving silently as the monotonous sound of the seaplane's radial engines wafts over him.

The pilot checks the time. Five thirty.

The thought of the rain forests doesn't worry him much, save for a vague apprehension that one day his turn may come to sink below the leafy sea drifting back beneath his feet. He forever hopes that, should it happen, he will survive the crash and be found. Maybe, he thinks, every pilot, every co-pilot hopes the same. Who knows, maybe every dead 'bush pilot', whose remains lie twisted and undiscovered below, had had the same hope.

His co-pilot blurts, 'Bar!' and opens his eyes to smile triumphantly: Bartica, a populated clearing in the green wilderness through which a great river courses, is coming up. A riverine settlement.

*   *   *

3

The eyes of the Amerindian child which, a moment ago, were watching two elderly men playing a game of draughts are now raised to the sky. The scheduled red and white seaplane moans across the sky above him. The movement of the boy's head follows it in its circling descent to the river – he runs off to witness the touchdown.

*   *   *

Fifty-five year-old Joshiah Smith sits at a game of draughts with his neighbour who is slow at deciding moves. Smith waits. His eyes, misty with cataracts, peer intently from the burnt, crease-lined landscape of his face and gradually shift from the checkered playing board to the great white house on the hill with the short-bladed, emerald green grass.

'You know something Mase'n . . .?' he says to his contemplative friend.

'Ow God, Smitty!' snaps Mason. 'Ah thinkin' man!'

Smith smiles mischievously and mumbles something apologetically. Passing a calloused palm around the nape of his neck he feels his grey Negro's hair and shakes his head.

A sound, rising and falling, a growling sound, almost animal, comes over to the two men at their game. They pay no heed. The sound of the seaplane, taxying on the brown-faced river, has become for them just another sound at this time of the afternoon.

Mason makes a move.

Smith makes a move.

Mason grins.

Smith's brows furrow.

'Watch dis Smitty!'

'Ah watchin' . . .'

'Bam! Bam! Bam! Three shot, Smitty!'

'You mean is done . . . the game done?' says Smith in mock amazement.

'You askin'?'

Mason filled at last with victory, closes his eyes and laughs like a story-book witch and then slaps his left knee with a thumbless left hand.

4

Joshiah Smith's home stands a little way from the shade of the old mango tree under which he and his friend pass away the time of another afternoon. It is a small, neatly built, unpainted, one-bedroomed wooden house standing on short thick wallaba-wood stilts. It has two flights of stairs with a maximum of four treads each. One stair leads to the back door and the kitchen, where bluish coal-pot smoke pours through the gable ends of the kitchen roof. The smell of breadnuts, steaming after being boiled, comes with it. The other stair leads to the front door which has a horseshoe nailed on it. Many of the locals believe that horseshoes ward off evil spirits. The windows are of wood. They have no glass panes and are like small wooden doors opening outwards. The thatched roof is made of neatly plaited leaves from the troolie palm.

There is a rebellious wailing.

Smith knows it is his one-year-old grandson Michael Rayburn Apata. It is not uncommon to hear Joshiah Smith saying: 'Michael Rayburn Apata ... yes ... that is a name ah really like.'

'Jane!'

His wife answers from the little house: 'Yes J.S.!'

'What happen to Rayburn?'

'Aw MAN! Play you' draughts and mind yo' own bleddy business! You too damn fussy over dis disgusting boy!'

'The woman too right,' puts in Mason.

But Smith is once more contemplating the great white house on the hill with the short green grass. It is a neatly built wooden structure that stands on concrete pillars. The roof is made up of galvanized sheet-metal that gleams under the sun's rays. Yellow light glints off the glass panels of the many windows. Each has a frame of mesh to keep out the large forest insects that are attracted by the light that will burn from the powerful lamp bulbs which go on when the generator, in the little shack at the back of the great white house, throbs at night.

Joshiah Smith remembers that he will have to get kerosene oil for his lamp.

A White woman with yellowish hair and a blue apron to her red-flowered dress, comes out on a back verandah of the executive house on the hill. She is taking bits of clothing off a line on a pulley. As fast as she unclips a few articles – she pulls ... and more dry laundry comes to her to unclip and drop into her yawning clothes basket decorated with Amerindian designs.

Joshiah Smith is unconscious of his slightly gaping mouth and the wrinkle of wonder on the humorous side of his face.

'Mase'n ...'

'Eh? Wha'?'

'Like you was dozin' off man?'

Mason yawns.

'Mase'n, you ever work at places like Matthew's Ridge, Tumatumari, or Mackenzie?'

'Man, Smitty, how you think mih lose mih big fingah?'

'But Mase'n ... you ever notice how in all them places the White people and the other uppertenths they's always be livin' on de hills?'

Michael Rayburn Apata screams again, shrilly

'Jane! What you beating dat boy for, eh?'

'Hear J.S.! They say grandmothers does spoil children! But I ent going to spoil dis one! Ah will clap hands on his little black backside everytime he slip! He like to play with fire!'

'Yo' right mistriz. Spare the rod an' spoil the chile,' mumbles Mason to nobody in particular. Then, with his palms resting in the small of his back, he raises himself with apparent effort. 'Smitty ... ah goin' home man ... ah goin' an' res' Gawd material lil', you know, dis body Gawd give me ...'

'A'right Mase'n boy ...'

And with that, Joshiah Smith takes up the draughts board and the little varnished box with the black and white playing pieces arranged within it.

1954
CHAPTER 1

And now, fifteen years have passed. Mason has long died and a seventy-year-old Josh' Smith peers up from under the shade of his calloused palms, to a brilliant noonday sky.

'But J.S.!' says his old wife in a hushed though reprimanding tone, 'Dat is not a sensible thing yo' doing! Yo' going to damage you' eyesight more than it damage a'ready!'

But he ignores her. 'Kite, yeahs . . .' he appraises to himself, then levels his magnified bespectacled gaze once more to the river glinting before them under the sun. Above the crowd of which the old couple forms a part, and in the breezy freedom of the sky, a black kite with red and white patterns on it in the shape of stars, hums and dances gracefully on the winds, but few of the people – who are arrayed like a rainbow, teeming along the beach and on a large wharf, now transformed into a grandstand this goodly Easter Sunday – seem to notice.

The beauty show has just wrapped itself up and the muscle contest is slated to commence after the power-boat race that will begin in five minutes. Music from the bandstand with the brick-red roof blares continually. Records by Sparrow, the Grenadian-born calypsonian, dominate the repertoire. As though only needing the encouragement of any patch of clean sand and a spot of sunshine, a few White tourists sunbathe. Bets have been made on many of the events that have taken place, and things of symbolic value have been lost and gained. On the events yet to come, the scale of chance will continue to seesaw and tomorrow's newspapers will compare today's regatta with regattas of years gone by.

Right now there are eyes . . . eyes . . . all looking towards the river. Seven motor boats are out there. Each has the power of eighty horses. Each contains a single contestant. Engines purr as the power of five hundred and sixty horses intermingle. Seven motor boats slowly edge to the 'start' area marked by a floating fifty-six-gallon oil drum held in position by a length of wire-rope down to an old paddle-steamer's anchor on the sediment-laden bottom of the Essequibo river. The boats bob on the choppy coffee-brown water, propellers idling, waiting for the thrust of full-throttled power.

In one minute's time the race will start.

On the sluggish looking barge, manned by the race officials, the 'starter' raises his red shirt above his head. His chest, the colour of pale gold, is exposed to the sun's warm glow that glints from the water's shifting face.

Waiting for the single downward chop of the starter's right arm, many spectators are now in quiet expectancy. The music from the bandstand comes to a stop and a shave-ice man not very far from Old Josh Smith and his Jane, holds his whistle before his thick creased lips. Tense for the moment, he stands ignoring the boy with whom he should have completed a business deal. So the boy walks away with a short shaft of compressed, crushed ice dripping guava flavoured syrup. And those children – those children from Georgetown City, who earlier had run, cavorted and made such a great show of being alive, are now staring-eyed and still, waiting for the single downward chop of the starter's right arm.

From high above, the droning of the black kite, with the red and white stars, filters down on the momentary lull ...

DOWN FLASHES THE RED SHIRT!

Seven motor boats snarl! Six grown men and one sixteen-year-old boy scheme for the lead positions. The onlookers, now one big intermingled mass, buzz in the wake of the deep-humming power-boats moving away to where another market drum floats as a turning point some distance beyond a little rock-bush islet outside the water circuit.

'Rias Lee leading man! Rias Lee in front skunt!'

'Stop fighting up you'self man. Apata gon tek 'e down!'

'They banking round now! SHEEEEET! Look leans deh . . .'

'BAASHY! Rias Lee turn over! WHA DE RASS IS DIS . . .?'

'What I did tell you man? Apata's me own boy!!'

A police launch, standing by as a rescue craft, growls out to the overturned boat.

The crowd on the grandstand will not keep still enough for Old Josh Smith and his wife Jane to see the river-line continually.

The boats are humming this way to complete the first lap.

The old man and woman shift themselves and are peering intently. At last the old man bares his strong teeth in a broad smile and the old woman begins to laugh whilst sticking her index finger into her ears.

'Same thing I did tell you'all!' he said. 'Mih boy Rayburn in de lead!'

'GO RAYBURN GO!'
'GO MOZE GO!'
'Throttle dem good Smally!'
'GO RAYBURN GO!'

The grandparents of sixteen year-old Michael Rayburn Apata, are smiling as the sounds of the approaching engines draw closer and closer to the grandstand. Michael's green boat meanly keeps half a boat's length ahead of the other two boats leading the rest. Through the spray arching back from the thrusting bow of the low, streaking, green craft with the name '*Jet*', the spectators see, hunched over the steering column, the head and shoulders of a dark-skinned youth.

The boats flash past the grandstand and the beach-stretch and then crash out once more for the second lap and the marker-float way off from the Bartica mainland shore and some distance beyond the little rock-bush islet off the water circuit.

'OH SHIT! THEY TRYING TO BLOCK ... THEY TRYING TO BLOCK MIH BOY IN!'

9

'God J.S.! You must have time and place for them kindza words!'

'Jane ... dis ent church you know, Jane ...'

Two boats are overtaking Michael Apata. One to the left, one to the right of him. They close in as if to block his path from each side. Just like that – in a quick second – the engine pitch of *Jet* falls in on itself and the boat drags as if held back, as if gently restrained by powerful invisible hands. The other two boats take the lead.

Apata glances behind him. Three boats are fighting to gain on him. Turning the wheel gently, Apata cuts a smooth diagonal away from the straight course and out of sight behind the small rock-bush islet off the true circuit. Now, out of line with the two boats leading and the three tailing, he pushes the throttle lever to its three-quarters full position and the engine gurgles in a surge of new power.

One of the leading racers glances behind him, but fails to see Apata whom he and his partner overtook by a ruse. He just makes out the three boats behind him, slamming and weaving through the turbulent backwash left by his own and his partner's boats. Suddenly he picks up an impression from the corner of his right eye. Whipping his head around he sees *Jet* as a dark shimmering shape hurtling out from the hidden side of the rock-bush islet. 'APATA's OUTA CONTROL!' he shouts to his lead partner.

'RAYBURN – JANE – AH MEAN RAYBURN OUTA CONTROL, JANE!'

'OH LAWD! DE BOY GOING TO CRASH UP WIT' DEM TWO ...'

But Michael Apata, hunched tensely over the wheel, holds his boat on a collision course. The two lead boats are running almost together and he is coming up on them quickly. 'Must time it right!' Apata whispers to himself as he makes out their wildly staring eyes and flailing hands shoo-ing him away. He can see their flaring lips too, with bared teeth. He can almost hear the string of indecencies. Apata smiles and

10

flicks the throttle lever to give maximum power as he simultaneously locks hard right and leans with the action. Thrown together the two other boats glancingly collide. 'SHIT!' someone shouts above the argumentative tones of the engines as control is sought, wrestled for, and regained. They separate from danger. The race lives on.

'CYANT WORK AH TELL YO'! CYANT WORK! DAT YOUNG CHAP GOT TO GET DISQUALIFY!'

'Aw McBean! Hushup you' mouth man! De boy lose lil control!'

'YOU WANT HUSH ME UP, SMITH?'

'HUSHUP YOU' MOUTH MAN! DE OL' MAN RIGHT! APATA YOUNG AN' LIGHT!'

'What happen? Ya'all fo'get skilful? Com'on man, SAY IT! Don't hold it back! Michael Rayburn ... my grandson ... is light! And skilful!'

'GO MOZE GO!'

'Ow man ... look how he pushing dat machine ...'

'GO PATA, GO!'

'Like a lil black joc' on a lil grass horse!'

'GO RAYBURN, GO!'

'Ow Smitty ... look how yo' smilin' ...'

'GO PATA, GO!'

'Ow boy ... ah wish Mase'n was alive to see dis spectacle!'

He's moving, moving.

With his left arm, Apata wipes sprays from his eyelids. Next year, he decides, he will wear goggles ... that is if Cornelius would let him have the boat. 'I'll get it!' Apata tells himself. 'I'll win this race and maybe get a picture of myself in this boat in the papers. Beverley will see it. I'll win for Beverley ...'

He's moving, moving.

Thoughts of his girlfriend nourish his will. 'YEA-A-AH!' he shouts above the undulating water, 'CAN'T CATCH ME NOW! CAN'T CATCH ...'

The engine misses, the boat jerks, drags, picks up speed, falters. Apata glances nervously behind his seat.

'LIKE APATA IN TROUBLE! THEY CATCHING UP WITH HE!'

'Oh tail Jane ...'

'NA NA! HE ALRIGHT HE ALRIGHT! HE GONE AGAIN!'

'Rass Smitty boy ... mih heart miss two beat dere ... YOU KNOW HOW MUCH MONEY I BET ON DAT LIL CHAP?'

'Well ... as I's always say ... all things does happen for a reason.'

He's moving.

But Apata has lost his lead. He doesn't mind now. His grandfather always tells him that all things happen for cosmic reasons. His grandmother always says that where there's too much speed there's always a bet-and-sure slowing down to come which is usually for the good. He is moving.

The lap marker rushes up. Soon they will bank around it and begin the run back. Bobbing, the marker drum rushes up.

'Take it easy son,' Apata tells himself. 'Don't rush the brush son ... 'relse you gon get daubed.' He is moving. Other boats are racing to take the turn. Apata keeps back ... holding away from the tightness of the race at this point. A pink man, in a red shirt, throws his white boat into a banking turn. The boat turns on its side momentarily and then flips over with a muffled 'BUFF!' Another competitor coming up at a deadly rate tries to avoid over-running the red-shirted figure treading the turbulent water. He succeeds but his boat runs up the marking drum-float, becomes airborne and smashes back, stern first, into the river. The engine falls off. The high-powered police launch grumbles to life and once more cleaves out to the rescue.

Seven boats started this race. The number now likely to finish is four.

'GO NOW PATA ... GO NOW!'

They are coming down the course in a shallow, aggressive

12

'V' formation, each taking a turn in holding the lead, thrusting and falling back, thrusting and falling back ... now *Jet* ... now *Manitu* ... now *Jet* ... now *Sea Bee* ... now *Jet* ... now *Zeus* ... thrusting and falling back.

'JEEZUS LORNA!' says a white tourist to her mulatto pen-friend, 'WOWEEE! – LIKE HELL THIS IS EXCIT-ING!'

'Wowee'?' butts in a coarse stranger, 'I ent know what language "wowee" is lady ... but dis is rass race in you' rikaticks!'

Old Josh Smith squeezes his wife's thigh. The old woman claps and claps and claps ...

But the river, for this aged couple, has not been a source of happiness. Deep down in the reservoirs of their minds float two bodies that made their grandson a "motherless-father-less".

*   *   *

There were three in the dugout canoe: Lilian and Harold Apata, with their four-month-old baby Michael. They were coming down to the Bartica settlement and it was night. Something happened on the way. To this day nobody understands what it was. The next morning the boat was found split in two and the only soul found alive was baby Apata. He was floating in a middle-sized wash basin that had belonged to his young mother. It was wedged below a thick growth of bamboo overhanging a silent part of the Mazaruni river.

Many people thought the finding of baby Apata was just like the biblical "Moses" and because of that Michael is also called "Moze". The settlement's most consistent necroman-cer dramatized the finding of baby Apata in a much more profound way. 'He go never die by water!' she had declared. 'He is a favourite o' de water people!'

*   *   *

13

'TWO MORE LAPS TO GO!'
'COM'ON MIKE!'
He's moving, moving.

* * *

Hardly any of the grown-ups present in this happy crowd would relish talking of the bodies of Michael Apata's parents, of just when and how they were found – not on the conventional third day after the event – but the seventh.

An Amerindian, now called "Crazy Kilran", went out early one morning to fish. That afternoon, around three o' clock, he stumbled back home a bruised, bloody and babbling man. He left his dugout canoe and came back overland, through swamps, thorn bushes and razor grass, making a straight line: the shortest distance between two points. The starting point had been where the horror that motivated his flight had suddenly surfaced; and from then on he had only one objective – home.

In a darkened hut, Cocorit, the village-wiseman, moved a battery torch over Kilran's sweating face. Kilran stared wide-eyed at the glowing bulb and with every movement of the shifting light Kilran's head moved. Then he was taken outside. Cocorit took a red-clay goblet of water which he dribbled out onto the ground before Kilran. The rays of the glaring afternoon sun were crystallized in the beady droplets of water ... and Kilran stared at them as if something terrifyingly demonic was slowly taking a repulsive physical form before his eyes. It was then that the old, one-eyed, ropy-faced Cocorit, brown as the palm fruit of the same name, declared his diagnosis: 'MAD ...' he had mumbled as he shook his grey head. 'De man gone staring mad!'

But what had catapulted the easy-going Kilran whom all the children liked, from one mental state to another? 'Where was his boat, then? His fishing tools?'

And so a group of men formed a search party. Three hours later, they found, on a silent part of the Mazaruni river, Kilran's boat with his three-pronged fishing spear laid in the bottom. They saw too, a pair of tightly swollen human corpses floating nearby. The bodies were greyish as with the regular drowned but they were not fish eaten. This was strange because the area where the bodies were was one where voracious, flesh-eating Perai abounded. Both the bodies were naked. One floated on the back, the other on the stomach. It is the quickest way of telling the males from the females in the category of the drowned. The females float on their backs due to womb-cavity buoyancy. Of course, the tresses or locks of a woman against the short-cropped hair of a man may clearly show differences of sex. In the case of Apata's parents, however, looking at their hair wouldn't have proven a thing because – and this was probably what unbalanced the calm, easy-going Amerindian – neither of the tightly swollen bodies had heads.

*   *   *

'MY-KEEEEE! MY-KEEEEEE!'

'GO PATA GO ... GO MOZE GO ... GO PATA GO!'

'LAST LAP!'

'LAST WHO? WOMAN WHAT YOU SAYING? Woman, dis is de finish!'

'J.S. Don't address me as "woman"! It ent proper!'

'THRATTLE DEM BACKSIDE APATA!'

'RAYBURN! RAYBURN!'

'O-O-O-O-OH RA-A-A-AAAS! ... don't tell me is lose I lose me Omega wris' watch?'

'COM'ON DA'SILVA! YOU COULD STILL TAKE 'E DOWN!'

'Wait man. You kunt doan know a loser when yo' see one?'

'Terrible language for a big man! Oh God J.S.! What kind-ah dirty mouth ...'

'GO PATA GO!'

'GO MOZE GO!'

Apata's moving.

The green boat hums and the bushes flash by.

He's moving.

The beach-stretch, the grandstand, shoutingly and pulsatingly colourful, flash by in a shimmering blur of sun.

He's moving.

More and more river rushes up to greet the vibrating hull of the motor boat *Jet* with the power of eighty horses behind her.

He's moving.

Soon the floating tank with the soggy white flag and the sluggish looking barge nearby with the race officials would flash by.

He's moving.

The official, who started the race, stands with both hands raised. He holds his red shirt above his head.

'MICHAEL APATA!'
'MICHAEL APATA!'
'MICHAEL APATA!'

But Michael doesn't hear the thunderous chanting dissipated by the wind and his speed. Apata doesn't even distinguish the hum of the engine, immediately behind him, as something outside of himself. Rather, it is as though the engine has become a part of his sixteen-year-old being. He feels victory now ... sees only victory now through eyes squinting from the sting of wind and spray. He picks up a downward-flashing redness off to the right side of his head.

The beach and the grandstand erupt in a cheering mass shouting a mixture of names ... PATA ... MOZE ... MIKE ... RAYBURN ... APATA – And they all mean the very same thing! 'He who wins like a water bird.'

CHAPTER 2

Two minutes to six o' clock and the light fixtures in the sprawling rafters of the Bartica stelling fade as the night's darkness gradually escapes them. Wharf timbers creak and make splintering sounds as a tethered steamer grazes and pounds against them because of the tide that washes in steadily. Scores of Coastlanders pass through the main gate and, after their tickets are clipped, the stream of people bent on embarking to the advantage of 'best seats' and deck chairs, shuffle in tumble-file down onto the main deck and up a railed ramp to the deck above. As they file into her, the faithful steamer, *M.V. Lady Northcut*, rises and falls negligibly on the dark-skinned river which is yet to be drenched by the rays of a new sun, while, in the distance, the growing light makes ragged-edged silhouettes of the distant shore-line bushes and forested mountain ranges.

Northcut. She's an old lady who served her youth some place in Europe. Her white paint-work is scratched, scarred, grimy and bruised and below her Plimsoll mark the accumulated barnacles guarantee that lots of man-hours will be spent on her in the dry dock in Georgetown City.

The figure of a short, thick-set, ruddy-skinned Negro shows on the bridge. He looks down briefly on the embarking passengers, then retreats into the wheel house. He is the Captain, Wesley Innes. Looking out over the water he discerns a tug chugging in from the misty shoreline of the Mazaruni mainland and Penal Settlement, way over from Bartica. Captain Wesley Innes watches with disdain as the small craft approaches through the dew-streaked window of the wheel house. 'I don't like transporting no bledly criminals,' he grumbles to himself then feels his throbbing forehead as if for a temperature. He turns his back on the approaching launch and closes his palms tighter on the steaming cup of hot chocolate. He sips, puts the cup down and holding his hands like a respirator in front of his face he breathes out warm air. The smell of the whisky on his breath has died. 'Bledly White people!' he mutters and wonders when they would arrive with their questioning children to irritate him.

The *Lady Northcut* rises and falls negligibly on the dark-skinned river, now beginning to gleam faintly under the sunlight that starts to burn the edges of the silhouetted shapes of the distant shore-bound vegetation. The wharf timbers creak and make splintering sounds as the tethered steamer grazes and pounds because of the tide that washes in steadily. Scores of coastlanders still pass through the gates in close order and after their tickets are clipped they shuffle onto the main deck and up the ramp to the deck above. 'OH CHRIST, MAN! YOU NEARLY PUSH ME IN THE RIVER, MAN! OH GOD, MAN, YOU BORN IN A PIG PEN? OR IS BECAUSE YO' RED?'

The Captain doesn't respond in any way to the loud voice. Such outpourings during embarkations are common. When the people get out of hand the wharf constables deal with them. On days like these, just after the regular Easter regatta, there's always a rush and a flurry to get back to the coast and the promises of Georgetown City.

The sun peers from behind the distant shore-line sending a swath of yellow sunlight over the Essequibo, bathing the ruddy face of the Captain and casting a soft, fat shadow on the clean bulkhead behind the helmsman's position.

Vibrations from the engine room, three levels below, tingle in the Captain's legs. He thinks they should throw away the bledly engines. Every time he suffers from a hangover he thinks badly of things, or people, close to him. He thinks that they should throw away the whole bledly boat for that matter. He sips his beverage, clears his throat gratingly and strikes it rich with phlegm. Stepping out to the wing of the bridge he spits into the river.

The blue boat from the Mazaruni Penal Settlement is cutting past Kaow Island and has set a true course for the Bartica ferry stelling and the moored *Lady Northcut*. Innes watches the approach. A policeman with a .303 rifle stands at ease on the low forecastle of the boat's raked bow. 'Bleddy criminals coming!' the Captain says to himself and feels the headache coming on once more. Footsteps are clattering up the steps that link the bridge with the second class deck below. Captain Innes turns his head and focuses his slightly bloodshot eyes on the chief mate with whom he drank four bottles of whisky last night. Morton looks fresh and as sober as a priest. Grudgingly Innes accepts that his first mate can really drink. That Morton 'is a real drink man!'

'Cappy?'

'Aye Morts.'

'Hangover in you' rikaticks Cappy.'

The Captain nods in agreement, laughs weakly, and grunts, 'The old system going down.'

'A man is as old as he feels Cappy!'

'Then I dead!' The Captain laughs deep in his throat. ''Cause that is how I feeling.'

'Them White people,' says Morton the mate, 'send to say that they ent travelling today. The message come in to the office just now.'

'First good news ah hear for the morning,' grumbles the Captain.

'They might travel out by speed-boat tomorrow,' says the first mate.

The Captain continues as if his first mate hasn't spoken, ''Cause I didn' feel like hearing them White people talking in they nose around me.'

Then he gestures with a careless palm over his shoulders through the window overlooking the brown-skinned river, 'But is bes' I had White people to bleddywell fret me than to worry 'bout two bleddy criminals going down to Georgetown to hang.'

The chugalugga of the police launch is below them now.

'I don't like transporting them kinda cargo on my boat, man.'

'Them chaps don't do nothing Cappy. Look how much times we carry criminals down to Parika and back? Nothing ever happen.'

'Crosses!' the Captain hisses, then on a lower note: 'Jonah-ites!'

'Ah think the number two engine acting up a little wrong – anyway, you going to get a report from Nedd.'

Wesley Innes looks at his thick Omega watch on his red, hairy left wrist. Simultaneously comes the sounds of the stelling gates being closed. Ablebodied Seaman Seals clatters up to the bridge and tells the Captain, 'Morning.' Then he takes his position behind the helm and the compass. The first mate leans over the wing of the bridge and gives scarcely needed cast-off instructions. His orders are followed by the sounds of the heavy maindeck ramp as it folds into place in the hull.

'Cappy!'

The Captain turns and faces Nedd the Chief Engineer. The grey-headed and lanky man with the gentle eyes is smiling. 'Everything alright. Number two kicking!'

'Those criminals aboard?' the Captain asks, needlessly. He knows they are.

'The police chap in charge coming up to see you now. Ah think Thom bringing him up.'

'Well ...' the Captain grumbles, 'here we go again.'

The Chief Engineer mocks a salute which turns into a farewell wave to all the men on the bridge, and moves off down the companion ladder and out of sight.

Two men, whose burnt-brown skins gleam in the new sunlight, hurl thick mooring ropes after the steamer as she moves under power, away from the wharf. Bells tinkle, the engines change their grumbling pitch and the water churns astern with flotsam swirling in the wake. Now the grimy, blackened understelling and the space where the *Lady Northcut* was berthed looks empty and forlorn as the vessel pulls out, heavily laden, for the main channel.

CHAPTER 3

Young Michael Apata, still filled with the calm elation of his victory at the regatta yesterday, meditates on the water washing back from the *Lady Northcut*'s bow. The muted grumbling of the steamer's engines come to him in hypnotic waves that have sent many to sleep even though it is only a little after ten o'clock. Teenage Apata's eyes, however, are clear and alert. He drops a banana skin into the water and the backwash along the ship's side whips it astern and out of sight. He looks up from the river's face and makes out a house between the bamboos. An Amerindian house? He reasons that it would be. But it could well be a Black man's house or, for that matter, an Indian's.

The shoreline breaks back into flat country past the house with bushes beyond the short run of plains. Just behind the house, its solitary partner is a great tree from which hang large birds' nests fashioned in the form of huge teardrops of straw. The water hisses from the crest of the waves formed by the onthrusting bow and even though that section of the shore is left behind, Apata cranes his head around and manages to see a flight of yellow-tailed birds burst from the variegated greenery of the background bushes to mill around the tall tree. He turns his head away and looks up. The clouds seem to stand still and to him there's one that's shaped like a Seagull outboard engine. He thinks of his girl friend in Georgetown City. 'If my picture gets in the papers,' he muses, 'Beverley will feel like a Queen boy. Maybe when I get home ... but home is behind me. No, I have two homes ... where my grandfather and grandmother is ... one ... where Bevy is ...

two. When I get home to her ... I'll kiss her forthwith ... if there's a chance.' Apata smiles to himself. The word 'forthwith', complete with tongue between teeth, always makes him smile. The verbal precision of his language teacher, Miss Frazier, who hates calypso and calypsonians, especially the Mighty Sparrow whose songs she says are ever vulgar, amuses him. And she never says 'vulgar' but 'vulgarrr'.

'But,' he chants to himself, 'I love Beverley Bailey, I love Beverley Bailey, I love Beverley Bailey, I love Beverley Bailey ...' and he is happy in the freedom and the privacy of his being.

Apata notices that the woman with the caged parrot next to him is staring at him and realizes, to his discomfort, that he has been smiling to himself. He re-opens the book he has been reading and finds that the sun makes the page too white to look at. So he seats himself under the forecastle to be in the shade and flips back to the title page. Then he decides that he has had enough of *Silas Marner*, rifles through his duffle bag and finds *The Thirty-nine Steps*. As he opens the book his attention is diverted by four men who step from the gloom of the third class deck. Between two armed policemen there are two men, one Black the other Indian, with their hands handcuffed behind their backs. They stare at the grimy deck. One lawman carries a .303 rifle, the other a single-barrelled shotgun.

'Excuse me miss lady,' Apata says to the woman next to him. 'Who are those two men?'

'Who are them jail buds?'

The policeman with the rifle fishes a packet of cigarettes from his tunic pocket below his nickle-plated serial number. He lights a pair and offers them to the handcuffed men. The Indian prisoner sticks out his neck and accepts one of the cigarettes between his lips. The other prisoner shakes his head then asks another favour. The policeman with the rifle nods and the prisoner sits meekly on a saltbeef barrel which lies on its side, prevented from rolling by wooden chocks. Blankly he gazes at the undulating shoreline. He breathes deeply and evenly and Apata notes that the prisoner's wide, flaring nostrils on his burnt-brown face open and close slightly in the process. His eyes are hooded, his lips pressed tightly together. Something about the man's massive head reminds Apata of a picture he once saw of the American boxer Joe Louis.

'Who them?' the woman with the parrot cage asks Apata who continues to watch the man sitting on the barrel. The man looks as if he might be thinking regretfully of his freedom and of days when maybe he shone his shoes in preparation for the Easter Monday dance at some public school or Parish Hall. To Apata, every district on the coast seems to have a Parish Hall and he thinks the prisoner he contemplates must be a coast man for if he came from the interior he, Apata, would have heard of him from his grandfather.

'Who is them two, you asking, nuh? AYE-YAGGA! Who is them two?'

Now there is a little ring of curious by-standers.

Apata reasons that the seated prisoner cannot be more than nine and thirty despite his weathered appearance.

'Who's them? Well ... you wouldn' know 'cause you was probably small when Chingarus, de coolie one, tek a hatchet and chop up he wife and two pic'ny dem like-ah the beef he uses to sell ah Mackenzie. When he finish he take them body apart piece-piece and stuff it ina wan rice bag and throw the bag ina wan creek at Wismar. Chingarus! Yes! That is the one smokin' the cigarette!'

The cigarette burns low and the glow stands less than half an inch from his thin lips. A bit of his hair has fallen over one of his eyes in natural hollows under a high forehead and thick black brows. He lets the stub drop and jerks his head around to correct the fallen wisp of hair. The movement makes a timid woman jump and the man she clings to laughs in her face. 'YO' FRIGHTEN NUH?' he says loudly, 'Chingarus ent going to bite you!'

'Who's the other one?' asks Apata.

'The other one ... wait! But mih know you face small bhai. You not Joshiah Smith gran'son?'

Apata smiles and nods.

23

'Bhai? You nah know me? All the same you won't remember me. Is good to see how big you grow though.' Apata scratches his head in mild impatience.

'Well the other one sitting there? Is passion have him where he is. He story lil' different from Chingarus story cause Chingarus story was a case o' blow, you know? He wife had a Black man with he and ... well, Chingarus find out. But that blackskin one sitting there? He name Parkinson but they's call he 'Nosegay Parkinson' 'cause he nose-hole big as you can see.

'They say he kill a man in front of a White man office. They say that he went to get a job with some White people and was plenty o' them there, and the White man had a Black stooge who uses to pick out who and who the White man should give work to. Is like the White man tell heself that since he don't know plenty 'bout Black people, who bad and who good, was best he get a Black man to tell him who must get work, which is the lazy kind and who is the boderation kind – you know?'

Apata nods his head.

'What the White man didn' realize was that once any Black man get that position he wouldah turn bigsass and wouldah want to show off on he matty Black man.'

The *Lady Northcut* changes course slightly and takes now to the river's centre. The parrot beats its wings and they smash into the water in its water cup. Apata shys away slightly. The narrating woman nudges the bird's cage – 'BEHAVE YOU'SELF LORA! Yes, I was telling you bhai ...

'The Black stooge uses to come out from the White man office ... he uses to look around ... he uses to take a good look 'round to the men waiting on two long wood bench in the front office.' The woman nods her head ... nods her head. 'He uses to look around good! And according to who is villager from he side, that man he go take on.

'Well, this day, Parkinson go to get work and when the White man stooge come out and look at the men who deh waitin', he eye fall on Parkinson – and when he eye fall on Parkinson, men say, that the stooge start to play like he

24

stiffling for breath as though he suffocating fuh air. Then he start to look around wild wild as if he ent sure who to look at and then suddenly he make he eye fall on Parkinson. Then he halla on Parkinson and say: "GET OUT OF HERE! YOUR NOSE SUCKING UP ALL THE ATMOSPHERE!"

'Anyway, people who know both people say that the stooge did know Parkinson and did never like Parkinson because even though Parkinson nah so good lookin' Parkinson used to give 'e stiff competition in a lil' rivalry they had over a certain brown-skin girl in the village where both o' them did come from. In the end Parkinson win the girl and marry she. So in the White man office this chap Parris, yes that was he name, he was only making insult to he old rival.' She takes a deep breath.

'So,' she continues, 'Nosegay didn' get the job. Men say that after that story Nosegay Parkinson stand up by a cake shop in Lombard Street and burst cry. An' when all them other men pick themself up and gone home, he wait round the office until was time for the White man and he stooge to leave. MAN? Dey say ... that JUS' PARRIS STEP OUT THE DOOR WITH THE WHITE MAN FOLLOWING CLOSE BEHIND, Parkinson fly up and without ONE GAWD WORD AH WARNING ... HE DELIVER ONE LASH in dat Black man head with a piece o' soft iron!'

'Dead?' Apata asks in a hoarse whisper, then as if not sure that it has come out, asks the question once more.

'DEAD? You askin' if he dead? Dead like a nit!'

'Where they taking them now?'

'They taking them down to brok they neck! De problem for a lil' time was that since the last hangman dead, say ten months back, they ent had no other till last week. An' yo' know we people. You don't get we men to do that work!'

'Why?'

'Woman doan accept man who does do them kind work!' Then the woman starts to laugh good naturedly but stops suddenly to prevent her plate falling from her mouth to the dirty deck. Apata smiles but it is a strained expression. He has borrowed the apparent misery he suspects emanates

25

from the man called Nosegay Parkinson. Apata tells himself that Parkinson's wife must be to Parkinson what Beverley is to him. If someone locks me away from Beverley, thinks Apata, What I'm going to do? Die? I don't know if I'm going to die. I don't think so. NO I WON'T DIE! But, at the same time, I won't be alive either.

Apata looks at the man hunched on the saltbeef and fantasizes, "If I were God, I would snap my fingers and Parkinson's trip to death row would be a terrible dream he wakes from to find his young wife lying close to his dark nakedness."

'What kind of man Parris was?'

'Wan red man!'

'A'RIGHT BOYS, ENOUGH FRESH AIR!' announces the policeman with the rifle.

'Ow offisah sah!' begs an old man from the ring of people severely inspecting the criminals, 'Ow man! Have a heart nuh? Alyo taking them two man dis fuh heng them – leh them get a good long look at life fuh last nuh? Ow man. Leh them look at water an' sky an' bush lil' bit more, nuh?'

There is a murmur of agreement from the by-standers. The shotgun-toting policeman laughs. The one with the rifle stares at the old man who stares back. 'OFFISAH! ME NAH FRIGHTEN YOU SAH!' he snaps. 'ME AH ONE BLACK MAN WHO NAH FRIGHTEN GUN … CAUSE ME HANDLE GUN AH NINETEEN FOURTEEN WAR!' The jutting chin badly shaved and the knotted brows tell that the old man has grown angry at the policeman's attempt to intimidate him.

'ME NAH FRIGHTEN POLICEMAN ONE BACK-SIDE!'

The rifle-toting policeman now smiles. 'Al'right old man … I'll let them watch at life lil' more.' Then he mockingly salutes the old man who, to the crowd's amusement, returns the salute as a proper English soldier should, 'Longest way up, shortest way down.'

*　　　*　　　*

26

The steamer blows a short note, to Apata, a mournful note. He looks over to the shoreline. A group of young Amerindians, like happy sea sprites, splash and frolic below the bushy river bank from which a frail landing juts out. Frantically they wave their hands above wide-cheeked smiling faces. Someone laughs above him and Apata looks up at the back of the head of a man who is also looking over at the children. Holding his gaze at the back of the head of the crew man on the bridge, Apata wills the man to turn and look at him. At last the head swivels and the first mate's eyes and Apata's make four.

The first mate turns to the wheel house and calls: 'HEY CAPPY!' But the Captain is downing diluted and hissing liver salts from a drinking glass. 'AYE!' he answers after the last swallow.

'Come and take a look at this young chap and tell me if you recognize he!'

The Captain moves forward to the wing of the bridge. As he passes the light-skinned, thin-faced helmsman he slaps him heavily and good naturedly on a shoulder blade. When he gets out on the wing of the bridge the mate asks him, 'You recognize that tall dark-skin young chap down there?'

'Since morning is only now I think ah finding mih head. That whisky have kick eh? Jeez!'

'You know that tall dark-skin chap down there?'

At last Morton gets through to him. 'Who that?'

'Next to that brute of a woman with the parrot cage.'

The Captain looks intently but apparently doesn't see who he has been asked to look at. He shakes his head. 'Is only sleep these eyes seeing. Yet I don't want go to sleep.'

'Wait man Cappy. Look!' The first mate points now. 'You ent seeing that chap down there with a book in his hands – '

'OH!'

'You recognize he?'

'Naw!' drawls the Captain and shakes his head in reinforced negative.

'That is the chap you bet against yesterday and lose.'

'WAIT!' exclaims the Captain, 'IS THAT LITTLE

RASS? JEEZE-AN-WEB! DAT IS THE YOUNG CHAP THAT DID PUSHING NELIOUS GREEN BOAT?'

The first mate nods his head. 'That is the man of the races, yesterday. And you know something, Cappy? I bet you that you know that boy more than you think.'

'Hear Morton, do something for me, CEASE TO USE THAT WORD "BET" AROUND ME FOR A LIL' TIME!'

The first mate laughs heartily at his captain's pangs from yesterday's misfortune at the regatta; whilst the reason for the Captain's misfortune sits hunched over a school text book down under the forecastle.

'You remember Apata?'

'Man, I know plenty Apatas!'

'You remember Harry Apata?'

'What kind-a question you asking me Morton? If I Wesley Innes remember Harold Apata?' Then the Captain laughs. 'Man, Harry Apata and me grow up so!' The Captain intertwines his index finger with the second finger. Suddenly he grips the polished railing of the bridge's wing. Staring down he says: 'JEEZE-AN-WEB! WAIT, MATE'O – DON'T TELL ME THAT IS HAROLD SON?'

'Aye, is Josh' Smith grandson.'

'Mih hear them calling the name, but for no reason I can blame, nothing didn't register.'

'Maybe is because you know more than one Apata.'

'JEEZE-AN-WEB!'

Then the Captain calls down to a sailor coiling ropes onto a pair of bitts on the forecastle. The sailor lifts his head sharply.

'THE YOUNG CHAP WITH THE BOOK ... BRING HIM UP TO THE BRIDGE!'

The Captain turns back to the first mate. 'Jeeze-an-web!'

(The *Lady Northcut* labours with a load of coastward bound commuters arrayed like the rainbow along her decks on this gay Easter Monday afternoon, a little after noon. A buoy, hands akimbo, dances by, lightly blinking a spot of red and directly above the steamer the sun prepares to sink slowly to the other side of the peak of the running day.)

*   *   *

'That man mad up to now.' The Captain shakes his head at the memory. 'Crazy Kilran.'

Michael has grown tired of hearing the story of Crazy Kilran. After all he has grown so far as to be synonymous with Crazy Kilran. He has grown to his present age hearing too many times the story of himself in the local bulrushes. But the Captain's finished.

'My father was what kind of man, Captain?'

'To begin with boy, you father was a book man just like you!'

The Captain wonders why the young man wants to hear about his father from him. Had not his grandfather or grandmother, or other people from his village, who had probably known the man, already told him about his father. But you could never be sure, the Captain tells himself. This chap looks serious and sensible. Maybe he wants to know deeper things which people doesn't want to tell, or couldn't tell since they probably do not know.

'Your father was a man of many facets, you grandfather never tell you?'

'Well . . . no sir.' Apata takes a deep breath. The first mate senses hesitancy in the youth and moves away. As he passes the wheel house the helmsman asks him for a cigarette and gets Morton's last. Morton moves to the opposite wing of the bridge.

'You father was something to talk about boy,' says the Captain. The breeze fills in through the neck of Apata's shirt cooling him from the sun and he thinks for a fleeting second of Beverley. Then he thinks for a moment of his grandfather back at the Bartica stelling. 'Well carry you boarding and lodging piece safe then, Rayburn,' old Josh Smith had said before he had kissed Michael on the forehead. Apata feels the pieces of raw gold, referred to as "his boarding and lodging piece" by the old man, in a miniature bag hung from a strong piece of cord around his neck. The precious bits nestle against his sternum under the blue-green terylene shirt.

'Captain, the things I want to find out are not easy to ask. I've heard of how my mother and father died in the

Mazaruni river. I hear that story many times since I was matured enough to remember things.

'If it is true that my parents' death is surrounded by some kind of sorcery, then some one of them, either my father or my mother, had to be dealing with those kinds of things.'

'Not necessarily so you know, boy.' The Captain takes off his cap. He tells himself that he should air his head a bit and dabs his palm over short-cropped red-hairedness.

'Boy, you father was a read man, but he used to read the wrong books.'

The Captain clears his throat. 'Hear me young Apata, you's a big chap and you're very intelligent from your questions. I think you can hear a bit of what many people never knew and doesn't know.

'Your father was a man who believed in quick money. He did believe in a quick dollar, me know 'cause me and he used to work on an old river tug in thirty-six. We was bachelors together.' The Captain laughs lightly. 'The false name he had was "Garvus" 'cause he was a man who did proper believe in Marcus Garvey.'

Apata remembers the two framed portraits in his grandparents' new home that overlooks where he grew up as a younger boy. There is the monarch of Ethiopia over his grandparents' Victoria bed and on a wall, that can be seen from any part of the living room and dining room, a picture of Mr Marcus Garvey.

'Your father was like myself a man who did believe in quick money. So one day we tell we self, why we don't work some magic and make some money? The first time the thought come out, the boys laugh, but one night Harry come and tell me that he got something to show me and he take me and show me a big black book he had wrap up in a brown paper. To this day I ent know how you father hand fall on that Black Arts book. But I could remember he tell me ...' The Captain turns the cap absentmindedly, round and round in his hands and clears his throat. 'He say to me: "Coolie cheap Wes! Coolie cheap!" You father take to studying the guarded mysteries, me and he together. We did believe that this book wouldah help we find gold cause we hear of men who used the dark secrets to tap the minerals of the earth and sea. So we studying and studying. Before you know it we allow one more into the fraternity. Was three o' we, me, you father, and a man that name Emelio Fiedtcou.' The Captain shakes his head. 'To this day Emelio mad as ass in Georgetown. Walking the streets and now and then he will bend pick up a brick and start to scream "Eldorado!"'

'Eldorado ... an old Portuguese man?'

'He and me, you father, used to study magic together until one night we go out in a boat at midnight to invoke an entity of the deep ...' The Captain's brows knit. 'Somebody do something wrong ... and suddenly the water start to bubble and churn up ... and Emelio fall in a faint and was never the man he used to be after he came out of it two days later.' The Captain brushes his hands together. 'From that time on – I washed my hands from magical quick money and start to study hard to be what I is now.' He gazes at the river. 'Boy ... I thought you father did wash he hands from them things too ... but the way I hear you father and mother dead ...' He shakes his head. 'I don't believe he really did stop.'

'What kind of woman my mother was Captain?'

Innes smiles warmly then says, 'I's never forget that Saturday in 'thirty-seven ... Was a August month ... Me and Harold spot she the same time ... a smooth, dark-skin girl with she old people ...' The Captain nods, then says to Michael, 'You born in 'thirty-eight, right?'

'Yes ... July, nineteen thirty-eight.'

'Ol' Harry did always faster than me ...' the Captain says with a reminiscent smile. 'Yes, you' old man marry Lillian in the April of that very year ...' He nods. 'Your mother was a good woman ... Plenty men did envy your father ...'

'You, for one,' Apata says within himself; then aloud: 'What my father looked like, Captain?'

'Is like if you' take father head and put it on your shoulders, boy.' The Captain sighs and adds: 'However, I only hope that you' luck different from he luck.' Innes shakes his head sadly. 'Is one hell of a thing that you' father and mother should die seven months after they marry ...'

Apata turns away and contemplates the river. The first mate moves into the wheel house and speaks to the helmsman then operates the engine telegraph and gives a blast on the steamer's siren. Apata watches the bushes that appear to be blocking the river coming up slowly. But really the bushes are far away and the river turns at that point.

Apata wonders if his father was a fool, or a dreamer and wonders if he would turn out to be like his father. Thinking of the necromancer of the village and what she had said about his dying, Apata wonders if he is associated with some sort of mysticism because of his father. His mother and father died strangely. Why was he saved? By the intervention of what or whom? Am I a spirit child or a spirits-favoured child? 'Rayburn ...' he remembers his grandfather having once said to him, 'always remember that you' father was himself and you is you own self. You and your father ent have to be the same person!'

The Captain stares glassy-eyed at the flat-bottomed mail boat coming alongside the steamer and the *Lady Northcut* crawls on the water while the bushes drag by and, from the landing from which the little boat has come, an Amerindian woman holds up her baby's arm and waves it. Apata waves back.

CHAPTER 4

'And you know something, Beverley? Even though I myself was on the steamer, I started to wish that the boat run up on a sandbank or something like that!'

Michael smiles whilst gazing blankly at the unlit cinema screen before them. 'I imagined the whole scene. The steamer going and going. Suddenly we grounding heavily on something and the whole boat starting to lean on one side as though it is going to capsize. People screaming and trying to kill each other to stay alive. Babies and children screaming, and women – I mean confusion! And the sailors wild – telegraph to the engine-room signalling wildly! The propellers churning up mud and sand. People screaming for help and the water rushing in! Fightings for life jackets, and people in the water and in life boats. Then the two prisoners jumping over the side and the policeman trying to shoot the escaping criminals but not getting a chance since there are too much innocent people in the way . . .' Taking a deep breath, Michael shakes his head. 'I imagined the whole thing.'

'But how they swimming? They hands ent tied . . . ?'

'Handcuffed,' Michael corrects.

'They hands ent handcuffed behind they back?'

'I could swim with my hands behind my back, girl.'

'But none of the prisoners wasn' a Black-buck like you?'

Michael ignores the crack, and completes the fantasy rolling from his mind: 'And in the end, Chingarus and Parkinson disappear, change they name, get plastic surgery, and live as free good men again.'

'Funny though,' Beverley says, 'life don't run like that.'

'You right. I think they got hung yesterday.'

After a few minutes of thought-filled silence, Michael begins to laugh. Says Beverley, 'Is true what old people say: "They have more mad people outside than inside".'

'You know Beverley, when we were small, we heard that the day on which they would hang a man he would get the option to call for any food he wants to eat, any food at all. But that's not what I laughed about. What I was laughing about is that we used to believe that the best thing a man waiting to be hung should call for is ochroe.'

'WHY OCHROE?'

'Because it's slimy and slippery and if you eat it then the rope going to slip off your neck!'

Beverley Bailey finds herself tickled and feels good to hear Michael whenever he breaks into his nonsense talking.

Apata's mood changes suddenly. 'I will never forget that chap Parkinson's face Bevy,' he says.

'He couldn't have get off Mike. It wasn't manslaughter, you know. It was deliberate murder with intent if what the woman told you is right.'

Michael smiles and shifts in his seat. 'I don't think she made it up,' he says, then turns and looks at Beverley for a while before watching once more to the direction of the unlit screen. 'Tell me something Bevy ...' he says then seems to change his mind about what he wants to find out.

'What Mike?'

'Don't worry.'

'I don't like people doing me that Mike, please tell me?'

'If you did red ... you-you'd like me?'

The girl's muted gaiety retracts, leaving in its place, a tender silence and Apata suddenly realizes that he shouldn't have asked such a question. Within himself, he doesn't even know why he asked it. It is as though a subconscious impulse threw it out. He doesn't know; but he feels immature and stupid now. He sucks his teeth and says in the tones of a fleeting unimportant after-thought. 'What nonsense questions I ask you sometimes Beverley?' He makes a disgusted sound in his throat and expresses embarrassment.

The girl smiles. 'Last night ... I dreamed me and you did making love Mike.'

Quickly he looks around. The section of the cinema where they sit is filling in quickly. Michael closes one eye and makes a roguish face at Beverley. 'Making love? I Mikus Raybunus no know what making love means. Tell Mikus Raybunus "common-nis", he understand!'

Beverley starts to laugh.

'Ssssh!' he says softly before turning her face to face his.

'Beverley, you think we're going to be together a long enough time for us to get married?'

'Yes Michael. But Michael, suppose you get a chance to attend King's College High School?'

'You want to know what would happen between us if that happens? Nothing would happen Bev ...' He takes her hand. 'Beverley, don't tell me you have Bajan in you?'

A brief smile flutters, founders, then breaks out once more, and blushing she says: 'My grandfather was from Barbados.' She giggles.

'Beverley, when I get that free place to King's College, I'm going to study harder. I'm going to win prizes and scholarships. I want to be like Mr Norman Cameron, Beverley. I want to go to the University of Cambridge.'

'I know you're going to get a chance to go to King's, Mike and I know you'll get to go away ...'

'And I'm going to come back and marry you Bevy. I'll never desert Guiana. I'll come back ...' he squeezes her hands, '... and make you my Elizabeth.'

Relief in her giggling. Calm settles on Michael. Inside himself he sings a song of sweet love and the warmth of Beverley's shoulder against his feels as if she is joining in the chorus. It's as though a gentle Ray Conniff breezes about in his inner being.

'When I return from England Bev I'm going to be a big man you're going to be my Queen. I'll have a big house like those in Kingston, and I'll personally plant a garden of roses for you.' She leans her head onto his face. The perfumed vaseline in her hair and her hair's warmth stirs him. He

35

takes a deep breath and feels drowsy with the ecstasy of their togetherness.

'Roses? Why?'

'Because every afternoon when I come home from the office I'm going to pick one for you.' He smiles. 'Everytime you answer the door and find a man offering you a beautiful rose, that man will be your husband.'

'All of us,' says Beverley whisperingly, 'now sounds like Bajans: Counting we chickens before they hatched. You ent even pass your exam yet.'

'Uh uh Bevy!' he stalls her. 'I'm going to pass girl and with great marks too. I know myself. I can feel what I can do and *know* I can do it!'

'Mystic?'

He taps his forehead: 'Brainstic!'

'"Mouthar an' guitar ah two different 'tar," boy!' she teases with a local saying.

'You want to bet that I pass that exam and get a free place to King's.'

He crooks a little finger. She does the same. They hook them together then disentangle them by pulling away. Sealing a bet. She blushes. Mike still senses a hidden fear, a disguised anxiety, so he playfully presses a folded fist to her left cheek.

'Wait, man Beverley, you believe if I go away from you, I would NOT come back?'

'In me family Mike, they say whenever a man leaves a Bailey woman, regardless of why they leave, they don't come back.'

'Aw man, Bevy – that's superstition!'

A bit of music which many associate with the starting of the show comes on. 'Picture will start anytime now Bevvy,' Michael says and squeezes her hand. The lights go off. She squeezes his hand between the folding seats that separate them. Michael turns in the new gloom and inhales her smell. Something about her breath always reminds him of the sweetness of slumber on a cold rainy night or of cows grazing where the branches of trees bend gently in the wind above green fields and rice fields turning gold under a one o'clock sun, or country skies with birds diving to dip briefly in the face of punt trenches and lily ponds.

'Kiss me Mike,' she says softly. She moves her face closer to his. He moves his face closer to hers. Their lips brush together. It is enough for both of them.

A huge silhouetted bell dominates the screen.

'What "toll" mean Mike?'

'When a bell rings in death-march time, Beverley, a bell tolls.'

'Oh ... Who's he Mike?'

'The star boy.'

'I know, I know, but he's which film star?'

Michael smiles in the gloom. 'Gary Cooper.'

Beverley squeezes Michael's hands. 'A'right Mike,' she whispers, 'no more questions.'

CHAPTER 5

The Sunday Crier

Sunday, July 14th, 1954.   *6 Cents.*

WHAT A REGAL REGATTA IT WAS!!

Last Sunday surely is a marked day in the minds of Regatta buffs who were there under the Bartican sun that streamed through the charged atmosphere of fun and water frolic spiced with the zephyrs of Easter.
The contests were good. The greased pole climbing competition provided much amusement; the swimming events, though not as hot and competitive as last year's, still held their own on the programme. The event that starred the show, and moved the crowd, was the eighty horse-power motor-boat race that was won by teenager Michael Rayburn Apata who placed in the said event last year.
The photographs taken by staff photographer Sahdoo tell the story in a way words can't.

'That's me,' says Michael, pointing to an almost silhouetted figure being mobbed by other figures apparently doing a dance of jubilation by the waterside. In the background of the shot, a White woman reclines on the flat sloping bow of a power boat.

'So how we going to know that is you Apata?' teases a school mate. 'We only seeing a black thing in the centre o' the crowd!'

'That black thing is me stupid!' answers Michael jocu-

38

larly. The boys laugh. 'Al'right then,' says Michael, 'what about this one? Eh?'

'Yeah,' agrees the Indian with the running ear blocked with a bit of cotton wool that fails to keep in the repulsive smell of the infection.

'Yeahs ... we boy look good in this photograph.'

'The smile of triumph you call it nuh, Mike?'

The photograph being discussed is a half shot of Michael with his grandparents hugged close to him.

'Who's dem ol' timers?'

'Old man look like Gabbianes.'

'That is my grandfather and grandmother, boy.'

'Hey Mike!'

Michael turns to Rodrigues who is cross-eyed.

'Ah want you to teach me to swim, man Apata!'

'So where I would teach you to swim Dreegs?'

'Sea wall, man. What happen to the sea wall?'

Apata folds the newspaper. 'Hear ... that ocean dangerous, you know.'

'APATA IS A BLACK BUCK MAN!' says someone from outside the immediate group. 'And once any buck man around, Dreegs, you can't drown.'

Apata turns and faces a light-skinned school boy. A stocky fellow with reddish brown Negro's hair. His bull-necked appearance lends him an air of a bully, which really he is not. But he's arrogant and boastful.

'Hear, Vanier,' says Apata, 'I have Amerindian blood in me, right? And anything in me I want people to respect. As far as I concern, "buck man" ent respectful!' Apata shakes his head, unsmiling. 'So don't call me that!' The corners of his lips tremble. 'You hear what I telling you?'

'Yes BUCK MAN!' says Vanier nonchalantly.

'WHAT HAPPEN WENDELL?' shouts one from the group, 'YOU ENT HEAR THE MAN DON'T LIKE PEOPLE CALLING HE DAT?'

The stocky Wendell Vanier smiles mischievously. Smirks. 'Wait-wait ... because he in newspapers you turn he representative? Hear Stephens ... I is ME! Right? And if I think Apata is a BUCK MAN, eh? Then he's a fucking BUCK MAN. None ya'all can't beat me, you know.'

The group begins to look disgusted. The atmosphere under the old sand-box tree, this time of recreation, begins to change. Henry, a fat boy mixed with East Indian and Negro, digs nervously into the old bark of the tree brutalized with school boys' grafitti and Michael Apata shifts loose dirt with a shoe tip. He knows that Vanier is prodding him for a fight. It has been like this a very long time. Their birth signs do not agree in any way. Vanier always tries to cross his path. Vanier always seems to want to find out how it would go if they came to blows. And Apata, knowing that he's only stopping in the City at the Bailey's, keeps trying to preserve his good conduct as he's away from home. But the chap's pushing him and he, Apata, is only human. This push against him has so far come from Vanier in all things. In school, particularly, the only student who ever beat Vanier, in terms of class grades, has been Apata. The "bush man" as Vanier and his kind have continually thrown it.

Standing before Apata, Vanier smiles mockingly.

'Hear Mike,' says the shortest member of the group, 'I think you should complain to Jaggy!'

Apata shakes his head.

'So why you don't run and complain BUCK MAN?' taunts Vanier, bent, it seems, on having it out.

'Because ...' And Apata folds the newspaper into a tight roll, 'it would be you who will have to complain now!' Apata slaps Venier resoundingly in his face with the folded paper.

'OH RASS ... FIGHT!' says an onlooker.

'DON'T CURSE BOY!'

'HEY, LEH WE PART DIS THING!'

'NO!' comes a unanimous response.

Vanier manages to free his head from an elbow lock of Apata's only to have his left brow lumped by a carefully delivered head smash from Apata's gleaming forehead. The boys jumping around argue that Vanier will gain the advantage once on the ground but it does not come out that way. Vanier reels to his feet and kicks out. Apata takes the blow on his head, makes a grab for the foot and misses. 'BLACK BITCH!' pants Vanier and comes in for another kick. Apata grabs Vanier's ankle and twists the foot. Vanier falls. Apata rises, plunges and smothers Vanier in a deluge of cuffs that rain on his forehead and down into his solar plexus. Vanier grimaces and tries a bear hug. Apata brings down his forehead twice and Vanier's grip slackens ...

'OH RASS! SHIT! APATA IS A BUTT MAN!'

'OH SHIT MAN, DON'T CURSE!'

Apata jumps up panting, and allows Vanier to scramble too to his feet.

'YEAHS!' says one of the boys, 'TOE TO TOE!'

The combatants circle each other, feinting and jabbing. Apata's head is dusty, and Vanier's face is red. His nose bleeds and the blood runs into the mean slit between his lips. Apata's lips tremble and his nostrils open and close, open and close. He licks his thick lips, he feints with a left and rushes Vanier who steps back into the tree's bole. Feeling cornered, he lashes out with a wild right that lands solidly on Apata's left cheek. Apata closes his eyes in pain and hooks wildly. The punch sinks into Vanier's stomach. He whispers a profanity and bends forward grimacing.

'WRANG MOVE!' shouts one of the boys.

Apata snatches Vanier's neck in a choking grip. Vanier plunges forward and knocks Apata off his feet. Together they fall to the twisted and bruised grass. The bell for the end of recess goes. Vanier rolls with Apata ... they just roll together. The group around the fight is quite big now, a pulsating group, a group giving incitement to both sides. Then, suddenly, 'JAGGY COMING OH SHIT, JAGGY COMING! LEH WE PART DIS THING LEH WE PART THEM LEH WE PART THEM!' And the exhausted pair still rolling on the ground like a boa constrictor and an alligator, are torn apart, both grateful for the fight's termination.

Jagnauth, the Indian Headmaster, tumbles his fatness over the field as soon as he spots the fight. Both boys hurriedly knock out their hair and brush broken grass from their bodies. At the same time, but with difficulty, they try to breathe easily and naturally. Now, as Jaggy gets closer, the timid witnesses disperse. Still he is not close enough to hear what is being said.

'Hear, Apata ...' says Vanier, breathing like a bull, 'I ent done with you yet boy.' He passes the palm of his hand over his face. A friend passes him a handkerchief. Vanier uses it to wipe blood from his cheek. He still glares at Apata who is buttoning up his shirt with trembling hands and knuckles that bleed. 'Yeah chap!' continues Vanier, 'this thing ent done yet.' Vanier spits. 'I ent have to tell me father, or Jaggy nothing! But I gon frig you up good some day!'

Apata nods his head with an action that seems to say: 'Anytime you're ready, jump Vanier ... I'll be waiting for you!' But only Apata knows the anxiety he, Apata, feels inside.

'Al'right boys,' wheezes Mr Jagnauth, coming to a stop. 'What has been going on here?'

The boys offer no answer. The Headmaster shakes his head, his lips tight with disapprobation. 'Well then,' says the big man, 'I'll give each pugilist the double dozen.' He nods his head for effect and looks around to see how it goes over. 'And it will be delivered on stage in front of the whole school this afternoon!' Jaggy looks intently at his pair of fighters. Vanier looks as though he has had the worst of it. Something about that makes Jagnauth feel good.

'NOW BOYS.' he booms, 'SHOULD I SEND FOR YOUR PARENTS?'

'No sir!' says Vanier quickly. Apata shakes his head. Vanier's answer surprises the Headmaster. The last fight Vanier had been involved in had brought his socially weighty father into the Headmaster's office and the dialogue that had ensued still upsets Jagnauth whenever he thinks back to it.

CHAPTER 6

'WHO GETS THE HIGHEST MARK? APATA? MICHAEL APATA?'

'Yeah man, "bush man". That boy from Bartica.'

'The regatta champ!'

'De man good on land as well as on water.'

'Yeahs ... WE BOY! Charlestown High! WE BOY, man!'

'From Bartica to King's College!'

'WHO ELSE WIN FREE PLACE FROM THIS SCHOOL? WHO ELSE?'

'Vanier.'

'VANIER?'

'Yeah.'

'OH TAIL! APATA BEAT VANIER?'

'The man get the highest mark in the whole country, girl.'

'APATA? THE WHOLE COLONY?'

'You can't take it, nuh?'

'But that chap so so black and ...'

'The boy face may be black, be he brains alright though.'

'I thought Vanier wouldah get that kind of marks Apata get.'

'Why? Because Vanier red and he father rich?'

'Vanier got all them new books that he's bring to school.'

'And Apata got all that brains he's bring to school!'

'King's College ... yes ... a break to be a Godling.'

'RAYBURN GET IT GIRL, RAYBURN GET IT!'

'Oh? He's Rayburn, now?'

'I like that chap a long time now.'

'But yet, when them girls tell you the other-day that you

like Apata, you tell them "NO!" How Apata face too black and shine and that he looking jus' like one o' them jujus in them Tarzan picture.'

'Them two boys going to fight at King's College. And them kind-a school is big shot children school. They don't have fight and them kind-a behaviour. OH SHIT, LOOK PEROUNE CRYING!'

'Not everybody could take failure with a straight face, boy.'

'But O'kunt boy ... that chap Apata is a real champ.'

'Don't curse man. We in the school compound still!'

'Mih boy Apata ... 'B' stands for blackman ... 'B' stands for brains. Ah wonder if this going to come out in the newspapers?'

* * *

'Only day before yesterday Beverley and me were talking of results. You did great Michael. You'll be attending my school now, soon. And I ...' Gerald sucks his teeth.

'Ah sorry to hear that man, Gerald.'

'Well, what I'm going to do Mike? If my father wants me to leave school and do farming with him at Parika, what can I do? Defy him? I can't do that kind of thing.'

'Well ask him for a last chance, nuh?'

Gerald shakes his head then takes the thin drinking straw between his heavy lips. He lifts the Pepsi bottle so that the end of the straw is deep into the cold drink and pulls until his cheeks balloon. Apata watches his number one friend's face. His eyes are riveted on the brown one cent piece nailed onto the shop's counter for money luck. Gerald holds back tears of disappointment. Apata turns away casually and studiously contemplates a poster that shows a crocodile with its body neatly severed into two halves by a gigantic razor blade of a most popular brand.

BACK-SWING OF THE PENDULUM:

Gerald Tross's sophisticated uncle looked at his brother, who was behaving like a peasant farmer, and felt angry enough to chase him out of his posh Georgetown bungalow. But the foundation of good blood prevailed and he swallowed his passion and listened. After all, the uncle told himself, Gerald was his brother's son, not his.

'Hif de bhai get first in de exam, LISTEN TO ME GOOD FREDERICK, HIF DE BHAI GET FIRST, mih guh leh he stay here in Georgetown wid you. But, hif he nah get first ah de exam fuh promoshan, well he gaffa come hom ah Parika an' help me at de farm. Fair enough?'

'Ulric ... Ulric ...'

'Mih hear yo' first time.'

'Please ...'

Gerald Tross's uncle took a deep calming breath.

'Must Gerald's academic future be balanced on whether or not he tops his class? Let's face it Ulric, Gerald's not the most brilliant boy in King's College. I teach there, my wife teaches there, we do know. There's a prodigy of a boy there named Booker and I know Gerald's not going to make it over that young man. First or not, man, is rather unfair to the boy. Gerald is your son and he's my nephew. He's making real progress in school. Last term he brought fourth – '

'AN' DIS YEAR HE GUH BRING FIRST, or he going to bring provision out de ground.'

'IT'S NOT FAIR ULRIC!'

'Well, I decidin' what is fair for me boy.'

'THEN WHY THE HELL DID YOU SEND HIM HERE?'

'Nah shout ah mih face, chap!'

'Jesus!'

'Nah get me vex, yeh!'

Frederick Tross rose to his feet. He wished he could have beaten his crude brother who sat in front of him with his feet most likely burning in leather shoes. It was easy to see the farmer's toes working away in discomfort below the leather. Frederick knew, however, that he could not beat his bigger brother who sat awkwardly in a Morris chair and emphasized his rough points by striking the arms of the article of furniture with calloused farmer's hands. And every time he brought his hands down he made a mess of the polish work done by his son Gerald.

'Why is it,' Frederick was saying, 'you suddenly want Gerald to do farming in the height of his high schooling Ulric?'

'Ah tellin' yo' that if he pass with first in class he going to continue, but if he ent pass what he going to do? Just keep going to school and in de end get wan office job? Fuh play bigsass pon he own country people? NOT ONE BACKSIDE FREDDY! De other-day some ah dem Georgetown office people come round tekking something dem ah call census and dem hinsult plenty ah'we ah Parika village! Office man? Me nah want Geral' foh turn office man.'

'Then why didn't you, in the first place, keep him in Parika and get him used to the cows and pasture life?'

'CAREFUL HOW YO' TALK CHAP!' the farmer threatened, 'NAH TRY TO HINSULT ME, YEH!'

'YOU SHOULDN'T HAVE SENT HIM HERE! BLOODY HELL, MAN!'

'Hear, hear. When mih see how you tek education and get scholarship to go away, mih tell mihself, mih tell mihself, "Ulric, you has a good boy ... Geral' making proper good marks in de village primary school, and he passing he exams good, nah hol' am back." Yes, dat is what I did tell mihself. Ah wanted mih boy to take in education like you Freddy, mih was always proud o' you, ah wanted mih boy Gerald to study and get bright and go away and come back with a lovely White wife. Dat is why when de opportunity show de way that I send Geral' to King's College high school as you help me do.' Farmer Tross took a breath.

'And what happened that made you change your mind like this?'

The farmer stood and his suit of crinkled, starched khaki fitted badly over his hardened muscular body. In contrast to his brother Frederick, who stood in well tailored pants of tweed and who wore a cream terylene shirt open at the neck, he looked a yard caretaker.

Frederick repeated the question but Ulric was firm in his

promise not to tell. The old family who lived on the West Coast, in the deep-country village of Parika, had promised not to tell. What good would it be to tell one's brother things that would make things bad between one's brother and his wife? Ulric Tross and the line from which he descended were Bible-embracing people. "Therefore shall man leave his father and mother and cleave unto his wife: and they shall be one flesh".

Frederick waited for an answer to his repeated question.

Even though it burned in the farming Tross's heart to let his scholarly brother know what his White wife did, he kept it hidden. "Who God has joined together, let no man put asunder".

'Don't look at me like that. I want you to tell me why, what influenced your decision to discontinue Gerald's high schooling?'

'"INFLUENCE" NAH?' the farmer said contemptuously. Then added in a scornful tone, 'Ah just' change mih mind!'

'You're being cagey, Ulric. I expected better from you.'

Ulric Tross sucked his teeth vehemently and said that he was going to catch the ferry. Frederick could have seen the anger behind his brother's expression. The mystery of it worried him but he tried to cover his worry by nonchalance.

'Well, it's your son's future you're going to spoil ... not mine.'

What the farming brother did as a retort shocked the scholarly brother. Ulric Tross, fifty years old and two years older than Frederick, turned, looked his brother in the face, and smiled as he sadly shook his head, 'Mih really sorry fuh you, me brother,' he told him.

Frederick laughed stupidly as he glanced away from his big brother's gaze. There was tenderness in it and the old care he knew Ulric had always for him. Something was wrong between them. He wondered if something was wrong between him and the old family. In himself he tried; he knew that he tried. But something *was* wrong. He knew that Ulric was just looking for an excuse to get Gerald away from the city. He wondered why.

'Man Freddoe,' Ulric said gently, 'I going, yeh.'

'You may give my regards to mother for me and tell her that Pat says hello too.'

On the way to the door, Ulric's face was set grim. 'When you' own fart wake you ... you well awoken!' he told himself when he heard the strange, quick-running slippery music that made his brother wave his hands effeminately in front of him whilst he closed his eyes. White man music! England! He remembered one time when his son Gerald came home from the city and was listening to the same kind of running, slippery music. Whilst he had listened he had done the same things with his hands as his uncle Frederick. Puzzled, he had asked his son, 'What kind-a music you ah listen to, and wave up you' han' like-ah dem woman?' And Gerald had replied, 'Symphony music Daady! This is good music, the *real* music!' He remembered that his son had closed his eyes like Frederick and like Frederick, too, uttered strange phrases that sounded like "Okrus", or "Opus eleven" and "Beetle-oven" and "Monzurt". But Gerald's father didn't mind. His son was learning new things that would have made the family proud. But now, he just wanted the boy home from the wrongness of his uncle Frederick.

As he walked through his brother's front lawn the gravel, that made up the footpath, crunched under his heavy shoes which were murdering his toes with discomfort. Off the path, he saw his brother's wife stooped at a row of little flower beds on the lawn. She waved "bye-bye" and her brother-in-law waved back whilst smiling from a head that said inside it, 'Smile yo' big teeth, long nose white bitch! Smile you' white rass! What ent miss yo' ent pass yo!' Then he wrenched his head away and concentrated on passing through the gate with frosted global lights on the concrete pillars.

'Freddy mih brother,' he muttered, 'yo' bright, but yo' ent have no sense. But yo' going to get sense in dat white woman hand backside!' And he repeated, 'When you' own fart wake yo' ... yo' well 'woken.'

Before passing through the gate, he glanced back at the pink figure stabbing the dirt with a little thing like a trowel.

Her husband, the farming man's brother was stooped with her now. Ulric burned within. 'Look at she! Ugly pink-faced bitch! Always telling the old lady that she jus' polish the front and if she could please use the friggin' back door. Always tryin' to explain 'bout de kind-ah polish rass! Then always skinnin' she blasted teeth and tellin' the old lady that she's part of the family and could come through the back door without minding ... RASS LIKE SHE! Me boy ent going to be no poonks to marry one ah dem rank rass. Is bes' me boy be a man like me than to grow to be a rass like Frederick! Don't even come to see the old people much. He wife can't stand de dust. Oh she's allergerick ... allerajic ... whatever the bleddy word is ... to dust!'

Ulric stood and waited for a yellow city bus that took him to the back of some place in Georgetown that he never saw before and, after having to pay a double fare, it took him to where he really wanted to go after having left Frederick's place – Stabroek Market square. There, he stepped off the short-bodied bus and trekked to the Transport and Harbours stelling to catch the ferry boat that took him over the Demerara to the other shore where he caught a train that jangled deep into the country.

FORWARD SWING OF THE PENDULUM:
Gerald Tross sets the empty Pepsi bottle down.

'As Bam-bam Sally does say, Mike, "Wha fuh happen leh'e happen".'

He smiles to himself. 'I like my father, and if he thinks that I should be back home and help him on the farm ...' He shrugs his shoulders. 'I'll go back home and help him on the farm. K.C's a great school Mike. When you start out, make some great grades in remembrance of me.' He rises from the tall stool.

'How much we have for you Sarge?'

'One shilling!' says the gravelly-voiced cake shop keeper, fatter than anyone could ever have imagined Shakespeare's Falstaff to be.

CHAPTER 7

On this night the Bailey's home is a place of modest gaiety. A borrowed spring-powered gramophone swirls music to Mike's, Beverley's and her parents' friends. A small gathering, but at the centre of it, one youth sits by the music machine and covers his apparent sadness by playing the operator, the record changer and the man who winds the crank. He deceives many, save those who know him best.

'Why you so quiet, Gerald?'

'I'm al'right man, Beverley.'

'Gerald boy, I don't like playing hypocrite. I know about it. Mike tell me.' She looks at his eyes and true to his Gemini personality, Gerald Tross looks away to the smooth surface of the ice-cream levelling to a fluid milkiness in the glass resting next to the turntable with the thick record turning. The music slows weirdly. Gerald leans over quickly from his chair and winds the little handle. The music picks up.

> *"As you sit by your window ...*
> *Bewitched by a star ...*
> *Are you really an angel ...*
> *I wonder what you are ..."*

Nat Cole sings and Beverley's head moves easily as she waits to complete what she tells herself she must tell Gerald. She values her consolation. And Gerald, too self-conscious to hear more "words of understanding" fights for something to say quickly, something to distract attention from himself.

'How far Mike and Keith gone for the ice?' he asks.

Beverley smiles. He wonders if she realizes that he's trying to change the subject.

'What you going to do now, Gerald?'

He laughs. 'Dance with you. May I?'

Dancing together, she feels the need to tell Gerald of herself and Mike. She wants so much to talk to somebody about her fears that are now rising like a high tide in her soul which feels so frail. Michael has indeed passed and will now go to King's College. He said that he would pass and he has. He has said other things. She'd talk to Gerald. He's one friend of Mike's towards whom she feels a sisterly attachment.

As they move through the little group of dancing couples she cannot see Gerald's face, but she knows that he's thinking, maybe, of how things have worked out for him. He doesn't want to talk about himself but she wants to talk of herself.

> "Cath-o ... Cathy-o ...
> Why do the flowers grow ...
> Answer me Cathy ...
> Only for you ..."

'I was telling Mike that ...'

'Um?' she hears from Gerald's chest. She sighs.

'Don't worry.'

He squeezes the hand he holds. To her it is an understanding gesture. Beverley wonders whether, if she tells Gerald of how she feels about Mike's eventual migration, it will remind him of his father's decree.

The music scratches to an end. 'You want more cake Gerald?' she asks as he releases her.

'After July ...' he says, and Beverley laughs before he can complete his statement.

'After July you would want more cake?'

Gerald laughs now. He picks his way over to the very short distance, from where they have stopped dancing, to the gramophone. He chooses a Billy Eckstine record and cranks up the turntable. He puts on the disc. Beverley stands and waits for him to tell her after July, what?

51

'After July, Beverley Ann Apata ...' Beverley blushes, 'I won't be going back to King's. God knows I would have had better grades now that Mike has gotten a chance to go there free. He would have helped me. We-we would have studied together.' He smiles at the turning disc, but the downpouring light from the light fixtures in the ceiling cast a foreboding shadiness under his brows. 'But he's coming when I'm going.'

'GANGWAY!' Michael's voice.

'They're back.'

'Yes,' says Beverley. 'I'll be back too.' She moves off to the kitchen. The song would soon end. Like Gerald's school life has ended. Like everything must end. The deep smooth voice of the singer soothes him and blurs the easy shuffling of the dancing couples not far from him. The aroma of the gin being drunk by Mr Bailey and the few friends he has invited, the sound of Eckstine, the trancelike movements of the dancers, and the perfumed smell of the colourless cocktail, take Gerald down into a numb reverie. He thinks of his uncle, his father and his uncle's wife. His uncle, his father and his uncle's wife: a triangle of conflict. He has noted enough to know that the reason for his father's abrupt decision to stop his schooling, thus pulling him away from his uncle's guardianship, has something to do with his uncle Frederick's wife.

She baffles him. Why? How is it she's married to his uncle when she apparently doesn't like Black people? From what he has seen of her Gerald has come to a conclusion. It relates to the growing coldness between his father and his uncle and it could have something to do with the fact that twice his uncle's wife has asked his grandmother to use the back entrance. Both times Gerald was at home. As a matter of fact, he was polishing the floor when the "both times" happened. He felt bad about the incident. He knew that his grandmother felt bad about them. He was sure that Pat, his uncle's wife, knew that asking her mother-in-law to use the back door might cause trouble. This was evident in the pains she took when she patronized the old, grey-headed lady with the tired gait. It is something which angers Gerald Tross even now. As he takes up the cheese cloth and begins to clean dust from the Glenn Miller disc that he will put on next, he wonders if her concern about the polish had not been used as a means of veiling her disrespect for a Black woman who was, probably, no more than a common native in her European estimation.

He cranks the turntable and puts on the record. *Tuxedo Junction* stomps from the speakers and the floor moves like be-bop.

Gerald is sure that there were many times when he only just missed the look of scorn on her face every time she had to hold his grandmother's hand in greeting. Maybe, Gerald thinks, I'm wrong. It would be good if I'm wrong for if I'm right I would be rather confused because uncle Frederick's a Negro too. Gerald takes a deep breath and is consoled that at least by going back to the country he will be leaving all this tension behind him. It had come to that. There will only be the schooling he will really miss. He will not miss his uncle's home and he knows that he is not ungrateful in his thoughts.

The party runs clean, even though Mr Bailey has been escorted to his bed by his wife who now comes steadily in Gerald's direction with a laden tray of food that is being quickly relieved of its burden. She turns back, but will come again. Soon she will be in front of him with a plate of cook-up rice with fried chicken laid on the side. Then what would he tell her? It would be in bad taste to refuse. Even if he has to force-feed himself he will take something. Gerald's the kind who finds it difficult to eat when upset at heart but refusing Beverley's mother's food would be wrong and ungracious. Besides, Mrs Bailey is a champ in the kitchen. His frequent visits to the home are testimony of that.

'AAH! HERE'S THE MAN.'

'What happening Mike?'

'Bevy says you need cheering up.' And he snaps his fingers towards a group of teenagers by the door. 'GRETA!' he calls through the party's din.

'What you calling dat girl for man Mike?'

'What happen, man Gerald?'

'Man, ah just ent feel like talking to Greta.'

Michael glances to the group by the door. 'A'right, she ent hear. But you al'right?'

'Yeah man.'

'What I could get for you?'

'Not Greta.'

They laugh. In the end Gerald settles for another glass of ice cream. Michael moves off after a quick clapping of his hands. He passes with a smile the plump brown-skinned Mrs Bailey with the thick eyebrows and heavy negroid nose that carries a conspicuous tip of which she is very self-conscious.

CHAPTER 8

Michael Apata shifts in the chair that is positioned in front of Mr Jagnauth's desk.

A gentle knock on the jamb of the open door. The Headmaster looks up and sees the son of Mr Vanier, an ex-pork knocker who as a pork knocker had enough sense not to squander his fortune as many of his counterparts, now poverty-stricken, have done. But his boy, in Jagnauth's estimation, is spoilt.

'Good morning, sir.'

'Come in and sit down, Vanier,' says Mr Jagnauth, wondering how the two boys before him would get along at King's College because of the bad feelings between them.

Having taken a seat, the Headmaster says: 'Now let me talk to you two. This morning you have to go to the office in Brickdam to have an interview with an Englishman, an Education Officer. His name is Mr Edward Carrington.' Jagnauth clears his throat. 'Now, I will talk to the two of you concerning yourselves and this thing you have to go to this morning – this interview.'

Apata takes a deep breath, and stares at the leading edge of the Headmaster's desk.

'Whatever it is that causes the two not to get along, conquer it! Start learning to forget! Hold one head as of now! You'all understand?'

'Yes, sir,' says Vanier. Apata says nothing.

'What are *you* saying, Apata?'

A fleeting knitting of brows, then Apata says, 'Nothing, sir.'

'What do you mean "nothing", Apata?'

'Mr Jagnauth, this chap is very insultive and vindictive!' Apata says.

'Now Vanier, if that is so then it is a short-coming. If such is true then it is something which you would have to overcome. For squabbling at a school like King's College could well be detrimental to both your futures. Do you get me Vanier?'

'Yes, sir,' says Vanier gravely.

To Jagnauth, it is not a surprising thing to hear that Vanier is insultive. Story has it, that when his father came home from the gold fields, the news of his good fortune had preceded him and as he came along the road from Parika, there were people along the way who hoped to see this great gold man. It is said that his old mother heard, too, and waited at the Georgetown Transport and Harbours Ferry stelling to greet her son because she was happy and guessed that her boy would be happy to see her. For he was her son after all and they had shared a lot of poverty-stricken times together. When the great man parted the crowd it is said that she opened her arms wide and rushed towards him. However, the great Gordon Vanier stuck out his palms, as a traffic policeman would to an oncoming unfit vehicle, and said in a clear voice: 'TOUCH ME NOT WOMAN ... FOR POVERTY IS CONTAGIOUS.'

Jagnauth wears a heavy, brown-framed pair of spectacles that would like to fall off but are prevented from doing so by the lumpy shape of his nose. He watches young Vanier intently and wonders if the boy's lightness of skin helps to spoil his mind. 'Vanier ...'

'Yes, sir.'

'I want you and Apata to shake hands like men before you leave this office!'

Vanier sticks his head out readily while Apata's comes up reluctantly because Apata feels that Vanier's eagerness is false. The instinct that Vanier may be playing games burns slowly inside the dark-skinned boy. Their hands meet and Jagnauth smiles. Then the smile fades quickly. It is said that Mr Jagnauth's face works like an electric switch: "KLIX!" A smile. "KLIX!" No smile.

The Headmaster continues to plead with them. 'And I expect you two to be just as courteous when you get to that office. The pair of you have gotten a chance in a million and such chances don't come easy. So, please, DON'T SPOIL IT.'

'No, sir,' mumbles Apata.

'Now you must go because you have to be there at half past eight and you must uphold the dignity of Charlestown Secondary – that dignity we have carved for ourselves by always being punctual.'

'Okay sir,' says Vanier.

'We're going, sir,' says Apata.

And so they leave together.

*   *   *

Whenever the question is asked: 'What does the Headmaster look like?' Time after time the answer ends up being worded thus: 'Is a fattish looking, dark-skin coolie man that does wear he glasses on he nose.'

Standing at his window, Mr Narish Jagnauth looks down the street until his boys have rounded the corner with the baker shop. He feels proud.

CHAPTER 9

Both look at the clock as they walk up to the floor above the main floor of the Education Ministry building that is situated in the street with the name Brickdam. It is minutes before the appointed time. This is the kind of punctuality that their Headmaster believes in. At the top of the stair Vanier asks an office boy, as old as his father, where they should sit to wait on Mr Edward Carrington.

'The White man?'

'Yeah.'

'You'all could sit over dere.' He points to a long seat, upholstered in dark brown, that already has one occupant, a heavily built Indian boy.

The boys glance around calmly taking in the office floor. Many desks are topped with covered typewriters and in-out trays. Only a few of the staff are around.

The heavily built schoolboy shifts and the Charlestown students sit. The Indian boy is smiling in his eagerness for companionship, with the result that in a short time the boys know each other.

The Indian boy's name is Cecil Gunraj of Berbice High and he is a sensitive young man and quickly senses the muted hostility between the lanky dark-skinned boy and the stocky light-skinned one, both from the same school.

Members of the Education office staff trickle in. Typing machines are uncovered and girls position themselves behind them. They dawdle and talk lightly of last night and this morning and even of tomorrow night. Then comes the sound of a car rolling over gravel to park in one of the executive spaces.

The girls who are dawdling change into alert responsive positions behind their desks, some pull open desk drawers, others roll sandwiches of paper and carbons into their machines. There are even a few who are honest enough to accept that they have nothing to do. They wait to be assigned duties. Finally, there are members of the office staff who have actually started working. There is the smell of coffee, too. From downstairs a coarse male voice orders someone with the name Welcome to fetch the "BLASTED!" ice from the dealer at the intersection; then the same voice says almost immediately after that, 'Yeh-yes, sir. N-no, sir. Around ten o' clock, sir. Right away s-sir.'

All these activities and events serve to distract the three youths who have been made tense by the waiting.

The tempo of the office floor increases.

Apata finds himself thinking of his own true friend, soon to leave the City, Gerald Tross. It's a pity that now, he, Apata will be going to King's College, his friend Gerald will be going back home to the country to become a farmer, a prestigeless country farmer. Apata realizes that he is playing a tattoo with his fingers against the wood of the seat's edge. Gerald *is* unlucky. What if I had a father, Apata wonders, and he decided something like that for me? What would I do? Apata thinks, then decides that he would do nothing. Like Gerald, he wouldn't do a thing.

Apata thinks now of his father and then he thinks of Captain Innes who claims to be a one-time close friend of his father, Harold Apata, Harry Apata. Lightly his fingers play a tattoo. He thinks of the telegram he sent home to Bartica: '*Rayburn. King.*'

A light-skinned Indian man is coming their way. He wears spectacles and the hair on his head is so sparse his skin shows through it. 'You remember him, Wendell?' Apata says to Vanier.

Vanier nods, sneers and turns to Gunraj to ask if he knows where King's College is. Gunraj says he does, that his father showed him the buildings which make up the King's College as they swept by on the way to the Stabroek car park.

59

The light skinned Indian Education officer walks past them. In his right hand he carries a case that has sides like a blacksmith's bellows. Over his other arm a long umbrella, cased in leather, hangs by an ornate handle. An inspector of schools in the city. In a clear tone of voice he tells the scholars 'Good morning!' before starting down the stairway up which they had come. Even watching his descent helps to kill the suspense of their waiting.

The office is really alive now. The staff are aware of the three students who have waited patiently to see the White man who now walks in by way of a special back-stairway from the parking space at the rear of the building. The time is twenty-nine minutes after eight o'clock.

The intermittent sound of the typewriters breaks the silence and it seems that whenever typewriters are not chattering, the brisk thumping of high-heeled shoes bridges the pauses.

'SO YOU'RE HERE AGAIN!' says a female voice that is filled with disgust and underlined with scorn. The three boys hear it and turn to see an old Negro woman with a swollen foot wrapped in brown gauze-like material. The voice belongs to a secretary, Miss Hamilton, before whom the Negro woman stands. The secretary, even though a Negro too, has a kind of skin hue of golden brown. Her hair is straight and piled high in a sophisticated style. Her face is heavily made up and lends a coldness to her personality. Without turning her head she asks, 'Which of you happens to be Wendell Vanier?' The woman before her clasps and unclasps the handles of a straw bag she holds in front of her. 'But-M-Miss Hamilton is long al'yo 'ave mih runnin' 'ere to get dis lil' money.'

'Listen woman!' snaps Miss Hamilton, 'I said! ... You have to come back tomorrow! I don't have time to waste now!'

Apata's brows knit involuntarily and he mumbles, addressing no one in particular, 'Some of these people in responsible positions really hoggish.'

'I don't know why them kinda people come into clean

offices like this,' says Vanier, referring to the old Negro woman who, walks away with dragging steps.

Apata turns directly to the light-skinned Vanier: 'What's so clean about *this* office, man?'

Vanier smiles. Apata's brows knit in irritation. Gunraj, as if prepared to make peace, watches them. 'What's so clean about this office, man?' Apata repeats, 'People like that painted-up red hog at that desk?'

Vanier rises to his feet. The heavily built Gunraj thinks that he does so to acknowledge that he is Wendell Vanier for the secretary had asked which of them happened to be Wendell Vanier. Apata thinks Vanier has risen for the same reason.

'MISS!' says Vanier. The secretary lifts her artificial lashes that sweep out above the open beige file folder before her. The lashes begin to flutter.

'Miss,' continues Wendell Vanier, 'this chap said that you are a painted-up red hog!'

'NO MAN VANIER!' blurts Apata.

'WHAT HE SAID?' asks Miss Hamilton tersely.

Apata grips Vanier's left arm and Vanier tries to wrench his arm away but Apata tightens his grip and jerks Vanier down, then sinks a deep punch into Vanier's solar plexus. Twisting from pain spreading out from below his sternum, Vanier falls on Apata and grips his head in a strangle hold. Apata pulls out of it and smashes a right to Vanier's face. Vanier falls back hard against the back rest of the seat and it topples over with a crash. The two grappling boys fall over with it with Vanier's arm cutting Apata's breath for this time he has Apata's neck. Gunraj dips into the scuffle and wrenches them apart. 'GOODNESS! WHAT HAVE WE HERE! I CAN'T BELIEVE THIS?'

It is the astonished voice of the White man they have come to see. He's quite red in the face, and understandably so. Mr Edward Carrington abhors indiscipline. His pale grey eyes drill into the dishevelled boys' faces. Vanier looks to the heel-marked floor. A spot of blood from his nose falls near the tip of his heavy leather shoes. He wipes his nostrils with the back of his hand while Apata looks out of a window that offers a view of the street. A twisted cripple in an old, baggy black serge suit slowly moves along with an up down corkscrew gait.

'FOLLOW ME, THE THREE OF YOU!' orders the White man, and whirls away to a roomy office with a large cream door. When he reaches it, he stops and adds, 'Would you also step in here, please, Miss Hamilton.'

*   *   *

'Friend . . . these things do happen, man.'

'Both of us should have been disqualified from entry, Gunraj. It wasn't fair.' Apata shakes his head. 'It ent fair, Gunraj.'

'I know it ent fair man Apata. Boy you ent got luck.' Gunraj feels stupid and inadequate for having nothing to say that might help his unfortunate acquaintance.

'I don't think is luck man,' says Apata. His face quivers and tears beginning to course down his cheeks glint in the mid-morning light.

They are approaching the Stabroek market and its yellow buses that wait to join the Water Street traffic flowing far below the clock tower. In Gunraj's heart he feels a great anxiety. Today he has seen how evil the world can be. He was there and saw what Wendell Vanier did to Michael Apata. Gunraj feels the hurtfulness of what has happened and wonders how, then, the dark-skinned boy must feel, having been unjustly victimized.

'Apata, my friend, this is not the end of the world and all of your chances. Everything happens for a reason. Never mind what your fellow man may do to you. Nobody can keep a good man down, never mind what race he is. No matter what colour his skin is.'

The heavily built Indian boy walks more slowly as they approach the intersection. 'Man Apata, I got to wait at this corner for my ol' man but since I will be going to school in town here, we will meet up man.'

Michael Apata looks at the paving under his feet. Crushed cigarette box, crushed soda cap-cork, broken pondfly. 'Nobody can keep a good man down, never mind what race he is. No matter what colour his skin ...' echoes encouragingly in Apata's head. A slight smile plays across his lips and he's silent and contemplative, until he muses aloud, 'Well, my grandfather always tells me that what is for somebody is always for somebody.' He scratches his left elbow and turns his head away from his new-found friend. 'I'm going to see you man Gunraj. We must meet again before we die.'

Cecil Gunraj watches him as Apata walks away. Soon he will be out of sight, lost in the pedestrian traffic.

A low wailing note sounds out and climbs steadily, then holds: The ten o'clock horn that reminds one so easily that it's Friday in Georgetown City.

*   *   *

'Mr Carrington has advised that the student Michael Rayburn Apata, despite his attainment of such high marks in the entrance exam, should not be granted admission into King's College.' Mr Jagnauth was thus informed immediately after it was verified that the fracas on the Education office floor was started by the student who, allegedly, struck the first blow.

CHAPTER 10

The gusty ocean breeze buffets their bodies and brings them snatches of the song being sung by the one-armed man sitting out on the stone jetty. Gerald Tross looks at Michael's face and sees bewilderment there. He pats his friend's shoulder ... then grips it and squeezes.

'That's a bitch you know. That White man's a real White man,' says Michael calmly.

'Well,' Gerald adds, 'this is British Guiana, you know. They hold the ropes, man.'

Apata nods his head. Cecil Gunraj's words come back to him: 'Nobody could keep a good man down ... never mind what race he is.'

'The boy Vanier ...' Apata says thoughtfully.

'It's hard to believe,' says Gerald, 'that after starting the whole thing in that office, his father came in to see Jaggy – bringing a police along on top the bargain.'

'They're right, man. I started it, not Vanier.'

'I don't see it so. I think the man acted like a snake.'

Apata shakes his head. 'I'm glad nothing came out of it. The police was understanding.' Apata shrugs his shoulders. 'Somehow the great Mr Vanier agreed that enough was enough and decided to let it pass.'

Gerald sucks his teeth then says, 'Maybe it was the satisfaction that his son's academic rival was ruthlessly debarred. Maybe he thought that that was enough punishment for touching his precious son.'

Apata pries a fragment of a little shell from the concrete showing between his thighs. 'People like myself,' he says, 'can't hurt people like the Vaniers. Cuff ent nothing in comparison to what they could dish out.'

'Don't worry with the Vaniers of this world man.'

'Jaggy feel wrong up about the whole affair boy. The man get vex with me, but I think he understand what happen at Brickdam there. He told me he would write a letter that I could give to my grandfather.'

'What kind of letter?'

'A letter explaining how I got blocked.'

'That's good.'

Michael smiles, scratches his head. 'Yeah ... at least it would take some of the heat off me.'

'Jaggy is an alright chap.'

'Listen to that one-armed chap singing over there. People would say he's mad, you know.'

'I don't think he's mad,' says Gerald.

'Something should be done about men like Edward Carrington!'

'Let's listen to the man singing. It's a nice song,' says Gerald, thinking that Michael should shift from his present stream of thought, since worry corrodes the mind.

'When I was small,' Michael says, 'I knew a boy named Matthew.'

'Amerindian?'

'Yeah ... how did you guess?'

'Kidneys boy,' purrs Gerald patting his right temple, 'kidneys!'

Apata laughs.

'That you can laugh is a good sign, boy,' says Gerald Tross and Apata decides not to talk of Matthew and the swimming times they had in the Essequibo river back home.

'I feel the evil in me retreating, Gerald.'

'You have evil in you? Evil's a dark bitter thing and it ent three cents ugly and smelly.'

'There's evil in everybody, boy. Since Eve ate the forbidden fruit she gave each and every one of us a little evil in our blood.'

'Hope I ent have much.'

'Naa,' says Michael, 'you ent have much.'

Mike hums along with the one-armed man singing out on the jetty that angles out not far from where they are sitting.

> "*Onward Christian soldiers* ...
> *Marching as to war* ...
> *With the cross of* ..."

'Suddenly I'm getting a don't care feeling,' Michael says.

'What you mean, Mike?'

Apata with a grim look, shakes his head. 'Ent know how to explain it.'

'Tell me about your grandfather,' says Gerald Tross, working once more at diverting his friend's thoughts from bitterness. He knows how much Michael's grandfather is interwoven with Michael's life.

Silently, Michael bends his head and gazes at a gnarled and twisted piece of driftwood below the stone wall on which they sit. Gerald feels a change of mood sweeping over his friend.

'I feel the evil coming back,' says Apata, knowing that it had never deserted him. Thinking of old Josh Smith ... he is sure the telegram of his success had made the old man uncork his bush rum.

The evening is cool and the sinking sun casts golden rays over everything unshaded.

Apata lays himself back and the sunlight gleams on the dark angular planes of his face as he gazes at the sky. 'My grandfather says he started poor – as a poor boy. He's no poor boy now. Neither is he a stinkingly rich old man. Our house at Bartica stands on good posts and there's a special room, a kind of guest room, that would make anybody I invited from Georgetown, welcome.

'He said that when I was small, we lived at another place, and that it was easy to see the hill, on which we now live, from that little place which was on the flats. His best friend, he always tells me, was a man called Mason. I knew him only a little. He and grandfather used to play draughts outside under a big mango tree that was not far from the little place we had.' Apata chuckles. 'He tells me that I always used to be giving my grandmother hell.

66

'Grandfather Josh is a gold man in a kind of retirement. He's got a little claim that still gives him something. He never really struck it rich, to get a name like Vanier's father, but he gets enough to send a bit down for my upkeep.

'Grandfather Josh likes to argue about politics. He's one old man I know who doesn't suffer from ... from ... you know that way most of our old people glorify and make demigods of the British royalty?'

'Yeah.'

'Well my grandfather is not like that.' Michael Apata laughs. 'Ol' Josh tell a man once that the queen goes to the latrine just like everybody and he wasn't going to make no promises to anybody that he'd turn into a pillar of salt if he sees the governor.' Apata inhales deeply. Gerald is glad that his friend is beginning to talk more calmly.

'From the front windows you could see when the steamer *Northcut* comes in from Parika and you could see the Grumman seaplanes coming in to land.'

Apata turns onto an elbow and contemplates a big-headed ant. It moves past his finger and gets into a crack on the solid concrete surface shared by others. Now Apata appears blank and Gerald feels his spirit tiring.

'But everything ent right with Grandfather Josh, you know. He's getting some problems with a Portuguese man who has a claim on the old man's gold works.'

'What kind of rights this man got?'

'Is a complicated thing.' The ant re-appears. 'Grandfather Josh and this chap father had some kind of a partnership going and the man died, and then a whole lotta fishy business start with the son. The thing tiring out the ol' man!' Apata sucks his teeth and crushes the ant with a thumbnail. Gerald realizes, that having set out to shift his friend's mind from worry, he has only succeeded in shifting it from the one worry to another. It seems to Gerald now, as though there's nothing to life but worry. He raises himself. Standing, he looks down at his friend.

'What you want to be when you grow up, Mike?' he asks.

'If I tell you,' says Apata, 'you won't believe.'

'What? A priest?'

'NAA!'

'What?'

'Let's go home man,' says Apata. He stretches a hand out to Gerald and Gerald pulls him to his feet. The ocean's breezes buffet their bodies.

'Well,' Apata declares, then yawns widely, 'not bad for a day's happenings. Fought like a fool in the people's fancy office, lost the biggest moment I ever dreamed of, made Uncle Joel leave his work to end up in Jaggy's office with Vanier's father and a big police. Not bad at all.'

'Closing week Mike. Going to school tomorrow?'

Michael laughs quietly. 'Yeah,' he says, and begins to run on the spot.

*   *   *

'Really . . . I do love Guiana,' says the White woman with the Grecian nose. Her Guiana sounds like "Goo-yan-nawh". But neither her perfumed presence nor the palm plants that grace the hotel's lobby, where they sit, affects any change in the way her husband feels.

Kingston, Georgetown. The traffic of Main Street is negligible, for it is after five in the afternoon. At this time, the city has become a haven for those who abhor pedestrian bustle and vehicular clatter and zoom. Edward Carrington dislikes mammoth cities like the one in which he was born. He has accepted a special posting to British Guiana for that very reason. He desired a country that was backward enough to have some peace. 'I never dreamt that Guiana would be like this,' says his wife. 'And I'm being honest, Edward. This morning, instead of sending Maggie to the market I went myself. Oh!' In her eyes there is a sparkle and her little lips, like a large cherry split in halves and pressed back together on an after-thought, holds a smile as she turns a swizzle-stick in her tall drink of gin and coconut water.

Her husband sits with his hands in his pockets and looks past the other tables to the street and across the street to whatever he could make out of the hibiscus hedge that flanks the open gate to the Catholic church. On the church the figures of the Virgin Mary and baby Jesus are just below the clock with Roman numerals. The clock tower grows from the belfry, and the ornate cross sprouts from the clock tower and it is below a sky flecked with clean cirrus clouds through which the dying afternoon sunlight gleams.

'"And I have done a hellish thing ... and it will work me woe,"' he says.

'What ails thee my dear Edward?' she responds playing a game they invented after they met at a drama club in London, a little love game. But the look on dear Edward's face suggests a real life drama. He smiles weakly and sips his drink. As he puts his glass down he shakes his head.

'I still cannot stand Kaffirs,' he says, 'especially when they're very dark and carry a savage Africanism about their faces, animal cruelty on their brows and thick grotesque lips.' He sighs.

'But Edward, you must fight against that part of yourself. OH, EDWARD!'

'That I know my cherry ... that I do know,' he says quietly. She touches his hand tenderly. A smile crinkles under an eye. 'This morning ...' he says, 'I broke the pen and hanged the chances of a brilliant Black who should have been allowed a chance to go to the best school here for boys ...'

'King's College?'

He nods.

'What was he like?'

'Like a terrible black jungle cat.'

Shaking her head: 'You do sound hopeless.' She isn't angry. On her face there's that amused look that a mother may give a son after a crisis moment of anger has passed.

He sips his gin and coconut water and feels calm sweeping through his mind. He closes his eyes. At that moment a tall dark-skinned youth with a companion jogs by, having come all the way from the sea wall.

CHAPTER 11

Mrs Bailey folds in her lips and bites in on them every time she comes down with the pressing iron to begin a smoothing run on Michael's short pants on the board. There's a hymn on her breath: *What a friend we have in Jesus*, she sings lightly. 'O what sins and griefs to bear ...'

'Beverley!'

'Yes, Mommy?'

'Don't put wares on that window sill, you know!'

'A'right, Mommy.'

Grumbles Mrs Bailey, 'Like you like to hear that man fret!'

Having made a smooth run to complete a neat seam she places the iron back on the little coal pot. She picks up a shirt and shakes it out. In the background Beverley is bent over the sink and from below the smell of the seedy glue being boiled comes up to them. Mrs Bailey wrinkles her nostrils. 'God!' she whispers to herself, 'I don't like how that thing does smell.'

'MIKE!' she hears her husband call from below.

'Coming, Uncle Joel.'

'Calculate this thing for me, man. You fast.'

Mrs Bailey shakes her head. 'But why Michael had to hit the red boy in the people office for?' she says aloud to herself.

'Why you like to talk to yourself so, Mommy?'

'Is only when you answer yo'self, yo' gone mad! So leave me alone. Plenty o' we does talk to we-self. And don't fo'get that you have to go for that milk.'

'No Mommy.'

Tomorrow, Monday, Michael goes to school. Mrs Bailey sucks her teeth. This week would have been the last week in

Jagnauth's school. Next term he should have started going to King's College. *Should have*. Not any more.

'Why Mike had to strike the damn red-man son?' She sucks her teeth.

'Mommy, I'm going now for the milk,' says Beverley.

'Take the enamel mug!'

'Man Mommy ...' she begins fretfully.

'I SAY TAKE THE ENAMEL MUG! WHAT HAPPEN TO IT? WE BLACK PEOPLE GOT TOO MUCH BLASTED PRIDE FOR ANYTHING GOOD!'

Beverley sulks away to the bedroom, but Mrs Bailey does not see her.

'Mike?' she hears Beverley calling from the bedroom window.

'Girl what you calling Mike for? Mike doing something for you' father!'

'He finish!'

Mrs Bailey wishes her husband had not said so. She knows that there's a tenderness between her daughter and Michael, but she doesn't like it. She's grateful to his grandmother Jane for bringing her up, but she still doesn't like it. She's a mother now, her own woman now, and no form of indebtedness should foil her judgement in something concerning her own daughter. *She doesn't like it*. Likes Michael, yes; but this deep attachment between Beverley and Michael she doesn't. She had told Joel her husband about it, but Joel saw nothing to it, sees nothing to it and would do nothing about it. The most he agreed on was that, at those times when they both would be out, Beverley would stay with his sister who lives in Albouystown.

But Beverley and Michael are aware of why this arrangement was thought necessary. Between them they have agreed not to attempt love making at this time. On that score, a few boys have tried to scare Michael. 'Boy, you stupid boy!' one repeatedly tells him, 'You saving up duh girl fuh somebody else to knock out before you!' But such taunts never did and do not now perturb young Apata. He loves Beverley and Beverley loves him. That he's sure of.

There's a boy who Mrs Bailey hopes Beverley would take to. He is the son of Mr Bernard the milk man. 'Girl?' the milk man's wife said one time to Mrs Bailey, 'Like my Dennis liking Beverley!' The milk man's wife had laughed at this point. 'But that girl don't even voonks on he. That Dennis liking Beverley is something strange. Even he father end up wondering if the girl got something special. Dennis is a boy who used to show no interest in girls. All Dennis friends got girl friends or some lil' girl they saying they like ... but not that Dennis. Leh me give you this joke.

'One day he father say to he, "Boy, when me dead you getting all them cow you see grazing on dat dam, you getting the butcher shop downstairs and the two in the market. And what? You ent even have a girlfriend. You ent going to get married?"

'Well Dennis tell he father that is not that he don't like girls, but is just that he didn' see no girl thet he like.' She laughed. 'But now is a different story. When Beverley come he does hussle to sell she milk and to give she extras too.'

'Well,' Mrs Bailey had said lightly, 'if Beverley don't like he, what we going do girl?'

Mr Bernard is part Indian part Portuguese part Chinese and a whole lot of Negro. His wife is a brown-skinned woman, mixed also, who was a runner-up, some years ago, in a popular beauty contest. Having come together they produced quite a handsome boy by a European yardstick of judgement. Dennis's skin is creamy. The pupils of his eyes are hazel. His hair is like an Ethiopian's and his manner is as tender as his voice is tender. To Beverley Bailey, there is something about Dennis Bernard that is effeminate. She doesn't like him for whatever it happens to be. She loves Michael for everything even though if she were to detail those specific things that make up everything, she would be stumped.

But her mother likes Dennis and wishes her daughter, who'd soon be grown enough, could see him as a future husband. Inheritance is lined up for him. The procreation of children with opportune skin hues seem lined up too. And those are things, main things, Negro mothers can find themselves hoping to happen to their daughters in this time.

Mrs Bailey watches Michael and Beverley as they walk out to the road. She feels the happiness they support between them. Mr Bailey watches too from where he works, and also feels the happiness they support between them. 'Twist it turn it,' he tells himself, 'King's College or King's College not, that boy will make a name for himself in this place, in this colony.'

The gimlet bites deeper into the mortice joint.

Mr Bailey thinks of his daughter, 'She likes Michael ... I thought they'd learn to see each other as brother and sister but ...'

The gimlet bites deeper into the joint.

'... things don't go the way we see things. Pearl wouldn' accept it. If Beverley like Michael and Michael like Beverley ...' He scratches behind an ear. '... we can't put him out or send him back to Bartica because of that.'

The bit of the miniature hand drill comes through. He pulls it out, makes the hole neat, then blows through it.

The thing that baffles Mr Bailey though, is Michael's calm settling to his fate after being denied the K.C. opportunity. To the man it just isn't natural. After it happened Michael was visibly upset and twisted about it. But now, three days later the boy seems to be his old self again, laughing and not at all reluctant to continue at the same school come the new term when he should have started going to King's College.

Mr Bailey takes up the thin saw that can cut around corners. He brushes the silverballi wood shavings from the worn and ready work-bench then clamps the panel of wood on it. He prepares to cut from the light panel of wood, the shape of a shamrock.

'If I say I understand that boy,' he mumbles, 'I'd be lying.'

The footsteps of his wife recede from that part of the house that faces the road and he knows that, like him, she had been watching.

CHAPTER 12

A telegram boy hops off his bicycle and begins ringing the bell as he pushes the duck-bellied contraption over a bridge.

From the open doorway of a bottom-house enclosure a middle-aged man in a string vest emerges.

'MORNING!' blurts the boy. 'TELEGRAM!'

'Telegram?' The man frowns.

'For Michael Apata in care of Joel – Mr Joel Bailey.'

'That is me.' Mr Bailey takes it, signs for it. 'A'right boy.' Mr Bailey opens it, scans and hustles upstairs. 'Pearly?' he calls out to his wife scrubbing a pot in the kitchen. 'Pearly! The boy grandfather like he sick bad!'

'Telegram just come?' she asks. He says yes, and she looks bewildered.

That evening Michael enters. He tells them good afternoon and gets a strained reply. Mr Bailey has a document open in his right hand.

'Something wrong, Uncle Joel?'

The man nods. 'You grandfather sick and you have to go home little bit.'

*   *   *

The *Lady Northcut* labours on to Bartica. From a wing of the Captain's bridge, a White man uses a spring-wound camera. From below the forecastle Michael Apata watches him casually then looks away to the shoreline on which he has trained his camera.

Someone within earshot says, 'Dat nah laugh story mate-o.

74

Hinnah awe dis fam'lee, everytime fowl cock put 'e head ina awe door an' mek suh: "COCKA-DOODLE-DOO!" Nah worry ask – COL' PORK!'

'It seems every family got their own death omens,' says the man he speaks to. 'In our family it always happens that glass somehow falls and breaks.'

Michael takes a deep breath. A rankness rises from the river. He has heard that when a rankness rises from the river someone is earmarked for Neptune's bosom.

'Ah going to see a sister I ent see for quite a long time,' says someone else to a companion.

'You' sistah ah live wheh life deh chap. Wes'Coas' Berbice nah gah life like Bartica.'

'MAN? AH HEAR OBEAH TEARIN' ASS AT BARTICA!'

'Obeah?'

'Yes man. Yesterday a man who does come down tell me that an old chap dying right now from obeah.'

'Obeah? Me livin' at Bartica and me ent know 'bout no . . . OH! JOSH SMITH!'

'Well de chap didn' tell me no name.'

'Yes . . . true, is ol' Josh Smith.'

*   *   *

Instead of his grandmother Jane, old Mrs Carey, a fifty year-old devout Christian friend to the home, greets Michael. She's basically Portuguese, but mixed with Chinese, Indian, and Negro.

'Rayburn child?'

'Aunt Carey.'

He comes into the house, walks to the lunch table and lays his duffle bag on a chair there.

'You' grandfather get worse this morning, boy, so I think the very same time you did travelling up to here, they did travelling down to the old village.

'Anyway, I going to get something for you to eat and afterwards you can catch Johnny launch and go up. You' grandfather done arrange it with Johnny.'

'A'right Aunty Carey.'

The woman moves away to the kitchen. 'Nothing my boy,' she says, 'goes unpaid.'

'What happen to my grandfather, Aunt Carey?'

But Aunt Carey sings a hymn of joy and peace-ables. Looking down from a window nearest the dining table Michael looks over the houses in the cross streets to the river which is silvered in parts.

Apata turns away from the window and over the song says: 'AUNTY?'

'Yes, son?'

'What happen to grandfather Josh?'

'Iniquity, boy.'

'And the claim, Aunty, what happen to it?'

'Ow boy, he lose it. He lose the whole thing.'

She comes out with food. She calls him to the table. She prays whilst he sits cold at heart to think of the old man sickened by loss. To Michael loss *is* inequity. If grandfather Josh has lost his claim, Apata thinks, it means that the rival party has done something legally strong. Maybe grandfather's partner wasn't honest in the original partnership to the point that the son could have taken over the whole claim from grandfather.

Inequity, Michael tells himself, may well be a losing blow, one too strong for the old man who always played fair with those whom he thought of as close to him.

'Rayburn boy, eat the lil' food before it get cold on you.'

Michael takes up the spoon.

*   *   *

The day is close. It is now minutes to three. Michael walks hesitantly down the slope of the hill. At the base he walks around a great embedded stone onto which he scampered as a child. Now Michael is blind to old memories. Having rounded the monument, he takes to the road that leads down to the river and Johnny's boat in which an engine, that used to be a truck's, grumbles.

CHAPTER 13

Storm clouds hang in Michael Apata's heart. He watches the Parika ferry stelling drawing nearer. Soon the steamer would brace and the lines would be hurled. Soon she'd be made tight against the pier. Soon the disembarkation.

'I'll find Gerald,' Michael says to himself. In the background, Captain Innes shakes his head and thinks that being a motherless, fatherless, grandfatherless, and who knows ... maybe grandmotherless soon ... is the most unfortunate thing that should happen to the strongest of persons and much worse to a sixteen year-old.

The first mate who went to the funeral and later spoke of it, said, 'Cappy, that young chap ent shed a tear.'

The Captain gives instructions for mooring and feels sorry for young Apata who gazes from the opposite wing of the bridge to the water. The Captain knows that there's nothing to fleece the flesh from the bones of one struck by grief like internal weeping. He feels sorry for Michael.

The engines grumble and the water churns muddy below the stern. Bells ring. The ropes snake out to the wharf that looks like a market, even a carnival; and in the background of the wharf's babbling the boat train squeals as it shunts.

Sunlight bathes the gangplanks.

*　　*　　*

Parika is a farming village. Here the land is sacred and the average person is a farmer and talks of the soil. The average person here is close to the soil and has no craving to speak

Queen's English. Here, at Parika village, it is known that the Georgetown city dwellers claim that they have fun listening to the broken-English speech patterns – the creolese of the deep-country dwellers. But here at Parika there's no great value to proper delivery. The only ones villagers here expect proper delivery from are the school people, the Headmaster and his teachers choked with bow ties and respectability. The villagers send their children to school for it is always a good thing to be able to read and write and it is a good thing if, through the magic of education, a man has a doctor or a lawyer in the family. But those are side things because farming and the land comes first. The Indians and the Negroes are farmers here; and the Negroes here, unlike those in the city, are not foolish as the city Negro who feels that to love the land and be a farmer is to be insignificantly *peasant*.

Here, at Parika, mud squelches between the toes of hardened shoeless feet. Here, at Parika, women know and show their strength in working along with their men and, though their skins aren't smooth, the men make life with their women, for the land marries them complete.

'Ah who yo' want small bhai?'

'Tross ... he have a son who uses to go to school in 'Town.'

'Oh-ho, YO WANT LIL' JERRY! A'right. Mih'ah guh ina de same direcshan suh fallah mih. Leh we guh.'

The road is flanked by canals over which bridges run to consecutive front yards, and yards without fruit trees are rare. Ask the city dweller why he has come to Parika and the answer can easily be, 'Fruits,' or 'Coconut water'.

The majority of the houses here are humble, shingled, one-bedroomed affairs. But, as beginnings, they are comfort for many and as endings too. Looking off the road of hardened dirt Michael sees a carpenter adding finishing touches to a coffin. A woman, head tied and face encased in her hands, sits in apparent misery on the short stair of a frail looking house in front of which the coffin-maker works.

Apata's companion waves solemnly and the coffin-maker waves back.

'Ow ...' Apata's companion says, 'mih really sarry fuh dah 'oman, mih tell yo'. Hymahrally snake bite she husban' ah train line. 'E dead yestahday a' de haspital.'

Apata thinks of his grandfather folded in a great pot in a cave in the old village.

Breezes blow through the trees, and the coconut palms whisper below the shrilling of a kiskadee from a mango tree not too long passed. Apata picks a blue flower from the roadside, crushes it, then sniffs at his fingers. And to him it's as though everything smells of death.

CHAPTER 14

'OH SHIT! MIKE?'

And Michael's hand is gripped in his. 'Mikey boy—' And Michael bursts into tears for his grandfather.

'The ol' man gone Jerry.'

'When he died, Mike?'

Apata shakes his head.

'Ease up, don't question he too much,' Gerald tells himself. 'He'll tell you eventually.'

The sound of farming tools under the house tells him that his father has come back from helping out their sick neighbour. 'Mikey, excuse me. I'm coming back just now.' Michael nods and Gerald moves off.

Downstairs, Gerald confronts his father and tells him about his friend.

'Well yes,' says Farmer Tross. 'Nothing wrang hif he stay a coupla days wid we hay. Mih sad to hear dat 'e gran'father dead.'

Gerald leaves the old man and goes back upstairs.

'How's life on the farm?' Apata asks easily, as if he has to fill the silence between them.

'I like it,' says Gerald, then adds, 'You don't want to stay here a few days? Pull your mind back together?'

'I would like that.' Apata tries to smile and finds it difficult. 'But what would your father . . . ?'

'I already asked Daddy. No problem. It's alright.'

Apata gets to his feet, looks through a window, and sees the section of a trunk of a coconut tree outside. 'I think I can climb one of these things you know.'

Gerald laughs. 'If I was still in Georgetown, I wouldn't have learnt how. But I'm going to teach you. We have some dwarf nut-trees at the back. You'll start by climbing one of those. But how's the city?'

'Don't know, boy.'

Gerald grins. 'How's Beverley?'

'She should be okay.' Apata takes a deep breath. 'You believe in obeah, Jerry?'

'Bunkum.'

'That's what I used to think, too.'

'USED TO THINK?'

'Yeah ... until I saw my grandfather on his death bed.'

'How he died?'

Farmer Tross comes into the living room where the boys are talking.

'GOOD AFTAHNOON! GOOD AFTAHNOON!' he says loudly and Apata turns to face him respectfully.

'Michael, this is my father.'

Michael moves forward and shakes the elderly man's hand. It is indeed a man's hand. 'Pleased to meet you, sir,' says Apata.

'Gerald tell me dat you is de best friend he gat, and in dat case, yo' mo' dan welcome hay. Yo' guh meet Gerald mother latah. She get lil narah so she gone ah she Nennen to get it 'noint'.

Apata smiles for the man hasn't yet released his hand and it seems that he must squeeze in encouragement with the weighty words in his welcoming speech, 'Well son,' he says gravely now. 'Jerry tell mih dat you' gramfather hexpire. Ah sarry to hear dat ... but all in all, ah suh life stay, and you has to stand up like a man-child!' He releases Apata's hand. 'Well den, Gerald guh make yo' comfuhtable.' He leaves and Apata sits in a chair made out of cane peel strips. 'I like the man,' he says and Gerald mumbles, to himself, the story of Solomon a' Grundy. Ask him why and he will tell you he does not know. Just some nonsense that can fill anyone's mind at times.

Apata thinks of his grandmother Jane. She won't last very long. He knows. But those ants ...

'I saw my grandfather die, boy,' he says to the chair's left side arm rest as he runs an index finger over it. Then he shakes his head. 'When he let out his last breath, a thick stream of big-head ants, red ants, poured out through his mouth and nostrils and ears and disappeared just so.'

'DISAPPEARED JUST SO?'

Michael takes a deep breath and says nothing more. Gerald Tross also says nothing. Only his slightly raised brows speak of incomprehensible mysteries.

*　　*　　*

It is night in Parika village. The moon is full and the dirt road, bordered by canals, looks cream-coloured under its glare. Michael and Gerald stand on the Tross's bridge. Like many others, bridge-standing is a leisure occupation in this village like many other villages on the coast through which the road runs, for there are no cinemas here, nor band-stands, only a dancehall for the occasional big dance or reception after a wedding.

'I like Beverley, man,' Mike says suddenly, 'But I'm not going to stay there longer from now.'

'What you're going to do?'

'Leave school ... work ... take care of my grandmother.' Smiles. 'Maybe persuade her not to follow old Josh in too much of a hurry. Old people go like that you know.'

Gerald nods a bit, then says, 'How you feel, man?'

'Tell you the truth, Jerry ... I feel lost. Like how we're here now, I feel al'right.' He sucks his teeth. 'I don't know how I feel.' He laughs like one embarrassed.

'Hear Mike, relax.'

'Beverley mother don't like me for her daughter, you know.'

'Why you say that?'

'I know,' says Apata.

'Hey man Mike! Relax as I told you.' He sees that Apata is crying again.

The gay voice of village boys and girls playing yard

games come to them: 'JOMBIE LEF' 'E PIPE HAY?' sings a piping girlish voice. 'NO-KANNO-KAH!' comes a mixed-toned reply in a chorus. 'ALTHEA!' a woman's voice pitches in. 'ALTHEA! GIRL HOW MUCH TIME MIH GAFFA TELL YO' NAT TO LEAVE DAT POE-ZEE UNDAH DE BACK STEP? ALTHEA! ALTHEA!! HEAR YEH! NAH LEH ME PUT DE RAHD AH COR-RECSHAN PON YOU' LIL RED TAIL, YEH!'

'You're going to get married, Gerald?'

'Don't know, boy. You?'

'Don't know too.'

'Why you ask though, Mike?'

Apata laughs shyly for an answer.

'Yeah ... why you ask?' persists Gerald.

'If I ask you to marry Beverley when you attain a good age ...' Apata tells his friend with a hold-don't-interrupt gesture. Then he finishes with, 'Would you do it?'

Gerald Tross scratches behind an ear then tells Michael that indeed there are more mad people outside than inside. Both break into laughter that's real but only Michael knows that the question he has asked is actually serious. Gerald would come to realize this a few years later.

'Ring game! Ring game!' chants a piping girlish voice.

'Coloured girl!'

'NO ... WE NAH WAN' PLAY DAH NO-MOE. DAT STALE!'

'Well wha' we gon play?'

The moon slips behind a dark patch of cloud.

'You speak well, you know, Michael, I mean good English.'

The moon emerges and the moonlight bathes once more.

'So why you thinking of leaving school, Mike?'

'What's in school for me, Gerald?'

The moon enters a long dark stretch of cloud.

'You don't want to make it like Norman Cameron no more?'

'What's to make anything in this country, Gerald?'

Gerald sticks his hands deeper in his trouser's pockets and gazes down at the dark face of the water below them.

The moon's journey through the dark stretch of cloud seems endless.

PART TWO

1958

CHAPTER 15

Beverley Bailey thinks of Michael Apata the schoolboy that he was four years ago. So much has happened since that time. Four years ago his grandfather died. Four years ago his grandmother also died. Beverley's father, too, has died. Three years ago by drowning. And Mommy's changing into something terrible. Things are bad and Beverley thinks of Michael somewhere in the interior. Through years past he has been writing to her from "my wilderness". That has been Michael's address: "My Wilderness". And then letters stopped for a seeming lifetime to Beverley, until yesterday. She presses her bosom and feels Michael's letter on her young breasts.

Her father's tools, in a box downstairs, lie unused. The saws long to grate their teeth against the sweetness of grains and an assortment of chisels think of days when they bit lovingly into the resilience of wood. The planes dream of rough surfaces to make as smooth as glass. The hammers miss their pounding moments and the gimlet his piercing times. The glue pot, smoothly lined with the brown residue, thinks of fire. Who knows the language of inanimate things? Who will tell them that their master's hands live no more?

The day is Sunday and her mother sits in a chair that faces the back of the yard and on to another street where pan-men practise the same love-lost piece they battled with last Sunday.

Pearly Bailey talks to herself and Beverley Bailey thinks its something that her mother should stop. First there's the self-talking then the tears that always follow.

'Mommy?'

'Yes Beverley?' her mother answers in a whisper.

'Mommy, stop this crying. Mommy ... Mommy it ent good for you.'

Mommy cries more heavily perplexing her daughter.

'Life bad to we Bevy.'

'To many people, too, Mommy. Not only us. But we got to try not to fold up, man Mommy.'

'Ow Bevy, you think if you father was alive I wouldav ended up selling bread? And you think you'd have to come out of Carnegie and work in an Indian people store?'

'Life ent fine, Mommy, but we got to make out the best we can, Mommy.'

Beverley pats her mother's shoulder and the woman ceases to whimper. It is always like this on Sundays. The self-pitying and the reflections. Beverley has grown to hate Sundays.

Beverley thinks of Michael and the way they parted after his grandmother died. He kissed her truly for the first time then.

'I will live at our house in Bartica. For a while I'll live there,' he had said, 'Though I really don't know what I'll do after a while. Maybe I'll get a job.'

'What kind of job you could get there, Mike?'

'River.'

'RIVER?'

'I'm good with boats, Bevy.'

He had kissed her and left but returned one year after because of respect and love when Joel Bailey died.

When Michael saw her, he had seen a well-grown girl. A woman, a ripe woman and that was the time he made deep love to her for the first time. One day after the funeral. Then he left, then a few letters from him, then nothing, until yesterday.

'Mommy?'

Mrs Bailey doesn't answer. Beverley unfolds the letter in her palms. She moves closer to her mother. 'Mommy ... Michael write.'

88

'How's he?' she asks in a dying mechanical tone. Defeatedly.

'He's working on a tug boat up the Potaro river.'

'Why he wasn' writing all the time?'

'He wasn't settled, Mommy.'

'You could have been quite somebody if you had taken on Dennis, you know.'

'Mommy, I couldn't take Dennis. I don't love Dennis.'

'Love, Beverley? You could have been something in that family.'

Beverley sighs. 'Yes, Mommy ... and you would have been something, too.'

Then she is sorry she has said it for Pearly Bailey begins to cry again.

'Ow Joel, yo' dead and leave eye-pass only for me,' she whimpers.

'Mommy, I'm sorry I said that. True, Mommy ... really sorry.'

But Mrs Bailey doesn't appear to have heard. She continues crying and Beverley turns and walks through the door.

Sitting on the neglected workbench she remembers it was there that she and Michael first made love. Bedding smuggled from upstairs, had made the love-nest less uncomfortable but the hardness had still come through. Though, as the workbench was hard, so Michael had been tender.

Beverley dangles her legs and gazes down to the open letter in her lap:

Dear Beverley, my love,

These lines you read are lines I hope will touch you as I want to touch you as I yearn to touch your tender sweetness that gives me faith as I daily ply this turbulent river which has taken lives and will take more lives. But this river cannot take my life because my life is for you. I love you Beverley Bailey.

Forgive me for not writing you for such a long time. I did not know what to write. I couldn't find myself. I was lost in the interior of myself.

I will be coming down to Georgetown sometime this month. I think it will be more to the end. I would bring something for you and something for your mother. How is she? Tell her hello for me. Beverley, I hope things are not too rough with the home. What are you doing? Do you still love me as I love you? Don't get angry girl. I am only joking. Remember that time when I asked you in the cinema if you would still like me if you were red?

I'm now working on a tug up the Potaro river. It's a big logging business tug. The times when you were not hearing from me were times when I seemed to have no fixed abode. I was all over the place. I was like a rolling stone that gathered no moss. I tried diamond diving, but wasn't very lucky at it. Going down was alright, but coming up was always funny. The pump always broke down and things like that. The last time I was trapped in an under-water cave, anyway, I came out. An old Amerindian man seriously believed that water people wanted me. (Laugh.) Eventually the boss of the outfit said that we weren't making much and that I had to be laid off. The other men told me that the boss really thought that I was a Jonah: bad luck. Anyway this new job seems to be working out fine so far. The money is good, and I am controlling myself and I am saving some of it so that I can bring something for you. We all need money Bevs so I'm not really planning to buy you. (Smile.)

When I come down this month-end I will be asking for your hand in marriage. I am praying that your mother agrees and gives me consent.

Do you write Gerald, Beverley? If you hardly do then step up your correspondence. Other than you, he's all I've got. He is my spiritual brother.

> *Yours Until Death,*
> *Michael.*

Beverley folds the letter and thinks of her mother's life. Pearl Bailey is acting faithful past death. Joel, she said, was the last man for her. 'Don't want no other man, Bevy.'

Countless times Beverley wanted to ask her what then *she* Beverley should do? Beverley wants to know if she must be her mother's nurse maid. She wants to know if she must be by her mother's side the rest of her life. She knows that her mother is being selfish, for Beverley knows that like her mother she, Beverley, is also a woman and a woman needs to be at the side of her man. As her mother had been by the side of her father. But if her mother persists on being the mourning widow, it will be hard for her to accept Michael's proposal of marriage or anyone else's. But, thinks Beverley, it seems that Mommy would allow me to marry a Dennis Bernard quickly. 'That is the part of you I'm beginning to hate, Mommy. You're weak, Mommy.'

Beverley leaves the workshop and walks through the tall grass converging on the workshop's door. She goes upstairs. Her mother still gazes through the window but on her face an evil reigns. Lately Beverley has seen this mean look on her mother's face, an evil kind of countenance. But why Mommy's changing herself like this? Why is she soaking herself in this whole self-pity thing? Beverley wonders what would make her snap out of it:

'Mommy . . . Michael write to say that he want to marry me.'

'NOT OVER MY DEAD BODY BEV'LEY!' Mrs Bailey explodes. 'NOT THAT MICHAEL!'

'But Mommy . . . I like Mike . . . love Michael . . . Both you and Daddy always know that I love Michael. And Michael feel the same for me, Mommy.'

'BUT BEV'LEY, YOU ENT BIG YOU KNOW!' warns Mrs Bailey. 'YOU ENT BIG YOU KNOW!'

'Mommy,' says Beverley quietly and without venom, 'is only Michael I would ever marry. And Mommy, you can't make me marry anybody else but who I want to marry.'

Mrs Bailey rises up with a rediscovered mother-fire, 'SO YOU GIVING ME RUDENESS?'

'No Mommy.'

'WELL I'M TELLING YOU, YOU ENT MARRYING THAT UGLY BLACK-FACE CHAP. AND FURTHER MORE I DON'T WANT HIM VISITING HERE!'

'Mommy,' said Beverley brokenly, 'Mike write telling you hello.'

'HE COULD KEEP IT! Oh, you crying. YOU AMBI-TIONLESS THING!'

'And he says ...' The tears course down Beverley's face, 'that he's coming down at month-end and when he comes down he's going to ask you permission to marry me.'

'NEVER!' barks Mrs Bailey.

'All right Mommy,' says Beverley.

From over the street drift songs from India.

*   *   *

Gerald Tross reads Beverley's letter then places it with the others, Apata's. Gerald looks at his hands. Farmer's hands now. He shakes his head slowly and wonders what life has in store for him. He wonders what life has in store for Michael. Michael, to Gerald, is one of the people who somehow reserve a kind of right to the destiny of their own lives. Unlike myself, Gerald muses, unlike me. I move by the proddings of circumstance and the tides of fate.

Ulric Tross has now retired. So now Gerald carries the burden of the farm. He has grown to love the land. He has discovered that within the blood of the Trosses there is a love of planting and watching things grow. Even his uncle in the city grows something, if only flowers.

'Beverley says,' he thinks, 'that her mother won't have Michael marry her. Michael asked me to take care of Beverley if anything happens to him.'

The old man's booted feet sound up a stair of the renovated house on strong stilts, pillars of concrete. Entering, he sees his son at his letters. 'Michael write?'

'Yes, Daady, and his girlfriend write, too.'

The older man eases himself down in a Morris chair. Slowly he undoes his shirt buttons. 'MILDRED?'

'ULRIC? YO' COME BACK?' answers a piping female voice. Gerald Tross's mother. A woman thin as her voice but as strong as a length of wire rope.

'But Gerald,' says the older Tross, 'yo' nah gat no gyal ah village.'

It is a concerned statement, not a question. The younger Tross shakes his head.

'Nat at-all, at-all? Dah haad fuh believe! Wait. Yo' nah want none ah dem gyal a dis village? Nuffa dem gyal like yo'. Mih know dat fuh shore. Suh wha' bhai?'

Gerald, smiling, scratches the back of his neck.

'I ent ready to choose none o' them yet.'

'Tell me chap ... you still innocent?'

'AW ULRIC!' snaps Mrs Tross from the bedroom, 'WHAT YO'AH ASK DE BOY?'

Gerald gets to his feet after closing a drawer with his stacked letters. His father watches at him all the time. Gerald knows that the old man waits for an answer. Gerald turns and the old man sees the twinkle in his son's eyes.

'Yes, Daady.'

'WHA?' blurts the old man. Gerald begins to laugh.

'It is a blessed thing to be innocent you know, Daady.'

'Wait chap ... ah pries' yo' guh turn to?'

'I'm already a farmer. It's too late to be a priest, man.'

The older Tross's brows knit slightly. He shifts himself as though uncomfortable. 'Come si' down wit' mih lil bit bhai.'

His son sits next to him. He places an arm around his boy's shoulders.

'Before mih had to bring yo' back to dis place, me an' yo' uncle Freddoe had a lil' row ovah you an' yo' schoolin. Tell mih, you does regret nat gettin' to finish high school?'

Gerald shakes his head. There's a smile on his face. He makes claws of his hands and holds them out. 'I wouldn't have had hands like these Daady and maybe I wouldn't have been at peace as I am these times. This time, there's only one person I find myself worrying about and that is my brother.'

The old man nods his head.

'Truh-to-Gawd! You an' dah Michael like'ah brother fuh-true. But ah when we guh see 'e?'

'This month-end. He's coming down to see his girlfriend.'

'Ah wan good gyal?'

'Yes, Daady. She's a good girl.'

The older Tross yawns. The younger Tross throws his head back and closes his eyes.

PART THREE

1959

1959

CHAPTER 16

The deep, throaty sound of the Grumman amphibious aircraft pulses in slow waves over to the two Negro men from the labourer's camp not far from the smooth-faced rocks on the sandy shore-line of the Mazaruni river, brown and shadowed by forest growth. The younger of the men, Apata, turns his head and looks.

In the Grumman are the pilot, co-pilot and two white Americans, Archibald Glenn and John Bolton, who are being taken to their rest house at Bartica, not far away.

The aero engines are opened for take-off and the sound waves they create diminish as the aircraft skims away to break its union with the river's face.

Apata smiles in silent awe, as the aircraft lifts off the river.

*   *   *

Below the silver-skinned amphibian, drifting back lazily, are square miles, square miles of turbulent rain-forest greenery. A clearing where the trees have been felled looks like a patch of material missing from a vast green carpet covering a ballroom floor.

One of the Americans looking down to the river sees it like a brown-watered irrigation drain worming its way through the forest which rolls away in all directions.

'"Water, water everywhere ... all the boards did shrink. Water, water everywhere ... not a gawddamned drop to drink."'

97

Turning to John Bolton, Archibald Glenn says: 'Bowl, just where the hell's the water you're purring about?'

'Think of the jungle as water and you'll understand what I'm saying,' and Bolton laughs wheezingly and tucks his fatness a bit more snugly into his seat.

'I see,' says Archibald Glenn.

From the port hole, by his left shoulder, he picks up a glinting of sunlight from off the galvanized roofs of the labourers' camp far below and smiles to himself as he thinks of one of the Negro workers.

'How many years before we'll see sky scrapers rising from that primitive greenery, Bowl?' he asks, but Bolton is fast asleep. The time is five o'clock.

*   *   *

The silvery speck disappears beyond the trees and Apata turns to his companion. 'I knew two chaps in school,' he says, 'who wanted to become pilots.'

'Black friends?' asks the older man. His voice is lazy, deep and gravelly.

'Yes. One was dark as myself. Black like me.'

'Dah's a ambitious young man. But fuh we people it guh be lil hard fuh he turn dat. Nah true?'

There is a chorus from the monkeys screeching in the great trees behind the huts from which comes, now and then, the exuberant tones of native workers being themselves away from the supervision of the White men.

'It's as though our only rights are to crave after rum, to shoot shit and chase pussy. It's as though we must be contented forever with mere existence!'

The older Negro glances at the face of his young companion then turns and continues to gaze at the dark green bushes hemming the opposite bank of the river which is wide at this point.

'And if people like us desires more than that then we don't know our places. "Oi say, oi say, Mike you're being jolly presumptuous! What? Eh?"'

Amused by his own mimicry of the English colonists, Apata shakes his head, laughs and says, 'Well then, I'm going to be quite presumptuous for I'm bloodywell tired of being "us humble people". I am tired of being numb. For a man to make an easy mark in this country he's got to be a European or a Yankee. In short you've got to look pink. Even an African albino can make it in British Guiana.' Then he continues in a softer tone, 'Do you know I won a free place to King's but didn't get to go?'

'Boy, mih hear people talk 'about what happen to you in 'Town, but me ent know much 'bout it.'

'Black stay back.'

'What we have here is a colour movement, not true? "White sees the light. Brown stick around, BLACK STAY BACK!" Think of it, Mr Alexander. And when you do, remember that we can make more for ourselves if we sail to England, spend seven years there then return White-minded and full of criticism of our own folk, culture, beliefs and traditions with a lot of bloody English mannerisms packed tight into our knotty nigger heads.'

'Boy, is suh life is – But talkin' 'bout life, mih hear de Queen comin'! Dat going be Christmas before Christmas, boy!'

'But let us suppose you don't fit shit into none of those opportune categories Mr Alexander. Then how can "us people" get any place? How?'

The older man smiles a beaten smile and his gaze moves downwards like self-pity. Sheepishly he looks at his gnarled hands resting loosely on his knees. He shrugs his broad labourer's shoulders.

'The sadness of ourselves,' sighs Apata and shakes his head. 'You know what's keeping "us people" down? It's our inability to come to grips with the anatomical fact that God gave each of us a brain. Provided you have a brain in your head, Mr Alexander, you can make life. And if you find you are denied the scope to make something of yourself ... You should do something about it.'

'Mih boy, lots'a we got sense. All o' we get brains. But where it puttin' we when we put it to work? Only a few places I know . . . like Mazaruni settlement jail and below the gallows.

'De had a man name Aaron. You couldn' 'ave known Aaron. Dead long now . . . but Aaron uses to stand up in 'Town during the Hitler war-years and talk out against the Governor an' everything 'bout de British Government . . . how they usin' black people youths dem, sending them to fight and then when they come back after the war finish they gettin' nothing but ingratitude.' Mr Alexander shrugs. 'In the end, what happen to the man Aaron? Dem nah lock he up at Mazaruni here? Eh? Mih boy, Aaron was a Black man with good brains and prophetical. You see where it put he? Small boy, hear. With all de sense we Black people might have is like one place it does quickly end we up. Dat is in front de wig an' de gavel!'

'It seems as though "us people" get quick recognition as criminals, especially if your skin is dark. It makes one wonder Mr Alexander. Doesn't it make you wonder?' Apata tilts his head contemplatively and smiles bitterly. 'Is it only when we become criminals they're prepared to take us serious?'

'Mih boy, I doan know what you mean by dat but me ol' man always used to tell a thing. He uses to say, "You mus' always learn to say thanks." He used to say dat a bird in de hand is worth two in the bush. What we should be saying now is "thank Gawd we have dis lil wok."'

Apata looks over to the three huts built primarily of galvanized sections. Camp. A man with dark skin and very curly hair has just entered one of the lowly shelters after parting the tarpaulin flap over the doorway. Another man, an Amerindian, squatting at the base of an old boulder, eats with his fingers from a tin plate. Apata turns his head once more to his old companion.

'Tell me, Mr Alexander. You're a big man getting down in age. You have a wife and six and a half children at Mabaruma village.'

Alexander smiles. *Six and a half children*. It is a witty way to say six children and one more on the way.

'But the house they live in,' continues Apata, 'is not much of a house. It is too small. So, tell me, are you satisfied with life?'

'Well ... I ... I must say, yes. I alive. Me wife an' children alive. So I must thank Gawd fuh small mercies.'

Apata, tall, compact, twenty-one years old, rises to his feet. The red-orange rays of the sun, this afternoon a perfect disc of deep yellow, highlights his burnt umber features, especially his receding forehead and high cheek bones below no-nonsense eyes which, when coupled with a downward-furrowing of brows, can be calculating. A smile plays on the left side of his thick lips below a nose which, seen full face, is all negroid. However, in the profile it is slightly aquiline. He smiles to disguise his contempt.

'Mr Alexander, I don't want to be disrespectful, but I bet you'll end up a poverty stricken Black man with a heavy weight in your heart or between your legs.'

'Boy, all man got seeds,' counters Alexander lightly, showing uneven teeth in a smile.

'Not me, Mr Alexander. No strains, no poverty for me Mr Alexander.' Apata shakes his head. 'No poverty for me Mr Alexander. You know why?'

'Well, you talkin', me listenin' ...'

'Because I understand something which none of you, Glenn, Bolton, you yourself Mr Alexander, understand.'

With bared teeth and open mouth, Alexander looks up to Michael to hear the revelation of a mystery. But Apata does not sound off. To understand, the older man would have to be in telepathic communication with the younger man for in his mind, the younger man's mind, there is a live picture.

A formation of gauldings wing their way in unison above the beautiful green head-dresses of coconut trees silently whispering in the winds. The gauldings are white and clean looking as they fly lazily. But high, very high above them all, a dirty, loathsome, black carrion crow circles, slowly circles.

'So is what you andahstan' dat me and the white basses dem doan andahstan'?'

'Some things, Mr Alexander, defy explanation.'

'Son,' Alexander smiles weakly down to the grass, 'son, you spend a couple years in Georgetown. High school you been to and all. Now you get good education and can talk prappah good English.' Alexander nods his head. 'Ah proud ah you fuh all dat Michael.' He scratches behind an ear. 'What ah wants to say is dat I doan andahstan' plenty of de things you talk since we sit down here gaffing. Not de words I mean, but something else, something from you' mind, a determination. Me ent know why you telling me all what you telling me. Maybe you want me to tell you if you right or if yo' wrong. Mih boy, what I want to tell you is dis. What evah you do! Do suh not to leh you' gran'parents dem turn in dem grave!'

'At least not the corpse of grandfather Josh.'

'Is true. You does talk jus' like how Smitty used to talk.' Alexander gets to his feet now. He stands as tall as Michael Apata. 'Well den ... 'til tomorrow son ... ah turning' in early.'

*　　*　　*

Lying in his hammock, Alexander listens to the voice of the camp's troubadour down by the river's shore. Away from the others the man sits on a smooth rock embedded in the sand that runs gradually under the brown-skinned river. He embraces the body of a darkly polished box guitar and caresses her strings as he sings above the harmony of their chords. His voice floats back from his bent head, back to the workers squatting on the sand and playing cards by the doorway of the largest rest hut where Alexander listens between the snores of a camp worker sprawled drunk on a folding cot.

> *"Captain, captain put me ashore ...*
> *I doan wan' to go any more ..."*

Mr Alexander gazes at the galvanized ceiling above his head and thinks of his Amerindian wife who is five months with child. He thinks of his six children ... *Six and half children.* He smiles to himself in the quickly encroaching darkness. Even though he doesn't understand old Josh Smith's grandson he admires something about the boy.

"E-tah-naa-mee gon frighten me . . .
E-tah-naa-mee gon wo'k mih belly . . .
E-tah-naa-mee gon drownded me . . ."

Old Josh Smith's grandson always tells Mr Alexander that he ought to expect more from life. It is one of the reasons Mr Alexander feels out of place, out of league when Michael talks with him. Mr Alexander finds it difficult to make favourable replies and comments. Sometimes his nervousness borders on fear wrought by anxiety for Michael. At times this feeling comes from something he senses below the cynical laughter. Something that does not swim in Michael's eyes.

This afternoon, Michael wanted Mr Alexander to agree to something that apparently tormented him. He is sure that he sensed a determination within the boy.

"One marnin' de captain wake . . .
Captain wake 'e wake de boat man . . ."

Before Michael came back from the city the only thing Mr Alexander could have written was his own name. Now he even tries to write letters to Marianne his wife. To Michael, he's grateful.

"Boat man wake 'e wake de bow man . . .
Bow man wake wid 'e paddle in 'e han' . . ."

But why the boy refuse to be like everybody else? As Mr Alexander courts sleep he senses that Michael is up to something that would land him in more trouble than Aaron had landed himself into. Many of the workers are stealing dynamite to blast fish. Two young men, Thomas and Barth, Mr Alexander knows, steal dynamite from the White people. Mr Alexander knows that they steal the charges for Michael. But what is Michael going to do with it? He ent blasting fish. 'Ah wonder what Michael planning to do with them things?' he thinks, 'Blow up the plane with Mr Glenn and Bolton? He did watchin' de plane in a strange kinda way dis afternoon.'

"E-tah-naa-mee is to' much fuh me . . .
E-tah-naa-mee! E-tah-naa-mee!
O-o-o-o . . ."

Lying in his hammock, Alexander wonders if it is true that
Michael was thrown out of high school in Georgetown
because he cricitized the colonial system openly in the city.
Apata knows that the Indian and Negro politicians in the
city do that kind of thing, but a school boy, born in these
parts, who had not even gone away and returned a lawyer? It
is true what Michael's saying about the chances Black people
have in this place. But, thinks Alexander, we have to thank
God for small mercies. Suddenly he feels ashamed: "Tell me,
are you satisfied with life?" "Well yes . . . Well I . . . I must
say, yes. I alive. Me wife and children alive. So I must thank
Gawd fuh small mercies." Alexander tells himself he should
not have said that. He feels ashamed for some reason he
cannot squarely name. Michael had not responded immediately. Alexander remembers that. It was after a while that he
had laughed and had said what had embarrassed Alexander.

A flight of parakeets screeches overhead and the first
marathon note of a six o'clock bee sounds out in high-
pitched monotony. Soon others would take up the call . . .
and others and others and others and others and others.

Dusk falls.

'SMALL BHAI! GAS LAMP BHAI. GET DE FOOP
WORKIN' BHAI!'

'ZANDER! ALEXANDER! STOP DREAMIN' 'BOUT
DAT BUCK 'OMAN AN' GIVE WE SOME JOKES
HAY, MAN!'

'WHAT DE RASS WRANG WIT' YOU?'

'Eh, eh, like yo' pull Zanda fret bone.'

'Ah does always tells al'yo, a man wife is a man wife,
yeh.'

'WHAT YOU KNOW 'BOUT WIFE, CRABAS? DAT
THING YOU HAVE IN BERBICE ENT WIFE. DAT IS
KNIFE!'

'ZANDA!'

'But small bhai, how you'ah tek suh lang foh light ah lamp, eh?'

'ALEXANDAH!'

'A'right nah try fuh deaf mih. Ah comin' to give ya'all a joke of Rayalty!'

'HAY, BHAIS? YA'ALL HEAR DAT QUEEN AH COME?'

'Hear, hear. Mih gaffa write Maisy an' tell she to tek out mih serge suit an' start to sun it fuh mih. When ah get pay ah plannin' to buy a new pair a Jahn White shoe, rass!'

'Boy me remembah when King Eze from Africa did come hay!'

'Man? We ent talking 'bout Blackman king. We talkin' 'bout de Queen o' Buckin'ham palace, man. We talkin' 'bout White people. Truh-to-Gawd people. We ah talk 'bout Rayal Yatch an' black car with shine shine body. We ah talk 'bout straight straight nose. Nothing like'ah what we have lump up on we black face. Hear, me uncle at numbah five gat a book wid all de Rayal fami–'

'Why don't you shut up your stupid mouth Walson?'

The man whose uncle possesses a book on Royal Families turns around and faces Apata who has just come up from the solitary spot by the waterside where he and Alexander talked earlier.

'Apata,' says Walson gravely, 'Apata, is not me you ah talk to!'

'Yes Walson, you.'

A vein has risen below the skin of Apata's forehead dully gleaming in the yellow light from the gas lamp hissing between the silence of antagonists.

'DAH NAH HINSULT FUH TEK!' goads a friend of the giant of a Negro known as Walson the Berbician Hercules.

Walson steps in and swings a knuckled backhanded slap to Apata's face. Apata, rooted, pulls his head out of danger and grabs Walson's wrist . . . pulls and turns away . . . twisting . . . bending from the hip. Walson yelps and hurls himself over so as to escape having his arm broken at the elbow. He lands with a heavy dullness and bruises his face in a patch of gravel.

Walson gets to his feet slowly then, turning his back to Apata, walks down to the river and takes a seat with the man on the shore who plays a guitar softly to himself.

'Wallo,' the guitarist says, resting a spell, 'you getting soft man. Apata high-fall you and you taking it just like that?'

Walson spits to the river.

'Dat is not like you Wallo. What happen man?'

Mocking laughter bursts from the camp circle.

'What happen chap?' asks the guitarist seriously.

'Nothing.' Walson wipes his lips with the back of a hand. He spits again.

'Well, me wouldah never believe I would'ave see what I just see happen here tonight. The Berbician Hercules, back down from fight.'

CHAPTER 17

The outboard engine is fixed and running well. Apata switches it off then replaces the cover. This afternoon they will be able to take the trip up the Cuyuni river. As he replaces a spanner in the little tool kit, he sees Thomas and Barth coming down over the sands to the huge flat boulders that rise from the water's edge.

Barth, twenty-four years old, squat and muscular, smiles his gap-fronted smile. He lost his teeth one year ago in a race to see who could bite through the tough seed of the greenheart tree first. At school, the children used to call him "juju" boy.

Thomas, the twenty year-old light-skinned youth with the thin face on which rests a lumpy nose, is laughing all the way over.

The morning sun rises confidently and spills its rays all around, lighting the foliage of trees and bushes. It also soaks into the mist which enshrouds the forest. Fresh vapour rises from the little plants nearby and the sands still bear the tracks of a jaguar that prowled there last night.

Thomas and Barth are both stripped down to their canvas trunks. Swim time.

'Hail the most skilful man on aqua!' is Barth's greeting as he extends a Nazi style salute to Apata who grins from the stern of the long boat painted in brown and cream. The brown on the sides falls all the way below the water line. The boat belongs to the company. Its name is *Star of Chicago* and Apata is the boatman respected most by everyone for his uncanny skill on water. Many call him "Aqua man".

107

'ACHTUNG!' shouts Thomas in imitation of a heel-clicking German soldier of World War II. His broad shoe-less feet clash together so that he hurts his ankles. He grimaces with a sideway flaring of his lips, 'Swinehound!' he sneers trying to hide the pain. Apata bends double with laughter.

Thomas and Barth are his only close friends. They are straightforward with him even though they are like the average Guianese Negro, timid and humble in the face of the colonial White domination. Nonetheless Thomas and Barth steal for him, time after time, sticks of dynamite.

'PATA,' says Barth, 'you ever notice how Glenn does watch at yo' crotch when yo' have on trunks only?'

'No.'

Thomas grins as if he knows something. Apata's face is calm. He does not smile or frown. Barth continues, 'Me no great man in anialsis but I believe that white bass Glenn does either give buggah or take buggah and I mo' believe is take.'

'OH MY LORD BARTH,' interrupts Thomas mockingly, 'speak good. The word is not "anialsis". It's analysis!' Apata smiles. The sun's rays gleam on his forehead.

'And the word "buggah",' continues Thomas, sounding like a headmaster, 'is derogatory to Mr Archibald Glenn's White respectability. It is best to say that Mr Glenn, the boss, so to speak, fervently wishes he had a vagina instead of a penis.'

Now, they are all laughing and the sound they make ripples over the river to an Amerinidan man on the opposite bank. He waves to the three young men.

'You'all hear Queen coming?' asks Barth.

'That would be big to-do in Georgetown boy. What you say about it, Mike?' asks Thomas remembering what he heard of Apata and the Berbician Hercules yesterday afternoon.

Apata shrugs as he wipes his hands with a rag.

'But why you assault the man, Mike?'

'That big fool, you mean?'

'But yo' wrang, yo' know. To each man 'e own belief.'

'When I was small,' Apata cleans grease from between his fingers, 'I thought Her Majesty never used to perform the excretory function.'

Thomas begins laughing. Barth is at a loss as to the point of the humour.

'Barth,' adds Apata, 'I thought the Queen, Her Majesty, never used to shit!'

'OH!' exclaims Barth and responds suitably to the joke. Apata's laughter dies first. He decides that it is time to clear a major concern from his mind. In a serious tone of voice he says, 'Hear, chaps. I don't need any more dynamite.'

Barth begins to scratch between his thighs and concentrates, seemingly, on the sign-lettered name of the boat alongside the rocks of the shore. Then he flicks a quick glance at Apata before dropping his gaze to the coffee-brown water, translucent along the shore. With his toes he gropes in the wet sand. 'TALK!' something within Barth commands. He lifts his head and says in a cautious way, 'But Pata ... you could trus' me an' Thomo.' Barth grins nervously before he continues, 'Pata, what you going do wit' dat danamite?'

Thomas pulls lightly but persistently at a strongly rooted reed growing out the water next to the rock on which he is stooped and, with his head bent slightly, watches at Apata. He and Barth had planned, last night, to ask Michael why he needed the explosive, but after they had spoken about that and other things, he decided that it was going to be wrong to ask Michael about his business. He had turned to Barth in the darkness of the camp hut and had said, 'Don't let we ask Mike nothing, right Bee?'

Like an answer Barth had yawned widely. Thomas had taken it for agreement. But now it turns out not to have been one.

'Man Bee don't ask the man 'bout he business!' Thomas turns to Apata gazing pensively at the bottom of the long boat. 'Mike, man, don't worry with that, yeh.' Thomas flicks a glance at Barth who is grinning stupidly and feels, like a turncoat.

'They are afraid to offend me,' Apata tells himself. 'They act, now, as though they have suddenly remembered that they must know their place, as though they must always remember to wait until I am ready to come down to their level. They act like most of our people do in the presence of White people.' Apata's brows knit.

Both young men watch the rise and fall of Apata's chest as he sighs.

He lifts his head and gazes at the trees he sees in the background between them. They freeze visibly.

'You want to know what I'm going to do with the dynamite.' A statement.

'Not really,' says Barth.

Apata smiles lightly. But only his lips fight to be true to the expression. His knotted brows betray inner turmoil. He gazes once more at the floor of the boat as one might gaze at the tombstone of a close friend.

'You are like brothers to me,' Apata says and stalls, remembering that afternoon, almost three months ago yet like yesterday within him, when he allowed himself to be consumed with the planning of what he will do. He remembers that afternoon: He was taking Jameson, Pocock and a woman who was a visiting freelance English photographer for a cruise up the Potaro river. All White, all strangers to the flora and fauna, yet Jameson the young engineer had postured as guide on the trip. The names of things and places along the river he did not know, nor the meanings of the names of things and places along the river. Apata remembers the two White men chatting and laughing forcedly in order to impress the woman. There was bottle of white wine between them. It was thrown from Jameson to Pocock and to the woman sitting between them when she was not taking photographs.

And through it all, Apata remembers, it was as though he was non-existent, as though he was not a human being but an extension of the outboard engine he controlled. He had listened to their bantering and outright laughter.

Apata remembers . . .

110

He had looked at them, pink as monkeys, and the old pain of having been judged and rejected by Edward Carrington swelled within his chest and brought back an old uneasiness, an old rancour. And link by link the chain that was wrapped times around the evil within him began to give.

Apata remembers when the sun was almost down and they were returning. When he had heard the Grumman overhead and knew that the big White bosses were flying to the resthouse at Bartica. It was then, he remembers, that he had thought of the ones he was taking back to the work-site camp. 'They will leave this boat,' he had said to himself, 'ignore Barth who I know will hold it steady for them to step out. They will walk past the huts we sleep in and the only thing that might make them stop might be that woman wanting to take a photograph of the natives after work. The men will suddenly be silent because White people will be passing on their way up the hill to that caravan thing.'

Then, he had remembered his grandfather talking so often of White men who acted as though the Negroes and Indians who worked for them and made them rich were savages to be isolated, hence, the White men living away on the hills and higher terrain. Living where they believed the stink of the natives would not be.

Apata remembers that evening some three months ago when he had felt the chain wrapped times around the evil within him breaking and chose not to do anything about it.

Apata feels the movement of the boat under him.

That evening, piloting James, Pocock and the woman, he had told himself that White men felt that all Negroes could have been symbolized as nails to be driven in with consecutive hammer blows until some great White thing began holding together. Nails to be driven, though, if by chance, buckle partly in, are to be clawed out and discarded without thought.

That evening, too, he had reflected on how he had become a true nail. It was after he had lost the house at Bartica to the very Portuguese businessman who had ruined his grandfather. It was after the years on the interior rivers as a diamond diver and later tug boat crewman. It was after he had been chased from Beverley's home and had walked away into a madness of a vagrancy of sorts.

Apata remembers ...

It was then that he had met an Amerindian derelict, a young man, creased and drawn and gaunt, who had said to him, 'APATA, LOOK AT ME! LOOK! LOOK GOOD AT DIS FACE! VERDICT: BUSH RUM. Never do it pardner. You to' looking bad and I believe is the same thing: BUSH RUM.'

'NO!' Apata had denied vehemently.

'Den is maybe because you not eatin' good dat you lookin' so blasted bad. WHAT YOU' AGE?'

'Twenty.'

'Yo' nah want a good work?' the derelict had asked finally.

At that time Apata had grown tired of drifting over rivers and bushy mountains and was beginning to reawaken.

'I don't want no more gold bush or diamond diving work, man.'

Then the derelict had told him of Archibald Glenn's outfit and Apata knew that he would have gone to try whatever it was. It was really falling low when a man as washed-out as the derelict could have called him pardner.

He had gone along with an old scrap book, his only possession other than the washed out suit of clothes on his back. In the scrap book were newspaper clippings of the nineteen fifty-four Easter Regatta when he had won the eighty horse power speed boat race.

'What can you do, darkie?' the recruiting man had asked him.

'Drive boat good, sah,' he had replied. Then he had shown the White man the clippings with the photographs.

'You've got a job,' the fat pink man had said. A true nail Apata had become.

* * *

112

The morning sun rises confidently and spills its rays all around lighting the foliage of trees and bushes and the river.

'There is something most common among Black people,' Apata says to Thomas and Barth. 'You know what it is?'

'Poorness,' says Thomas. Barth nods.

'Poverty,' agrees Apata and remembers Mr Alexander, how he had expounded above the simple man's intellect and social awareness. He still feels ashamed.

'Grandfather Josh used to say poverty is a sin. Right now many of us live from pay day to pay day. I don't want to live like that any more.'

'Yo' gat fuh born wit' silver spoon in you' mouth to live otherwise, boy.'

Apata laughs. 'You know that is not necessarily true Barth. A man can make his own silver spoon, you know.'

Thomas laughs.

'I am serious,' says Apata. 'I have decided that I will live as big as any Portuguese businessman in Georgetown.'

'How yo' going do dat, Pata?'

'I am going to rob the first big Post Office down from Parika.'

'Hoop Village?'

'Hoop Village, yes, as a beginning.'

'WHY PATA?' Barth is clearly disturbed.

A stupid question because he's afraid for me, thinks Michael.

'Because I want capital, Bee.'

'But you ah work, man Pata, yo' could save!'

Barth's brows raised slightly in bewilderment tells Thomas how much his crude-looking friend cares for Michael who has taught him to read and write properly.

Apata chuckles. 'Everything will work out without no problems, man Bee. You and Thomo don't have to worry.'

'They going catch you, Mike,' Thomas says soberly.

Anger sweeps through Apata but he manages not to show it. 'I will be too clever for them.'

'The Crime Chief is a White man, Mike!'

'SO WHAT?' snaps Apata.

Barth is once more scratching between his thighs.

'Mike man, I know that you getting vex, but I think I got to satisfy me self that you know what you doing,' says Barth.

Apata feels an emotional warmth for the two men before him. He smiles. 'I know what I'm doing,' he says quietly.

'Good, Mike,' follows up Thomas quickly, 'but suppose they catch you, what then?'

'No White man will be able to catch me,' Apata says tersely, then as though feeling obligated to lighten the tension he feels growing between them, adds, 'They won't even be able to find out who it was until I get old and write my own life story.'

Thomas sighs. 'Fair enough, Mike,' he says as though finally giving consent to a headstrong son bent on setting out alone on a hazardous quest.

'And that is why I need Glenn's rifle.'

'Lil tricky to get that, man. Hard card thing that, Pata.'

'I need the thing, man. What you think Thomo?'

'Seriously Mike?'

'Seriously.'

Thomas is squatting on a great slab of rock dropping pebbles into the transparent water. Not very far away a fish, a lone tilapia, idles as though on sentry duty. 'What Barth saying is true, you know, Mike?'

'What you mean Thomo? That getting the Winchester would be difficult?'

'No, not that.'

'What?'

'That Glenn looks as though he likes you.'

Apata searches Thomas's face for the gist of a joke to come, but does not see any. 'What has that got to do with my possessing that repeater rifle, man?'

'Men of his sort, Mike, would give anything to a man they like. I could see Glenn giving you plenty of things if you give him what he want and keep quiet about it, you know. Once you in man you could get whatever you want.'

Thomas notices that Apata is listening with a flare of scorn on his lower lip.

'But just one thing, Mike,' Thomas stalls and tells himself that if Apata is interested he will urge him on. If Apata doesn't urge him on, Thomas decides that he will swim over to the opposite bank in the hope of seeing and maybe, even, succeed in talking to Elizabeth the Amerindian girl he tells himself he's in love with. Even though Barth, in his own rough way, tells him that it is just a long-hair infatuation.

'You say there's just one thing, Thomo. What's that?' says Apata.

'Those kinds o' people dangerous and like hold on, play leech,' continues Thomas. 'Take a man like Glenn. American. Yankee dollar. A man like Glenn would give a man cash, and believe that he buy a man. So when a man think he get enough money and ...' he shrugs his shoulders, '... leh we say get fed up with doing *that* thing then I can see a man like Glenn killing somebody. And of course if a man like Glenn kill a man like we, you know, he won't get wrong. He White. That is number one. And we is just natives from British Guiana, number two. You get me, right?'

'Dah truh,' says Barth.

'I get you,' says Michael, thinking of Mr Edward Carrington and remembering:

'My dear young man, Apata.'

'But sir ...'

'Have manners,' scolded the secretary with the heavily made up face. And the light skinned Vanier, with the swollen left nostril had smiled slyly. While the heavily built Gunraj who sat sombre in the background of it all after having given his unbiased version of what took place outside, had stared blankly.

'My dear Michael Apata,' had continued the White man, 'I give you my word: your savagery would not be tolerated at the King's College for boys and neither would you. I'm terribly sorry.'

Michael Apata takes a deep breath, raises himself from the little padded seat by the outboard engine. 'I heard that when I was found as a baby, floating in a wash basin, an obeah woman said no water would kill me. She said that my undoing would not be by water.' He nods his head. 'But I am adding, now, NOR BY ANYBODY WHITE!'

'WHY YOU SEH SUH, PATA?' asks Barth scratching between his toes.

'No White man can't kill you Mike?' says Thomas. 'Chap, what you saying?'

'No White man can kill me,' repeats Apata.

Barth glances at him briefly then plunges into the cold river and swims under the surface for a few yards. Then he comes up spouting water noisily. Thomas wades out and throws his body forward to begin swimming to the other shore.

CHAPTER 18

Archibald Glenn, a fifty-year-old American with a mat of brownish hair atop a thin, sharp-chinned face, sits in one of the folding chairs in the six-man tent used by himself and associate John Bolton. Glenn delicately strokes a can of tomato juice with his fingers. Before him stands a collapsible table. On top of it there are little stones and a few fist-sized rocks. On the larger areas of the surfaces of specific rock samples there are little crystalline deposits which give those parts a rough, sharp texture. The little stones and rocks rest on thin strips of paper that are carefully marked with inscriptions.

Close to the table's edge that faces away from him rests something else. Not a rock. Not a pebble nor a stone, but a handsome utilitarian article of metal and polished wood.

In the other chair, beside the little table in front of the White man with the creased eyes below vertically lined thought furrows on his broad forehead, sits Michael Apata who has accepted an invitation to enter the tent, given by Glenn himself. Apata had been walking past the White mens' tent and Glenn was standing in the flapped doorway. The dark, native worker wore very short pants that gripped him tight and created a marked bulge in his crotch.

How was Glenn to know that Apata's shirtlessness and close-fitting pants were designed to attract his attention?

Glenn, looking serious, had beckoned the young native to enter the tent.

*   *   *

Apata drops his gaze. The White man's lips tightly pressed together, bend upwards now at the corners into a benevolent smile. He drinks daintily from the can of tomato juice.

'You're one of the first Guianese in this part of this gawd-forsaken bush who ever looked me in the eyes for three straight seconds, Apata. I like you, yeah, I like you very much. A man with a positive mind and a good worker.'

The portable fan, spinning from the top of the little filing cabinet in the corner, spills cool air around the tent's interior. The sound of the little generator at the back does not intrude. It has become an acceptable sound, as normal and inconspicuous as a man's heart beat.

'Tell me about your name. Sure sounds queer to me.'

Apata, head bent, smiles his simpleton smile.

'Anyhow,' Glenn continues when Apata does not reply, 'I like you ... and I know what you like.'

Glenn stabs a finger at the semi-automatic rifle with the telescopic sight. A handsome, utilitarian article of metal and polished wood. 'You like my rifle. And you can bet your ass I'm right about that!' Glenn laughs, empties the can of tomato juice and drops it carelessly on the ground. He shifts in his chair and places his right index finger on the commissure of his lips and looks speculatively at the native, who Glenn muses, is dying a dozen deaths from being in the awesome presence of a white man. Glenn knows that the Guianese locals see White folk as superior beings.

'Tell you what Mike, I'm going to teach you to use that rifle. Yeah, I'll teach you. Really, I don't get to use it much and someone should. Pick her up, Mike!'

Apata picks up the sophisticated weapon and the way he does it says something to the white man.

'You've handled a rifle before, haven't you?'

Apata smiles whilst looking down to the rifle in his hands. 'Is jus', is jus' from watchin' you sah.'

Glenn smiles and runs his eyes down Michael Apata's torso and the smooth, burnt evenness of his shoulders, his arms, his pectorals, solar plexus, abdominals. Crotch. Almost imperceptibly he nods.

A pink hairy hand parts the opening into the tent. A plump bespectacled white man enters "Chri-sayking" about the tropical heat. Already on his feet and in apparent respect to Mr Bolton Apata blurts: 'GOOD AFTAHNOON SAH!' but the newcomer appears not to have seen or heard the native yet. Resting the rifle back on the table, Apata leaves.

Bolton "Chri-sakes" about the heat outside as he mops the sweaty chinfulness below his face. At the same time he slides a little haversack off his right shoulder. 'You like him, huh?' he asks matter-of-factly of Glenn who interlocks his fingers, raises his arms up and behind him and rests his head in his cupped palms. He grins at Bolton who dusts the chair Apata sat in. There's no dust there, only, to Bolton, the unwanted heat left by a native.

'Yeah-a-ah!' he says in restive tones as he lowers his bulk into the seat. 'I can see that look in your eyes Glenn. You do like him. Say, listen, we've worked together a long time, eh? And I've always wanted to ask you something.' Glenn does not respond. So Bolton, with his face twisted in distaste, ploughs on, 'JESUS CHRIST GLENN, WHEN SOME NATIVE'S WALKING INTO YOUR END, HOW DO YOU FEEL?'

Glenn smiles. Bolton shifts irritably in his seat. 'I guess it's some feeling ... always takes me back ... I have a brother. When he was a kid I caught him with his finger up his butt.' Bolton blows down into the neck of his shirt as if the fan's breath is inadequate. '"How do you feel doing that, you bum?" I asked him, "Nice ..." he said, "nice."' Bolton laughs and shakes his head.

'To each his own Bowl ... to each his own,' says Glenn in a sing-song tone. Bolton now looks concentrated.

'Suddenly, pal, I'm really thinking of that Apata character,' he says.

'What about, Bowl?'

'Man, I've watched him work. Doesn't talk much. As a matter of fact today, a moment ago, was the first time I heard him speak. As to that I must say I'm a bit surprised and a damn lot disappointed ...'

Bolton wriggles uncomfortably in his seat. Takes a deep breath of the fan-pushed air, deeply in, evenly out. Clears his throat. Swallows. Continues, 'I expected him to sound unlike the rest. But his speech is the same as all the rest. A great battle with Elizabeth's language. Creolis it's called, huh?'

'KREE-O-LEES!'

'But I've seen that kid handle a boat. Yesterday he was making a trial run on his own ... WOW!' Bolton shakes his head in remembering ... 'He's a virtual whizz on the water. And when I say whizz I mean whizz-z-z! Not double-u 'i' zee as in wizard.'

Bolton chuckles then his expression changes, 'But I don't trust him. If I were you Glenn, that's one native I wouldn't mess with.'

Then Bolton becomes conscious that he is getting too involved in another man's private business. Uncertainly he begins to laugh, falters and tries humour to atone for his intrusion, 'What makes you think he'd agree to your motherly embraces Glenn, huh?' Emptying the content of his haversack Bolton "Chri-sakes" again about the "fucken" tropical heat that's so difficult to get used to.

'I think you're stretching your sensitivity too far Bowl,' Glenn tells him. 'Mike is alright. I'll teach him to shoot then he will be all mine. You know, he likes my "Chester repeater".'

Nodding his head and making his tone business-like, Bolton points to a new collection of samples emptied from his haversack. 'What do you think?' he asks.

'We'll give this area a one-more-month over, right?' Glenn replies, 'Especially since the findings are so far positive.'

'Uh huh. O.K.' Bolton reaches for one of the local brand cigarettes Glenn has taken to smoking profusely in the evenings.

A dull boom comes from afar off. The White men feel the accustomed vibration. The aerial, extending from the small transmitter-receiver set on the little filing cabinet, shivers slightly.

'Let Jameson keep an eye on the dynamite, Bowl. Let him

keep a continuous and tight check! Those bastards steal em to blast fish! And keep an eye on Jameson himself because he likes fish, too.'

Bolton laughs and looks like a jolly round fellow. He remembers what happened two months ago. One of the bastards had stolen a few sticks of dynamite but not enough detonation wire to touch the river's bottom. If the wire-lengths had been long enough the dynamite charges would have anchored on the river-bed and the bastard, in his little boat, could have been far away from the actual point of eruption. Since the wires were too short the charges on the trailing end didn't touch the river's bed and the sticks of dynamite simply swung like a pendulum then hung directly under the boat so that when he activated the charges, fish, boat and bastard were blown out of the water.

Bolton laughs hugely and Glenn begins to grin.

'You're a sadistic sonofabitch, Bowl. I guess you're remembering what happened to that stupid nigger and his too-short wires, huh?'

Choking on his mirthfulness Bolton coughs a little then tells Glenn that he's enjoying British Guiana.

'Some fuckers here could give Charlie Chaplin lessons in comedy!'

Glenn laughs outright now, and shakes his head as if to say, "true, these people are really funny". But the man he is really thinking about is Apata.

CHAPTER 19

Tross, now a bearded young man with a habit of wearing khaki, long boots and a quick smile, arranges before him months of unopened, returned letters.

Where's Michael? What has happened to Michael?

Gerald places the letters on top of each other until the pile topples back onto the writing desk with the agricultural books, farming machinery manuals, and accounting ledgers.

What has happened to Michael?

It's too long since he has heard from him, or of him. Over many months he has written letters and read the daily papers, afraid of coming across news of Michael's death. It has been the same with the radio. And Gerald will listen again tonight. He will comb the news tomorrow. The deaths of unimportant men are found in very small columns.

In each letter he had told Michael, among other things, that he, Michael, is the father of a baby girl and that:

> *'Her name is Michelle. She's just under one year old. She's dark with a beautiful powdery darkness that is rare, boy. I think you should see your child, Mike. I know it would be hard for you to come back but I think you should see your daughter and Beverley who has grown thin because of missing you. I'm saying these things, Mike, with the understanding of wood, as Mr Bailey used to put it, 'Wood does explain life boys'. You remember how he used to tell us Mike? 'Small days is like soft wood, silverballi. But hitting manhood and going through it is like greenheart and knotty wallaba that can blunt and break good tools.'*

Along with that, Gerald wants Michael to know how drastically some things have changed since he, Michael, has last seen Beverley, since he last saw her mother, being that time when she chased him from her home. The letters before Gerald tell of those things.

Gerald Tross remembers Michael stopping by on his way back to his wilderness. 'Jerry,' Apata had said, 'nothing ent make sense anymore.'

It was the first conversational thing he had said on that day which seems so very long ago. Michael had saved up quite a sum of money during a long sojourn in the Essequibbean hinterland and thinking of it now, it seems to Gerald that he must have given all of it to Beverley after her mother insulted him. On the way back to his wilderness it seemed to Gerald that Michael had changed radically.

But where's Michael?

Since that time, much has happened. Mrs Bailey has twice had a nervous breakdown and it was Michael's money, left with Beverley, that was in both instances, spent to get her back together.

Tross gazes at the letters which tell Mike the whole story. The first breakdown came when her mother learnt that Beverley was "in the family way". The second came about when the young man Mrs Bailey thought was the perfect mate and match for Beverley got married to the daughter of a woman whom Mrs Bailey thought was a commoner, in the vulgar sense.

In her frazzled state of mind she denied Michael's child his surname. Mrs Bailey stood on it and crushed it like a black repulsive roach.

But where's Michael? Why have these letters never found him?

Gerald has visited the Baileys countless times during Michael's absence. He knows that Beverley's attachment to her mother is complete even though the union is a miserable one for the daughter.

'*Mike*,' one of the letters reads:

'If I could have persuaded Beverley to come to Parika and live with my parents she would have been here now; but she won't leave her mother's side. The woman's cruel to her, but she won't leave. She tells me that if she leaves her mother it wouldn't make sense because, if something happened to her mother when she's away, she would blame herself.

The most I can do for her, then Mike, is to visit her at least once every month and to take something for them whenever I go.'

A Parika night of darkness reigns outside.

Listening to the crickets and frogs from the canals that border the road just outside, Gerald begins to feel as Michael must have felt when he said that nothing made sense any more. He remembers Apata walking away to the ferry stelling. For days afterwards conch shells, the lowing of cows, the hooting of owls, everything, after that day, sounded mournful to Gerald. It was as if every sound embodied the sadness he felt for his friend. It still is that way. Now, Gerald tells himself, he should have followed Michael, he should not have allowed Michael just to walk away to the ferry stelling the way he did. But that one-year-ago time, Gerald was afraid to follow his own friend. For some strange reason he had been afraid. But now Gerald tells himself that probably if he had, the letters before him would not have been returned unopened and unanswered. Solomon a' Grundy born on a Monday Christened on a Tuesday ... 'If I live to be five hundred,' Gerald Tross mutters to himself, 'I will never understand why that "Solomon-a-Grundy" shit flies into my head like this.' He reaches for the closest envelope, tears it open, slips out the letter, unfolds it and reads,

'Dear Lost Brother Mike,

This is my eighteenth letter, hoping to let you know that Beverley has gotten a beautiful baby girl for you. Her name is Michelle. Yours truly is the God-father. Mike the baby is a sweet mixture of yourself and Beverley. The enclosed photograph will tell you much and, man, everybody missing you badly.

For some reason, all of my other letters before this one, have returned unopened. Mike, missing you is a painful thing for me. Just imagine then how it is with Beverley. Oh God Michael why don't you ...'

Gerald Tross folds the letter, sighs deeply, and forces himself to think of the government's marketing outlet for which he has a contract to supply farm produce.

But where's Michael?

What has happened to Michael?

CHAPTER 20

A female praying mantis eats off her mate's head whilst he's locked into her as they copulate on a broad leaf in this forest glade surrounded by great trees rooted in firm ground. Nearby there are swamps.

A little creek runs through this seldom-visited spot that is heavily layered with years of fallen leaves. It is some way from the camp site of the American Ore Prospecting Company.

Not far from the creek two naked men recline in a roomy cleft made by the roots of a gigantic tree. It is a cleft that looks like a gap between the splayed fingers of a hand pressed, palm down, on a flat surface.

Not long ago, Michael Apata and Archibald Glenn were swimming and the White man was childishly playful. He had splashed and spouted water at Apata who had acted the role of the happy playmate.

With her mate locked into her as they copulate, the female mantis finishes eating off her lover's head and continues eating down the slender neck.

To Apata, the White man lying next to him brings back scorn-filled memories of young, soft, blind pink mice lolling amidst chipped bits of paper in the corners of cardboard boxes in unswept nooks. He fights within himself for a thought to force his mind from what will be expected of him. But why do I have to do anything? he wonders. Why do I have to do anything? The gun is over there ... just over there. I can kill him. Kill him? But I don't have to kill anybody. I can just get up and take the damn rifle.

A calm fills his chest and, for no reason that Michael can consciously pin-point, Beverley comes to him this moment. It is a vision of her in the sweet softness of her flesh. And to think he has felt triumphant, time after time, that he has ridden himself of love for this girl whom he was forbidden to have. He thinks now of the last time they were together. It was midway through nineteen fifty-eight, for him a sad and sensuous year. Pulling the workshop's door close behind them, he had hurriedly made up a bed of sawdust ... and there were piles of it in an old box. Over the sawdust, Beverley spreaded an old clean bedspread folded twice.

He went down first and left her to stand above him. She began taking off her Spanish-style flared dress. As he gazed upwards, excitement tore through his body. His nervous system's needle flicked wildly. Pulling the garment over her head he saw her breasts rise like smooth nut-brown hills with raisin tips. Michael gazed from a paradise within his being, loving Beverley's whole being, inside and outside.

She knelt to him and he ran his trembling palms over her plump nut-brown thighs and their hairiness heightened the anxiety that affected his breathing. She went down with him and the smell of her skin stirred him further and further.

Lying, now, with thoughts far from the white man by his side in this forbidden Eden, Michael remembers their love-making. Beverley's uncontrollable orgasmic vibrations and her whimperings. He remembers, too, how, after they were both spent, she lay beside him in total abandon like something happily dead. His penis begins to fill.

Glenn notices and leans over to rest his head on Michael's thighs. Something sharp and murderously cold lances through Apata's system. A hellish internal uproar follows. 'KNOCK HIS FUCKING HEAD AWAY!' something screams hysterically within Michael's head. But he resists for this is no daydream but reality and Apata fears a fight. He fears a scuffle, he fears that the White man could well get to his feet first and gain the advantage of the rifle. The White man would kill him dead. Relax, relax, Michael Apata tells himself, relax ...

Glenn greedily grasps Apata's sexual member, and slowly begins to masturbate it. 'I'll kill him. Jesus I'll kill you dead Glenn. I'll kill you. Dead, man. Dead. "And of course," he hears Thomas say, "if a man like Glenn kill a man like we, you know, he won't get wrong."

'I'll kill you Glenn . . .

I'll kill you dead, man . . .

Dead . . . DEAD!'

And the precious seeds spill to waste on a carpet of broad fallen leaves.

'I have something for you Mike,' says Glenn at last. Apata forces a smile. He feels dirty within himself, as though he has ruined himself. 'I don't deserve Beverley's love now. I'm dirty enough not to. If Grandfather Josh and Granny Jane never turned in their graves, they're turning now. I'm no good now. Why should Beverley want me now. I'm no good.'

He watches the White man through narrowed eyes and can tell that he thinks the game is his but, Michael tells himself, it's *his*. One hour of perverted sex has passed and gone to the Devil.

Glenn points a finger to the rifle. Four weeks ago the same rifle was strange and fascinating to Apata. Now it is still fascinating but it is no longer strange. Now he knows it well. Glenn has taught him all there is to know of the weapon. There have been many hours in practice sessions.

'When we leave Guiana that will be yours. I'll see that you get a permit, or whatever legal stuff will make your ownership of it alright.'

'Thanks sah. I very glad 'bout dat sah.'

'But until then is, well, until then. Right now I have something else for you Mike. Go get the haversack.'

Apata gets to his feet in all his ebony beauty. Glenn watches blissfully. Slowly he closes his eyes and smiles.

'Whatever you find in that left side pocket belongs to you Mike.'

Apata reaches into the pocket and brings out a gold plated wrist watch. Glenn opens his eyes, clears his throat.

'Night dial kid. With a wrist watch like that you can see the time in the dark of hell. Some watch, huh?'

Apata smiles and nods his head.

'You're worth every tick from it. Mike?'

'Yes, suh?'

'What's between us is between us. For the records I've given you that watch because of your ability on the water. Huh?'

'Yessuh! Nobody gon know suh!'

'Yes,' says Glenn, half-closing his eyes. 'If anybody does, it won't be very good.'

*　　*　　*

The sunlight sieves down through the forest. Between the high foliage of the massive trees tangled together by creepers and parasite vines and many tones of greenery a few bright birds can be seen. A lone monkey hangs as in limbo. The animal begins to swing in the graceful way that only monkeys can.

'Can you hit him Mike?'

'I think suh, sah.'

'Big deal. Com'on then, let's see you hit a moving target!'

Apata gets up, moves over, picks up a rifle, braces the stock firmly into the crook of a naked shoulder and leans the cold flatness of the breech against his face as he peers through the telescopic sight. Temperatures, that of the rifle and Apata's body, are now one. Very slowly he curls his right index finger around the trigger. Through the sight the monkey is all that Michael can see as it hangs slightly pendulous. Apata holds his breath and squeezes without jerking, three times.

Against the close echoes rippling through the forest comes the sound of the monkey's dead body falling through the network of boughs. In its fall the body flattens a broad leaf on the stout limb of a tree. On the leaf a female mantis, with her half-eaten mate still locked into her, is crushed. The monkey's dead body lands with a light thud to the leafy ground.

'JESUS CHRIST!' Glenn whispers in sharp-toned amazement. The White man slowly gets to his feet and takes a step in the direction of the fallen animal with the clipped tail. 'Jesus Christ, Mike . . .' He begins, shaking his head in unbelief, then he turns and looks towards Apata and sees the meaning of John Bolton's words: '. . . If I were you Glenn, that's one native I wouldn't mess with.'

On Apata's lips there is a smile that seems to say, "How stupid of you to think I'm just another native?" But the White man does not even see that. All he can see is the barrel of the rifle levelled at his pink chest with its short golden hairs.

'OH GOD! OH GOD!' something screams inside him. 'For Chri-sakes, Michael . . .' he mouths. '. . . for Chri-sakes, don't shoot.'

Apata pulls the trigger.

Archibald Glenn screams sharply as he crumbles to the sperm sprinkled ground carpeted with layers of rotted leaves. Apata stands slackly above the body of Archibald Glenn that is alive with the fear of death, a fear that makes him only half aware of the pain in his bullet-shattered left knee.

'Put your kind heart at ease, Mister Glenn,' Michael smiles scornfully. 'No, Mister Glenn, it is not by chance that my pattern of speech differs from the way I usually speak. Nor is it due to poor marksmanship that you are alive.' Apata shakes his head. 'Pure design.' Apata's body begins to shake with silent laughter.

Glenn's chest heaves with effort. With his head bent, he grits his teeth. Blood spreads below his thighs.

'Please Mike. PLEASE! Don't leave me here to die, Mike. No one ever comes along this way. We found that out, didn't we Mike?'

'We did.'

'HELL MIKE! DON'T LEAVE ME HERE TO DIE!'

'You perverted White sonofabitch. You're also clairvoyant. You can read minds good.'

Slowly Archibald Glenn begins to get a hold of himself.

Apata lowers then leans the rifle against a rotted stump near by his leg and begins begins to cover his nakedness.

130

'I'll give you anything Mike. I'll make any deal with you. Just don't leave me here!'

Apata puts on Glenn's corduroy trousers.

'FOR GOD'S SAKE MIKE! I'M BEGGING YOU! YOU CAN SPIT ON ME IF YOU LIKE!'

High laced leather boots that are reddish brown in colour. Bush jacket with green and brown camouflage patterns. Ammo belt filled with shells for the rifle. Haversack with compass. Four heavy slabs of chocolate and a small tin of lubricating cream which Apata hurls away contemptuously. All these articles were all Glenn's. Now they are Apata's.

'IF YOU WANT, I'LL KISS YOUR FUCKING TOES!'

Apata stamps his booted feet. Good fit! he tells himself. Then he picks up the rifle. 'I hope someone finds you, Glenn. After I'm gone the thing you should do is shout at spaced intervals. That would be sensible.'

'YOU MURDEROUS FUCKING BLACK SONOFA-BITCH! I'LL MAKE IT BACK, YOU SOFT-DICKED NIGGER!'

But after that outburst, Glenn, even grown as he is, breaks down whimpering like a lost child in a hostile crowd.

'APATA-A-A-A!! – APATA-A-A-A!!!'

But the owner of the name being shouted has long disappeared into the jungle. Glenn violently shakes his head as a dog shakes its wet body. His damp hair hangs raggedly over his forehead. He looks around and sees Apata's clothes. He sees his own pair of underpants lying two arms' length from where he has fallen. Glenn sniffs sharply and begins to drag himself over to Apata's clothing.

Knowing that he must stem the bleeding in his knee he tears a strip from Apata's cotton shirt and bandages the wound. The bullet has passed right through the flesh splintering the bone. Telling himself that he must get some clothes on, Glenn turns to his shorts and, grasping a fallen leafless branch, he hooks them to him and drags them on, being careful when pulling his underwear past his damaged knee. Deciding against Apata's trousers he puts on the torn shirt. Crutches! he tells himself. To move about he needs crutches. 'No Gawdamn knife,' he hisses. It was in a sheath fixed to the trousers now being worn by Apata. He decides he's going to get himself crutches somehow.

He hears a sound.

A premonitionary fear grips him. It thrusts reasonable thoughts out of his head. Then he realizes that he should not lose control of his faculties and gets a grip of himself.

He *hears a sound*! A moaning, ending in a prolonged sighing. Sudden fear again grips Glenn and he fights to control the panic which floods his mind. It's just a bird, he tells himself. IT IS A BIRD! He feels a tightness in his chest and he lets his breath out. He listens. The strange sound doesn't come again. 'Think as though everything's normal Archibald,' he tells himself. 'Do normal things.'

Staring at the water bottle in a cleft, beside the gigantic root where he and Apata had been lying, he decides that he's thirsty and drags himself over. He drinks the bottle dry. There is no shortage of water around. Patterns of pain dominate his left leg and thighs then invade his abdomen.

He sees a little tree entangled in a tight bush, a little tree with fist-sized yellow fruits. 'I'd better eat something,' he tells himself. To him the fruits look like guavas which he had eaten once from a city market when he first came to Guiana. He drags himself over to the tree until he gets within hand-reach of one of the fruits. He picks one. He decides he's really hungry. He bites deeply into it. It tastes good to him ... tastes good. He swallows. Yes! I'm calm now. I'm in control now. 'I'll get him!' he says between mouthfuls. 'I'll live, I know I will live!' But something is wrong, something going wrong. There's a strange numb feeling in his mouth and his tongue. 'WHAT THE HELL?' he tells himself and spits, vehemently. He's feeling funny inside his chest and out. For no apparent reason, since Glenn admits to being non-religious, he remembers a sign a peach farmer back home had painted and nailed up on a high post on part of the fence that went around his orchard. Of course many people thought that the peach farmer was mad. As mad as Archibald Glenn appears to be, now, as he screams shrilly, wildly, stilling the sounds of the birds and other animals. As mad as the peach farmer came across as being because, on a board nailed upon a fence post, he had painted verses sixteen and seventeen of Chapter Two of the first book in the Holy Bible:

"And the Lord God commanded the man saying, Of every tree of the garden thou mayest freely eat. But of the tree of knowledge of good and evil, thou shalt not eat of it: for in the day thou eatest thereof, thou shalt surely die."

CHAPTER 21

Police Constable Elwin Boston pushes down with purpose on the pedals of his big-framed bicycle: a type referred to as "duck belly" and "preggy" by the Guianese children. From under the weak glare of the dented headlamp the road below the bicycle's worn tyres stretches out like a grey ribbon thinning down to a vanishing point which, when reached, will offer another vanishing point destined to give view of yet another vanishing point and then Hoop Village.

The wheels of the bicycle hum along and with every full crank of the pedal there is an accompanying scraping sound from within the crank case.

On the rear carrier of Constable Boston's transport there is clamped his long, wooden truncheon. It is his night stick and day stick. It is his weapon and because of it his three children often are heard bragging that their father, "is a mastuh at throwin' duh staff between dem bad-man foot when dey runnin' 'way!"

A lone sea bird hurtles overhead squa-a-aking at spaced intervals and something inside Boston runs cold. The lid of the box of superstition opens a crack and he feels a tingling of fear. Placing a hand inside his tunic he brings out a crucifix hung from a delicate gold chain around his neck. The emptiness of the road ever approaching and slipping away behind creates an expectancy of horror resurrecting mental images of some of the demons his dead grandfather told of time and time again. For many of the coast-dwellers there exists a local dread of lampless country roads at nights, especially of reluctant moons and dead night-air's silence.

The crucifix lightly brushing against a nickle plated button on the Constable's tunic assaults his ear drums with its metallic jingling and Boston begins to hope desperately that light will save him.

On the left and right of the inert road there are trenches where alligators and snakes live. Cane-punt trenches. The cane fields begin from the opposite banks and stretch out and away from the bisecting road and lone cycling figure, tall and thin in the saddle. Boston pedals faster hoping to depart this stretch of cane growth, that threatens to crush him from both sides, as quickly as he can.

*   *   *

Having left the last of the cane fields Boston breaks into rice lands. Hoop Village lies not far away. The road runs above the dark, low plains. Now and then the silhouetted roof of a thatched shed, standing on sturdy stilts, drifts by. In the distant backgrounds, preceded by middle-distance dams, it is possible to make out the silhouette of coconut groves. Between the long dam now running by and its distant background of bushes, Boston makes out a light. Then two spots of light, rising and falling. He hears no sound but knows it is a tractor and that it has on board an Indian who is a descendant of an East Indian.

Constable Boston begins to think of how prosperous Indians seem to be and this leads to a stream of thoughts around the word "promotion". Boston has denied himself promotion from third class constables, the rank that he now holds, to something higher. *Denied* himself thus far due to a case of unproductivity in the line of duty. Boston finds it difficult to send traffic-law breakers before the wigged head of Rajaram the village magistrate. Boston, as a constable, would stop such a person riding a headlampless bicycle at night but, on the verge of writing the person's name down in his charge book, he would think, 'If I were in this chap's place ...' And the concept would dominate the compassionate compartment of his mind. In the end, the defaulter often got off the hook with a stern warning. It has even turned into a kind of mantra for one guilty of traffic-law default, on beholding the lawman on his bulge-bellied iron steed, to repeat to himself, 'Boston don't charge nobody. Boston don't charge nobody. Boston ...'

It is not, however, an unfailing truth because Boston does charge traffic-law breakers occasionally. Take those who buzz over the night roads on headlampless bicycles. Such offenders he charges whenever he catches them, usually after sweaty, chest-pumping chases. One such chase took him through a long uneven yard path, over a rickety back-yard bridge over a salt-water trench that empties into the coastal waters and on to the local railway line where the fugitive fell and was apprehended by a panting and furious Boston showing a rare temper that his wife did not know he possessed.

His wife ...

To his wife he forever seems to be giving criminals chances. 'KEEP ON THINKING OF HOW PEOPLE FEEL AND YOU WILL SOON FIND OUT HOW HARD THIS WORLD IS! LIKE YOU WILL NEVER GROW UP AND REALIZE THAT IT DON'T PAY TO BE NICE ON THIS PLANTATION!' she hurls at him.

The wording changes from time to time but the essence is always the same. Boston finds it hard to explain to her that he cannot help being the way he is.

From under the weak glare of the dented headlamp, the road below the bicycle's tired tyres stretches out continually like a grey ribbon thinning down to a vanishing point.

I would like to be a Corporal! Constable Boston says to himself and remembers the way his wife flirted with Stephens a fellow Hoop villager who was promoted to the rank of Corporal. Stephens had celebrated his promotion at a Constabulary dance where he had openly flirted with Constable Boston's wife. But how far the new Corporal had gotten with Mrs Boston? On the night in question Mr Boston could not tell whether or not things climaxed. He was in no state to miss his wife when she and the new Corporal slipped out to compare passions under the Constabulary building which is raised on short, concrete pillars.

Boston's cheeks are hollowed. His forehead is furrowed with permanent thought creases. Boston doesn't bother any more to get irritated when called Bagabones and he has no head for strong drink. But that night, seeking a place to hide from his wife and his arrogant associate he had hidden within a bottle of vicious Demerara rum. How far did the new Corporal get with Constable Boston's wife? Boston found out by hearing of it a few days later. The villagers said, and still say, that Constable Boston is a good man, a nice man who make one big mistake which was to marry that girl who grow up in Georgetown City.

Pushing down with purpose on the pedals of the big-framed bicycle, Boston assaults the slight-angled grade of the huge wooden bridge. From its highest point he ceases to pedal. Coasting down, easily now, the gravel that makes up most of the road's surface at this point, hisses below the wheels.

Boston loves his wife and the thoughts of Stephens wrench his emotions into tearful paths. But Constable Boston would not bow to their satisfaction. He tells himself that he will always be himself. He will always be what he thinks he is. He tells himself that sometime his day will come. How soon or how late he doesn't know. He just believes that sometime his day will come. He sighs. Enough of desolation.

The lights of Hoop Village show before him. He grins through the lessening darkness.

Enough of desolation.

CHAPTER 22

A night bird, squa-a-aking at spaced intervals, arrows over the gloomy compound of the Hoop Village Post Office which is hemmed in by an aging wiremesh fence. The night watchman sits and reads. He looks up but doesn't see the night bird. His gaze moves down from the lead grey sky and falls momentarily on the overhanging leaves of the great mango tree that dully reflect the glow from the doctor's gate posts which carry orb lights. The long leaves stir in a slight breeze that is a carry-over from the winds blowing along the not too distant stretch of beach where there are granite rocks waist deep and humbled before the great Atlantic. The sea is darkened but alive under an overcast night sky.

In the area where the Post Office stands there are few houses and save for Doctor Benn's residence, the others, that make up the few, are separated from the Post Office and the doctor's house across the road by great acres of open land covered with short-cropped lime-green grass. Two pairs of crude goal posts jutting from the ground can be seen during the day.

A nocturnal commuter along the road, or from the railway line, would see the Hoop Village Post Office as a silhouette rising from the low level landscape planted with short pea-plants and wild clumps of berry-bearing bushes. The nocturnal traveller's attention would be pulled to the Post Office by a rectangular patch of yellow light at the base of the silhouetted structure.

Hoop Village's Post Office looks like a little cabin with a V-shaped roof that grows from the roof of a larger building with rectangular sides. The bottom floor is raised by a concrete foundation from the gravelly ground on which it sits. There are two concrete steps in front of the main entrance door. From this first floor level and straight up along an outside wall, shared by top and bottom stories, there is a stairway that takes a visitor upstairs.

On the stairway sits night watchman Munesh Singh. He is on the third tread from the concrete base. A long constable's truncheon rests across Singh's thighs. The elbows of both his hands are propped on his knees, and his palms are tucked into his fleshy cheeks below a forehead wrinkled with concentration. Singh's eyes are hooded by thick, shiny black-grey brows. They attempt to pierce the pages of a translation of the Kama Sutra. The type is difficult for his sixty-three-year-old eyes and the barred pattern of light shining from the bottom floor's window does not help much.

Hanging squarely above the thick-walled metal safe, that is embedded in the concrete floor, is a single forty watt filament bulb which does not provide enough light through the barred window. The bulb goes out. 'SHIT! ANOTHER FUCKING BLACKOUT SKUNT!' The experience to Munesh Singh is as if unexpectedly he has walked into a cold, hard, black wall. He puts his book down and gets up thinking of candles inside the Post Office above a side door inacessible to the regular public. There he fumbles for the bunch of keys in the pocket of his terylene shirt, still startled by the suddenness of the apparent power failure. Eventually he singles out the right key for the door. Then he experiences difficulty in finding the key hole. He misses the aperture twice before he is successful. The hinges of the door squeak, rattling the contents of Munesh Singh's box of superstition. Inside the building he stretches up and feels above the door for the candles, selects one and shuffles over to the little desk next to the heavy iron safe. There he takes a box of matches out of a back pocket of his trousers and gripping the matchstick between a trembling index finger and thumb he pulls it against the sensitive side of the match box. In the momentary flaring of the match and the simultaneous pungence of ignited sulphur, the night watch-man glimpses a blurred movement before darkness envelopes him.

The rectangle of light has disappeared from the silhouetted shape of the Hoop Village Post Office. Pedalling back, Constable Elwin Boston thinks that another blackout has occurred. He squeezes gently on the brakes then realizes that the gate lights of the vacationing Doctor Benn are still on though they are dim. He slows down and hops off his bicycle and walks forward pushing it. Something does not feel right to him.

When he was a boy, the crone of a necromancer who lived next door told his mother that Elwin had the gift of the third eye and could see far into the future. Mrs Boston, though by no means a woman who held any abhorrence for natural magic, did not take proudly to the old woman's prophetic pronouncement. Natural magic was natural and Mrs Boston believed in it. But the works of many of the people whom she knew "saw far" were works of evil. 'I ENT WANT NO OBEAH MAN GROWING UP UNDER ME,' she had declared after the old woman's prophetic pronouncement. She felt even more strongly about the prophesy after she had been cautioned on giving salt to Elwin. 'Salt, Baasy!' the crone had said in a crackling, hoarsed voice, 'Salt guh spoil de power wha' deh deep inna dat lil boy Elwin dat you have dere.' For Elwin Boston's mother the crone's dietary hint could not have been more acceptable and immediately after the old woman turned her back to shuffle back from the fence to her home that reeked of occult ceremony, Mrs Boston took Elwin inside and sat him down on a wooden bench in the kitchen. On the spot she mixed a small glass of salt water and forced Elwin to drink every bit of it.

Maybe this dose dried up the greater portion of his innate mystic qualities but left a trace in his psychic sensibilities. For as long as Constable Boston can remember he has always sensed things before they happened. Now, as he pushes his bicycle slowly along the road, and gazes at the dark shape of the Post Office, a tightness in his throat tells him that something is not right, cannot be right. He trundles his bicycle over to the bole of the huge sandbox tree that his grandfather has often talked about and lays it down by the ancient roots. He looks at the Post Office, solitary and to him, now, ominous. He breathes carefully, taking very deep, very deep breaths at spaced intervals.

A black car approaches from out of the gloom. To Boston it is narrow and looks as if the back seat can hold only two persons in comfort. It is a high topped cab that gives Boston the impression that once seated an occupant would not be able to raise his arm and touch the cab's ceiling. It is a dark and ungainly car and its headlamps are dimmed. It moves forward very slowly, even stealthily and stops on the part of the road directly outside the doctor's gate. There it is almost opposite the lightless Hoop Village Post Office.

Boston knows that Doctor Benn is on vacation. He knows that the resident caretaker is probably asleep in a drunken stupor. He knows that the car's stopping at the doctor's gate is a ruse of some sort. The engine idles. A figure steps out of the driver's door that faces the post office.

GUNSHOT!

'Oh God! What is this?' A tremor passes through Boston's lanky frame.

The figure has disappeared. 'DO SOMETHING! DO SOMETHING!' shouts Boston's inner man but his limbs refuse to be moved by mere subconscious commands.

'I WISH I DID MARRY A MAN! AND NOT A MATCHSTICK!' taunts his wife.

Constable Boston passes the back of his palm below the hairline above his forehead. His hand comes away greasy wet as if the sun burned down from a glaring noonday sun. 'MATCHSTICK!' He feels his own hand groping at the bicycle's carrier that carries his truncheon. He releases it from the carrier lock, takes a firm grip on the ribbed hilt and slips the leather thong around his wrist. Then he takes another hold of the ribbed hilt but is unaware of the ferocity of his grasp.

'I WISH I DID MARRY A *MAN*!'

He moves off, down the embankment.

'MATCHSTICK! MATCHSTICK!'

The embankment runs past the stationary car and the figure that has reappeared out of the driver's door. It is a man. He is facing away from Boston's line of approach and towards the Post Office.

'MATCHSTICK!'

With the surface of the road above him Boston, crouching, slowly stalks the car seeing it from a low vantage point. The figure disappears. Boston freezes. Like a wraith the figure re-appears. Boston is still frozen.

'OHO! IS THE TRUTH YOU WANT? YOU THINK YOU IS MAN ENOUGH TO HEAR DE TRUTH?'

Boston moves on. The car is just a few yards ahead now.

'STEPHENS IS MAN. AN' IS MAN AH WANT, NOT MATCHSTICK!'

Boston stealthily moves until he's crouched below the port side of the car directly above him. He cannot see the driver now. Boston's heart labours under his tunic and the perspiration of fear bathes his flesh. All that he must do is to climb up, stalk around the car, and surprise the man. But Boston is thinking of death.

'IF I FUCK WITH STEPHENS, DON'T BLAME ME! BLAME YOU'SELF QUIET MAN, BOSTON, DON'T-LIKE-CHARGE-ANYBODY BOSTON!'

Boston crouches now and climbs on to the road and then moves on all-fours along the port side of the car, past the back fender ... edging round the trunk ... edging around the trunk. The figure spins. 'NOT A MOVE! O-OR I SHOOT! POLICE!' Boston holds his long truncheon as one would a rifle. The hands of the figure jerk upwards in a gesture of surrender and then, abruptly, the arms of the figure fall to the waist as he rushes at the scared Boston. Boston hurls the long staff between the legs of the figure. The man crashes to the ground and Boston, motivated by fear and terror, steps in delivering a kick at the man's head and feels a hand, hands around his ankle. Boston feels himself going down and lands on his hands, palms splayed. He scrambles to his feet as the man does. No face. He dips to pick up something. 'KNIFE!' a voice shouts in the constable's head and he dips too and brings up a handful of loom dust, flinging it as he comes up. The man staggers back spitting and Boston rushes in and sinks a kick into the man's stomach. He goes down sucking air. Boston crouches and kicks the figure once more in the stomach. The figure whimpers and the air grates in his throat. Boston scrambles for what looks like his truncheon. It is. He swings it back to come down on the head of the grovelling figure.

The sound of a thunderous explosion rends the silence of the pre-dawn gloom. It shakes Boston's rabid, murderous intention. It has been brought on by his fear. With his truncheon still upraised murderously something within him shouts, 'RUN BOSTON!' Boston crouches and scurries down the embankment back to the base of the old sandbox tree where his bicycle is laid. From that point he braces and tries to get control of his lungs and of his senses driven wild by the blood pumping furiously through his veins. A band tightens around his head making him breathe deeply in order to aid a return of calm within him.

'IF I FUCK WITH STEPHENS! DOAN BLAME ME!!' screams his wife.

But the quaking of Boston's limbs continues. Now he believes, as he watches the Post Office, that he hears a distant mechanical fretting. He thinks it is coming from behind him but he's afraid to take his eyes from the Post Office building. There's someone, something in there.

A bomb went off in there just now.

The mechanical sound is indeed coming up behind him. He sneaks a backward glance and sees a pair of lights emerging from a bend of the road not very far away. Boston wrenches his head back to watch the Post Office and sees a figure with a bag running out of the Post Office compound. The mechanical fretting sound is clearer. The fugitive slips into the back seat of the car and slips out again. Boston sees a powerful torch beam lance out. It slashes the tree. Boston ducks. The light catches the car's body and it momentarily reflects light onto the planes of the fugitive's face. The light dips to the ground and the figure from the Post Office, seemingly startled, jumps back. The clattering, Boston realizes, is being made by a tractor. The fugitive figure's head whips up. TRACTOR! Torch beam lances past Boston's tree. MUDDY TRACTOR!

A shot rings out and pieces of glass from the machine's shattered headlamp clink to the road but no one can hear it above the nasal song of the engine.

ANOTHER SHOT!

The other headlamp goes and the Indian farmer bales out and dashes over to the old sandbox tree. Boston sweats. The figure with the gun stands with the weapon raised once more to shoot. The tractor clatters on menacingly, a blind, berserk contraption. The night marauder fires again. Compressed air hisses. Slowly the tractor veers, canters, crashes on one side and lies kicking in its death throes. The Indian farmer grips the bole of the tree as a man might grip an obese lover, and trembles and babbles Hindustani mixed with bad English. The man with the firearm has now ducked behind the car. Boston's trembling fingers unconsciously squeeze the crucifix dangling from the delicate chain around his neck. He feels that the gunman will now come to hunt the Indian. Boston is sure the gunman saw the Indian dash behind the tree for safety. And he knows the gunman is crouched behind the car. He knows that the gunman has seen his mate on the ground. He tells himself that the gunman is angry, so Boston tells himself that he and the Indian will both be killed. He thinks now of his only daughter. The grating of the tractor's engine, like a death rattle, comes from the bottom of the embankment on the side of the road from the tree. He thinks of his only daughter. Sons will be able to make out.

CHAPTER 23

A shaft of new light slants in through a broken section of a kitchen window that carries glass panes made semi-opaque by coats of bottle-green paint partly impaired by scribbled black lines. The window faces the sun as it crawls up the sky. As he passes through the intruding beam, an old man defensively shades his eyes. The villagers contemptuously refer to him as Old Fool Tobin for it is well known that the large two-storied house he now lives in, was offered to him by a White estate overseer in exchange for a rusted canister of dug-up, blackened, Dutch gold coins. A veritable fortune.

He shuffles to a pot-bellied cast-iron stove that stands on legs that terminate in the form of cat's paws. The stove is positioned next to a long cupboard in which there are an assortment of labelled bottles and jars. The labels on a few of them should not be taken as gospel. One heavy, glazed-pottery jar, though labelled "YEAST", contains sugar.

Tobin takes an aging teapot, with a broken spout, down from a wooden rack above the cupboard. He handles the bulbous container as one would a day-old baby. As he puts it down the rimmed bottom crushes spilled sugar grains from last night. He turns to the stove, pats himself on the chest, mutters inaudibly, shakes his bald head and scratches his sternum through the string vest. It over-rides the baggy grey tweed trousers that hide his toes. He shuffles over to a dirt-stained kitchen safe and pulls open a drawer. Set free, a large cockroach scuttles over the old man's hand and drops to the floor with its cold, worn linoleum of an indistinct pattern and colour. The roach crawls under the safe.

Tobin takes a battered box of matches from the drawer and lights the stove. With trembling fingers he opens a compartment under the sink and takes out a covered pot that is thick with soot. Sniffing at the old coffee inside, Tobin wrinkles his nostrils. He places the pot over the stove's feeble flame. His wrinkled-nostril expression twists into a smile then, as Tobin turns away, he knocks over a heavy jar.

*   *   *

Startled to alert wakefulness by the sudden crash somewhere on the floor above his head, an uninvited guest grabs his rifle and rises to his feet. He looks carefully around the large guest room and bit by bit the waking terror sinks back into and disappears from his eyes.

The room, chosen before last night fell, faces the main road of Hoop Village which is now coming alive, at intervals, with humming traffic to and from the Vreed-en-Hoop-Georgetown ferry, six miles away. The jangling of a just-passed morning train dies into the distance and the whooping of its engine, saying farewell to the village, trails off weakly. The train's last stop will be the village of Parika, ten and a half miles away.

The guest peers through an unpainted patch in the window. It was scraped of its paint only last night. It is a sunny morning.

The room is furnished, though unused by Tobin, and the wall that faces the main road from which the hum of the traffic has died, carries seven windows. Each has twelve panes. Save for the uppermost panels of each window, swirling bottle-green paint masks every pane and makes it impossible for anyone to see the unkempt lawns, or pathway, below. Daylight lances in through the dusty uppermost panes. Daylight strikes the aging papered walls where pink petalled roses once were red and provides fading evidence of a woman's touch. There is a simple double-bed that is made up with dusty chequered spread and a pair of mildewed pillows. In a shadowy corner there is a tarnished vanity-piece its drawers pulled out, its mirror draped. By the head of the bed stands a small wardrobe with its easy key in its easy lock. Close to the single door from the room, there is an American lazy-chair of a kind that converts into a recliner. A haversack, with bulging pockets, leans against the back of the chair. The pockets bulge because they are filled with Queen-head bills and the haversack itself is filled with canned foods. Under the bed there is a portable V.H.F. transmitter-receiver. The haversack, the V.H.F. and the high powered rifle he is standing with, now, in his hands all belong to Apata. More daylight filters in to brighten the room.

'I wonder what has happened? What happened to Tony while I was inside?' Michael wonders, remembering his dumb accomplice lying on the ground by the car that should have gotten them both safely out of Hoop Village hours before the sun poked above the horizon of this new day. 'I think somebody clashed with Tony and gained the upper hand. If I could have handled a car, that car ...' Apata, uninvited guest in Tobin's house is full of regrets. 'Tony's dumb,' he tells himself. 'He won't talk.' Making a sound of disgust, Apata begins to feel the pangs of his own incompetence as he sees it and feels it. The blast, he reasons, that opened the safe should not have been so wide and loud. Too much paper money destroyed. I could have killed myself. I could have killed that watchman with that rifle blow. Even the grip I had on the gun, even that was wrong. The gun should not have gone off. Scared ... I was scared. Admit it man. You were scared shitty! He sighs. 'I'll be better next time. I'll be better next time, if they don't discover who I am this time!'

On the wall to his left, which makes a right angle to the windows that face the road, Michael notices a cut-out, magazine portrait of Doris Day. A strip is torn out of her right cheek. His brows knit. He lifts his weapon and sights along the barrel aiming right between her eyes. Then he whips his head away from behind the breech of the rifle and walks over and peers through the aperture he scraped in the painted window pane. A tractor from a nearby ricefield clatters past pitching clumps of mud high into the air. It is followed by a car that roars by leaving a churned fog of yellow dust to settle back to dust. It is the dry season.

CHAPTER 24

A crowd thickens quickly on that part of the main road outside the gates of the Post Office that has never had so much attention before. Sad faces dominate, muscles of woe that never expected to be pulled are, today, working their tendons off. There's a kind of deep, remorseful silence of meditation from those who stand around, an interweaving of shaking-headed-nodding-headed-teeth-sucking dialogue:

'Yes, somebody knock out Singh and blow up the safe wit' all de money.'

'You ent hear, too, dat Boston catch one'ah dem?'

'Who Bostan, dah?'

'You nah know Constable Bastan? If you nah know P.C. Bastan then you nah live ah dis village!'

'Eh eh ...dis colony turnin' like'ah wan republic!'

'Wha' ah wan republic, Chachee?'

'EH? WAN PLACE WHEH YO' CAN BUY GUN, RASS AN' KILL WHOEVAH YO' WAN' KILL!'

'Wha' happen to Munesh? He dead?'

'No, Mr Singh ent dead. He in hospital for shock an' concusshan.'

'Dah ah true. But dem seh dat Singh seh whoevah lash 'e ah 'e head, pull 'e out before de bomb guh off.'

'Dah lie! 'Ow Singh could seh dah if 'e deh in a shack?'

'Anyway ... 'e pull Munesh out befo' de bham guh aff an' whoevah de skalewag be, he really considahrate!'

'DAT GAT TO BE WAN COOLIE-MAN, RELSE HE WOULDN'AH SAVE SINGH!'

'PAHSAD! YOU TOO RACIAL RASS!'

'This is what I would call a black Friday!'

'No penshan rass.'

'ALL DE MONEY GAWN FUH CHANNA!'

'No. I don't share your view. If not today we will get it tomorrow, or by Monday the latest.'

'True wha' teacher Davis ah seh.'

'The government won't see the elderly folk go hungry. They would do something.'

'Yes. Dem guh bring money from Georgetown tomorrah! Yo' wan' bet?'

'Mih agree with you on dat. But mih hear de thing go off las' night. Mih did dreamin' when de fuck ... excuse me Pars'n ...'

'That's alright. I heard it go off too.'

'Mih hear de thing guh off, too. But I did frighten too much to come out to see what it be.'

With a torturous squealing of brakes a Pontiac, sprayed in grey, stops on the road behind the curious crowds. The dust it disturbs settles slowly. Out of the car steps a strapping, grim-faced White man with a handle-bar moustache. He slams the door shut behind him. In his wake two Negro detectives emerge from the car.

The driver sits alone now and watches the two Negro policemen as they move up quickly behind the striding White police officer. The trio makes its way through an unreasonably wide passage-way made by the roadside locals for just three persons.

'RASS BOY! Who's duh?'

'That is the Crime Chief. They's call 'e Bloody Jesus!'

'DAT ENGLISHMAN DAT? EH? DAT MAN DOAN MAKE JOKE!'

'Sandhurst man, yeh.'

'PURE BUSINIS' DEM WHITE PEOPLE! TRUE! DOAN MAKE JOKES ATALL, ATALL!'

As a man reputedly not given to humour, Assistant Commissioner of Police and Crime Chief Maurice Adolphus Plumb, forty-nine years old, jokes well enough with his fellow police officers in the officers' mess in Georgetown City. His cold expression, which gives rise to the comment on his non-tolerance of jokes, is often used by his tribe in the colonial ruling-race farce. There's a probability that the cold-cruel no-nonsense expression is necessary to remind the natives that the pink-skinned ones are in charge and bent, for their own satisfaction, on enforcing the God-fearing submissiveness of the colonized natives.

Plumb's five feet eleven inches adds to his inherited show of racial superiority this day and the correctness of his movements, too.

Then there are the Negro detectives: Braithwaite and Gittens.

Detective Sergeant Kenrick Alexander Gittens' scornfully puckering lips protrude from a grim face. Should he tip his Panama hat over his brows he would look very much like a stereotyped North American gangster. His jawline is as squared as Dick Tracy's and his brows are heavy-set and knotted with slight furrowed lines on the forehead above them. He has light brown skin. On his haunches before the blast-torn metal door of the heavy Post Office safe, he shakes his head. A smile, known by many of the seasoned criminals he has arrested without the assistance of a firearm, kills the self-important puckering of his lips. 'Nitro,' he mutters then, raising his hand, he announces, 'Dynamite, Chief!'

The Crime Chief grunts and repeats the word. Then he turns and stares into the violated safe. It yawns back emptily as the open-mouthed dead would. In its empty stomach lies the debris of shattered paper money and shifted towers of coins. A shelf breaks the safe into two compartments, upper and lower. On the lower section's base there are sheaves of business papers, forms and more shattered paper money. Every bit of it would have to be gathered.

Plumb turns away while Gittens proceeds to make a note of his findings and Braithwaite, the other Negro detective, dusts for fingerprints.

Plumb mumbles that something is 'bloody interesting'.

Through a blast-shattered window he sees a few children intermingled in the crowds on the road. The main group that converges on the Post Office compound's gates has grown bigger. He looks at the steeple of the old Anglican church and a windmill in the vicinity of the steeple which turns slowly. It has part of a weathercock that is painted in red. Plumb moves over to a wall where a board has been blown loose. Below the wall, the portrait of Her Majesty the Queen lies disrespectfully on the floor. The glass, protecting Her Highness from the filth of moths and other insects, is shattered but her Royal Primness is not disturbed. The Crime Chief picks up the portrait and places it gently on top of the Post Master's desk.

CHAPTER 25

Crime Chief Maurice Plumb glides his palm over his bald cranium. His palm comes away a bit damp. Then he lifts the receiver, 'Lovell?'

The officer from the ballistics department tells the Crime Chief that the evidence is unshakable.

'You're quite sure?'

'Yes, sir.'

'Very good, Lovell!' Plumb replaces the instrument. The little tinkle stands out like an asterisk set to mark off one stage of his investigation.

Enumerated on the desk before him are the elements of the case. A brief description of the Post Office robber provided by one, Constable Boston. A typewritten report on two men, one White the other Negro, lost in the forested Essequibbean hinterlands. There are two photographs. One is of a high-powered rifle the other of a very dark Negro youth. There's also a rifle bullet pried from the Hoop Village Post Office ceiling. A bullet from a high-powered rifle. Plumb pushes his chair back with a scrape, then steps from behind his desk.

He moves to a grey filing cabinet and takes out a folder. He looks once more at the American he has studied half an hour back. He returns to his desk and places the American's photograph next to the photo of the dark Negro and the rifle.

The sounds from the hand-cranked duplicating machine filter down from an open-doored room at the upper end of the heel-dented lino-covered corridor. Plumb imagines the clanking of newspaper presses stamping his conclusions and photograph on the front page, stamping the manhunt, and

153

the capture. Yes, he thinks he's got something concrete on the elusive Hoop Village Post Office robber.

Brisk footsteps draw near, pass, disappear from the corridor and clatter up the stairway that leads to the floor above. The unbroken rhythm of the footsteps tells Plumb that it is the Commissioner's Portuguese secretary.

Plumb would report his conclusion to the Commissioner but not immediately. First he will discuss his findings with his friend, Robert Taylor, the office-bound Deputy Commissioner of police. Plumb places the articles that give rise to his conclusions in a large manilla envelope and tucks it under his right arm. He then puts on his officer's cap and moves to the door.

Before he opens it he makes sure that his White officer's no-nonsense countenance is in place.

CHAPTER 26

'Boston ...'

'Yes Corporal?'

Standing, Corporal Charles Stephens smiles but the expression does not reach his eyes. They are cold and hard and they do not meet Boston's who has answered in the tones of one seasoned in inferiority. At this moment only Stephens knows.

Corporal Stephens is in charge of the Hoop Village Police Station, a building painted in cream and blue. One and a half months back he told the wife of the man before him that her husband was not ambitious enough and therefore would never get anywhere in the police force ... It was a statement he made at the Constabulary dance when his promotion to Corporal was being celebrated. It was a statement he had made to the man's wife after he had already made love to her. That night, he had found out, Boston had made himself drunk in order to brace himself to the painfulness of the humiliation. Stephens heard that Boston sat the whole night silently drunk. Stephens felt bad after he heard it but was able to console himself with the thought that a man ought to be able to hold his wife and if his wife was willing to give a piece of her matrimonial cleft to someone else, so what? All in all, there is something about Boston that Stephens has always despised and still does. He feels this even more strongly now that he must tell the lanky man before him, 'Orders have just come through. You have been promoted to full Sergeant.'

'ME?'

'Congrats.' Stephens sticks a hand out to Boston but Boston's vision has suddenly grown selective. He deliberately chooses not to see Stephens' hand.

Boston had sat out the evening of the Constabulary dance as a specimen of jest and Stephens, the man of the moment, had been smiling a lot. The lights from the hall had glinted on his polished gold-capped teeth.

Now Stephens' teeth are dry. Making a congratulatory face is difficult, especially in the face of Boston's cold snub. He licks his lips, swallows as if to make sure his salivary glands have not deserted him and sheepishly retracts his hand and uses it to fiddle with a fountain pen on the desk behind which he sits. A little desk now. Before Boston's promotion the desk had been a mahogany roll-top.

'Superintendent Franklin,' continues Stephens, 'will be here at three o' clock.' Boston does not hear the rest of it. When Stephens' lips cease to move Boston tells himself he will thank him for delivering the message. 'And you're expected to be presentable. There will be an inspection parade.'

'My children,' Boston mutters, 'will feel glad. Especially my big boy.'

'And what about your wife?' asks Stephens.

'Well, she has a Corporal on the side so she must be happy with him.'

Watching the trembling fingers of the man before him, Boston suddenly feels embarrassed and at the same time elated and triumphant. What he does not feel, is the ominous envy which envelops the mind of the Corporal standing, now, dry-mouthed before him. And he will never know that, before the day passes, Charles Stephens, seeking to bring him a spell of misfortune will consult a sorceress. Then again, Corporal Stephens does not know that his evil scheme is destined to fail because all the sons of Isabella Boston are protected against any of the forms of necromancy in which the Corporal believes.

CHAPTER 27

The Hoop Village highway stretches away into a moonless night. Along that part of the road which runs on the outskirts of the village, a medium sized car frets and occasionally farts. Mr Barnum sees the old colonial Dutch sluice coming up. Soon he would pass Old Fool Tobin's house with the rich yellow gas-lamp glowing from a window on the upper floor. Barnum sucks his teeth and begins to grumble below his breath something about 'Black people'. Barnum is sixty-three years old, a bachelor, a ladies man and, in his own eyes, the safest taxi-man in Hoop Village.

The car rolls past coconut trees which stand like sentinels of the night. The road slowly comes forward, slinks under the car and stretches away behind it to Parika, ten and a half miles away. The car drops into a rut and something scrapes below the chassis. Barnum sucks his teeth and again begins to grumble below the aged rattling of his vehicle with the name *May May* sign-lettered on the rear window. 'Ayo does laugh at Barney an' 'e *May May*, nuh?' people say. 'But dat man deh pon it fuh over nine years an' 'e nevah yet had a accident! NOT A DENT BY BAD DRIVIN'.'

Barnum takes the shallow turn easily. On his left he sees Old Fool Tobin's gift mansion coming round. Soon he would pass the rusted iron gate. He shakes his head, grumbles and spits off past his right shoulder away from the building. He passes it.

In the glare of *May May*'s headlamps, Barnum makes out the figure of a woman. She waves as if she wants him to stop. Barnum shifts down and glances at the face of the alarm clock conveniently wedged into what used to be a glove compartment on his dashboard. 'She can't catch no train at this time,' Barnum tells himself. 'Somebody at leas' couldah tell she so. Anyway she can still catch the late train. It got to be late train she want cause other than me all them other boys finish work. Wonder where she going, though?'

He stops.

The woman comes over. He leans over from his right-hand drive position to listen through the window on his left.

'Good night Mr Driver. You could please drop me to the train station?'

'Miss lady, where you going?'

'Ow Mr, I really want to get to Parika tonight.'

'You late fuh every other train but late train, Miss lady, which is ten o' clock. You gon have to wait at leas' one hour after you get there.'

'I realize that but I rather be at the train station and wait 'cause I have to get home to my sick mother. A chap riding down, bring the news not long ago.'

'I did going home, anyway I understand how it is when you have sick and you want to get home quick. Ah will drop you at the train station and have faith, man, the ol' girl going to be a'right. If Parika wasn' so far away ah wouldah take you all the way. But ah lil tired. You understand?'

'Ow, only a hard hearted person wouldn' understand something like that.'

Barnum gets out to place the woman's suitcase in the car's trunk. He lifts and almost strains his back because of the unexpected weight. He puts it into the trunk which closes after two slams that resound harshly, but briefly, in the night. The woman stands with a cloth-wrapped paddle-like object in her hands.

'Sit down, Miss lady. Leh me turn the car 'round.' He opens the rear door for her. She gets in, and the suspension whimpers.

'Mr Barnum? I was frightened as I did waiting for a car to come by. I was telling myself: 'Ow God leh the car that I see first be Mr Barnum car.'

Barnum laughs modestly then closes her door successfully with a single slam. 'Why you did praying to meet Mr Barnum?' he asks, as he gets in.

'Don't laugh Mr, but I frighten car men at nights bad! Plus all like how you'all have a gunman at large ...'

'You new here?'

'Yes, but people tell me 'bout you.'

The cab light is on. Mr Barnum takes in his passenger. Her hair encased in a fine net under a broad-brimmed hat fashioned from a lacey material, doesn't hold him neither does her face which he really can't vouch for since it is heavily shaded by the down-casted shadow of the hat's rim.

Too much lipstick! Is the most Barnum can say for the face. All in all she comes over to Barnum as a real country-don't-know-how-to-dress. Puff sleeves and ruffly-ruffly collar. For Barnum there is one thing that's right about her that being right makes everything else forgivable, her breasts. Good bust line! Thinks Barnum in lustful appraisal. Good bubbies them. I could live between breasts like dat.

He throws *May May* into the appropriate gears and points her, after turning around, back the way he has come.

Barnum could clearly be heard at times declaring to his fellow taxi drivers that he is a breast man.

'Yeahs,' he says to his breasty passenger, 'is home I was going after finish working for the day. But one more job won't kill. On second thoughts Missis, I ent going to charge you for this drop.'

'Thanks Mr Barnum. Also, I ent married.'

'Man,' says Barnum to himself, 'she got one helluva a voice dere, though is not the voice that matters.'

'Well, Misses,' he says aloud, 'well how you like ahh what is going on in this village here: Hoop Village gets like a cowboy town. Post Office robbery with nitro-glycerine, that is dynamite by the way, and getaway car ... GUN ...' Barnum clears his throat, grunts, shakes his head and dips his lights so as not to dazzle a tractor driver. The farm machine clatters by in the opposite direction.

'Missis, I bet you that this guman won't be easy to catch! From what I hear is a young man who put good brains to bad things. British Guiana police ent used to that kind of criminal. They used to cutlass criminals! BUT A BRAINS BAD MAN? DEM PORTFOLIO ENT WRITE UP TO DEAL WITH THAT! HARD TIME! I am sure that this gunman will get the attention of the criminological sophisticates.'

Barnum loves the use of tricky diction especially in the presence of women.

'Already the Crime Chief using this gunman to make a big name for himself, you know, by trying to figure out things like where the man is who he is and if he still in the village. BRAINS BAD MAN. Hmm! This gunman will give dis colony a hard time to catch him. Mark what I say Missis. BRAINS BAD MAN!' He shakes his head, laughs in his throat. 'If you ask me, I think that chap done cross over the border!'

It dawns on Barnum that his passenger has not, thus far, contributed a single word towards making his monologue into dialogue. So, thinking that his passenger may be worrying deeply about her sick old mother, he cuts his gaff and proceeds to think of her breasts and how he might feel wedged between their toothsome softness. Words of an old man and dead alcoholic friend brighten in him: 'Baby bottle, man plaything ... WHAT IS THAT?' Lackraj, Barnum's late friend, once threw that quiz question.

A late prowling dog takes its time to cross the road before *May May*. Barnum honks his off-keyed blaring horn. The dog startles and bolts yelping.

He smiles to himself. 'Baby bottle, man plaything: breasts!'

The red-spot glare of a storm lantern at a police check-point shimmers ahead. Barnum gears down. In the middle of the road stands an Indian law man like a colossus. He lifts a hand the palm open towards the approaching vehicle. Barnum stops.

The policeman bends and peers into the car. He sees a sleeping woman, a woman now stirring in her sleep.

'Thought you finish for the day, Barney.'

'Las' train to Gun Hill, Comar boy,' says Barnum jovially. 'By the way, how long you'all got to keep this checking-ah-cars on this road?'

'Crime Chief think that the gunman still hiding in the village, so 'til he decide that the gunman lef' we got to keep up this.'

The lights of a vehicle coming up behind *May May* cuts into the conversation.

'Ah will see you tomorrow Barney!' The matchbox is waved on. From the corner of his right eye Barnum sees another lawman in the shadows. Unlike Comar, with whom he just spoke, this other one holds a .303 police rifle at the ready.

*   *   *

Barnum shifts gears to take the turn in to the Hoop Village train station and sticks his right hand out the window to signal.

'Old man,' says the calm voice of Michael Apata, 'Take me all the way to Parika or I shoot your head clean off with this gun.'

Something cold and metallic jams against the back of Barnum's head. Something cold and metallic stays pressed to the back of his neck. Signal arm retracted speedily, Eleazar Barnum continues driving straight on whilst his hands tremble, whilst his sixty-three-year-old frame grows weak, whilst sweat beads on his forehead and runs down into his eyes.

The road comes forward, slinks back under the car and tails back to Hoop Village now become background.

CHAPTER 28

Gerald Tross thinks of Michael Apata. Last night he dreamt of Michael and Michael was covered with blood. Where is Michael?

He turns from the window and looks to the red clock on the cabinet of cutlery and expensive ware that his mother uses only when there are visitors. The time is five minutes to nine o' clock. There will be news to come. His thin mother sits in her rocking chair being courted by sleep. Ulric Tross reads an old newspaper. The radio plays and Gerald knows that the old man's ears are cocked to hear of the gunman of Hoop Village.

Outside an owl hoots mournfully. Gerald peers up in the Parikan dark and believes he sees the owl's silhouetted shape perched on a coconut tree's branch.

'Something is going to happen tonight,' he tells himself. 'I can feel it. Something is going to happen tonight.'

'Mih nah hear you,' says his father. Gerald turns. Old Tross folds his heavy brown-framed spectacles.

'You were talking to me, Daady?'

Tross watches his boy.

'A was asking you what you think 'bout dis robber man ah Hoop Village?'

'Well, Daddy, what can I tell you?' Gerald then shrugs.

Old Tross folds the newspaper he has been reading and puts it away.

'Is what bothering you son? Ah watchin' yo' fuh some time an' everything nah right wit' you. Mih sure ah dat.'

'For a long time, Daady, I was worrying about Michael. All the letters I wrote him have come back.'

162

'Life ah wan strange thing bhai. Yo' mother an me binnah talk 'bout Michael las' night. She nah think Michael dead. She seh dat if 'e dead you fus guh know. Mih nah know wha' she binnah talk 'bout, but she seh how you an' Michael ah spiritual friend a-an' if 'e dead you mus' know.'

The owl hoots outside. His haunting solo is backed by night's orchestra and spreads foreboding in Gerald's chest.

'You think Michael dead, Jerry?'

'THE TIME ... NINE O' CLOCK ...'

'Eh? You think Michael dead?'

'NOW, THE NEWS.'

'I don't feel so Daady.'

'UP TO NEWS TIME THE POLICE ARE STILL CONVINCED THAT THE GUNMAN WHO ROBBED A POST OFFICE ON THE WEST COAST OF DEME-RARA IS STILL AT LARGE IN THE VICINITY OF THE CRIME. TODAY, CITY DETECTIVES HAVE COMBED HOOP VILLAGE WHERE THE ROBBERY TOOK PLACE FOR INFORMATION LEADING TO THE POSSIBLE WHEREABOUTS OF THE GUNMAN. POLICE ROAD BLOCKS ARE STILL PLACED AROUND THE VILLAGE. ALSO, TIGHT SECURITY MEASURES ARE IN EFFECT AT THE HOOP VIL-LAGE TRAIN STATION. CRIME CHIEF PLUMB IS CONFIDENT THAT SOONER OR LATER THE MAN WILL BE ARRESTED.

'A RECENT POLICE STATEMENT SAYS THAT THEY ARE LOOKING FOR A YOUNG MAN WHO MAY BE ABLE TO ASSIST IN BRINGING THE INVESTIGATION TO A CLOSE. THE NAME OF THE YOUNG MAN IS MICHAEL RAYBURN APATA WHO ALSO ANSWERS TO THE NAMES "APATA", "RAYBURN", "MOZE", and "ROCK".'

'OH JESUS CHRIST!'

'WHAT HAPPEN ULRICH?' asks Mrs Tross, shocked awake. But the old man stares with his lips moving silently at the radio.

'Geral'? What happen Geral'?'

163

But her son too just stares at the big dark radio.

'GERAL', WHA' HAPPEN?'

'Police ...' her son manages to say in a voice that takes on a hoarseness he does not intend. So that his mother can hear him, he repeats: 'Police.' His face twists with emotion. 'Police looking for Michael.'

Her eyes open wide and stare at her son's face. Gerald's lips tremble, and his eyes glint with tears.

'OW GOD, WHAT IS DIS?'

As Gerald turns away from her and heads for the door, the owl hoots again outside.

She turns to her husband who folds and unfolds the handles of his spectacles with hands that tremble. 'ULRIC?' Slowly he turns his head to her. 'ULRIC, YO' THINK HE GUH COME HAY?' Ulric turns his face away from his wife.

'Is Jerry friend yo' know ...' he says, quietly.

'ME ENT THINK,' she says breathlessly, 'ME ENT THINK MIH WANT 'E FUH COME HAY!'

The old man sucks his teeth, swings and glares angrily at his wife then looks away abruptly to suck his teeth again.

*   *   *

'Solomon a grundy ...' mumbles Gerald Tross standing on the bridge in front of his home when the news ends and is followed by the announcements of deaths and messages. He gazes down to the water, stagnant water, deep stagnant water. Slowly he sits down allowing his legs to dangle in space. And his mind, strangely numb, spins in a void of emptiness for a moment. 'GERALD!' He hears it cleanly and clearly within himself. Remorse suddenly swamps him. 'Solomon a grundy ...' he mumbles and seems not to care that tears course down the cheeks of a respectable young farmer who would be unable to answer with an unwavering voice should a fellow villager pass a greeting of the night. Gerald Tross, however, seems to be beyond social convention and the farce of manhood. It's as though, he thinks, all men are children, all children are babies, and all babies cry.

164

'What happening Gerald?' says someone who stands next to him in the gloom. But to Gerald it is still the voice of his subconscious breaking in to chat with him as part of the inner madness of love and care that have been affected by the police news.

'Gerald,' says the voice clearly, edged with impatience. Gerald twists his head and realises that there is someone real outside of him who is speaking to him. 'Gerald, IS ME. Mike!'

'Mike?' Gerald slowly gets to his feet. 'Is really you MIKE?'

'Could I sit down?'

'M-MIKE?'

'Hey man, you're crying. Shit man!'

Gerald laughs, throws his arms around Michael's shoulders. 'Yes and funny, I can't stop the thing.' Gerald laughs. 'The news didn't say it until tonight but I felt all along that you were the Hoop Village man. I wish I could see you, see how you look!'

'Feel my face. You'll see how I look. Feel it.'

Gerald reaches out, feels, laughs. 'BLUE BEARD!'

'Black Beard,' corrects Michael.

The owl plagues the reunion of friends with its haunting call.

'How's Uncle Ulric?'

'One year we worried for you chap.'

Apata says nothing.

'Is one year I'm writing letters to you ... but all come back.'

Apata says nothing. He sits down on the low bridge. Gerald looks down at him then sits, too. 'Mike?'

'Yeah.' His voice is flat, emotionless.

'Beverley got a daughter for you, Mike.'

Apata begins to shake his head like one enduring agonizing pain.

'Is a real nice girl, Mike. Beverley named her Michelle.'

'I have something I want you to do for me Gerald.'

Apata takes a rectangular parcel from inside his shirt.

165

'You were always good at managing money. You made the smallest amount of money between us in Georgetown, do big things. So, master of financial management, take this.'

Gerald takes the packet. It is a tight parcel.

They sit silently.

The owl is silent. Probably he has flown away while the night's orchestra is taking a rest. A lone cricket does a solo some place nearby. Clouds, dimly seen above seem motionless and for the first time it becomes clear that the strains of a wake-house hymn float on the soft winds of the night.

'Gerald, I-I'm a fool you know.'

Gerald does not reply.

WANTED

Police Offer $500 Reward for the Arrest of
Apata.

$500.00 is offerd for information leading to the
arrest of Michael Rayburn Apata, also called
Rock, Moze, and Pata; who is wanted for the
following:

- Questioning in relation to the disappearance
  of North American national, Archibald Glenn,
  whose weapon, a high-powered rifle, is
  believed to be in the unlawful possession of
  the said Michael Apata.
- For robbery with accompanying destruction
  to State property.
- For being in possession of an un-licensed
  fire-arm.

DESCRIPTION:
Negro/ 5 feet 10 inches tall/ Medium build/
High cheek bones/ Reclining forehead/ Com-
plexion: dark brown/ Age: Twenty-one. Now
probably bearded.

Last seen on Monday 8th., wearing a blue
organdy dress.
May be travelling in the Bartica area.

Appeals are made to wood cutters, farmers and
boat owners to report to the nearest police
station or outpost if anyone resembling the
description printed above is seen.

Members of the public are cautioned: DO NOT
TRY TO APPREHEND THIS MAN. He is armed
and extremely dangerous.

CHAPTER 29

Daylight has sunk into dusk. Dusk has given way to a moonless cold darkness. There are no streetlamps for there are no streets, just an old dirt road bordered by canals.

In the few houses, separated from each other by dense dark acres of bushes, women and children make no fuss being alive. They breathe carefully and, when drowsiness overpowers fear, they sleep while the men folk stay awake on guard. Windows and doors are barred and soundless prayers for the waking sun rise to heaven.

A night-bird's droppings hit a house's galvanized, sheet-metal roof and a man starts and grips a shotgun tighter yet in his trembling hands. Now and then fireflies light up parts of the darkened home. The man gets up from his vigil and looks around, moves to the kitchen and presses an ear to the door there, moves across the floor in a flat-foot glide. His shoeless feet make no sounds. Through the slats of the jalousie which faces the old dirt road, he stares from darkness to darkness. Searching. Then he thinks he hears something. Something?

Holding his shotgun by the cold barrel he eases the wooden stock down to rest on the floor boards between his feet, turns an ear to listen, presses the side of his face against the slats. Above the usual nightly music of miniature nocturnal creatures comes a sound. To the man it might be that of a diesel engine. Harsher and clearer it rises getting closer. He turns his head at an oblique angle to look through the horizontal slats. He sees glaring monstrous eyes pitching about. Soon they will flash by. The man watches the lights coming closer . . . closer. Then, with thundering vibrations, it passes.

'HARRY?' It is the man's wife. 'WHA' DAH HARRY?'

'Police truck.'

'Harry, you believe dem guh ketch am?'

The man shrugs his bowed shoulders and, with a sideways jerk of his head, corrects some hair that had fallen over his brow. Fatigue shows on a face wretchedly lit by the little kerosene lamp in his wife's hands.

The sound of the truck fades. A dog howls far, far away and a zephyr ripples and rustles the branches of a coconut palm outside.

*   *   *

So far it has been a matter of following the run of this dark corridor through the dew-wet, body-brushing undergrowth that is cold and startling to the face and uncomfortable against bare arms. The police, however, have become used to it. The repeated susurrus of leaves being brushed aside has become just another night sound and their eyes have become more or less accustomed to the gloom.

The trail opens onto a plain. Far beyond it waits the black uneven wall of another forest. Here in the plains the grass grows high. The advancing policemen, faces grim under riot helmets, think of snakes. A man moving a foot forward cannot see his own boot. Nor does the man see his fellow pacing ahead of him. He sees a shape and finds solace in the knowledge of the amassed presence of the others.

An invisible attack from biting flies or mosquitoes draws a little blood, and a lot of cloth-dulled slaps and muttered indecencies.

A deep-toned moaning, a weird bassy sound fills the forest gloom they have just left. The sound rises from below the incessant screech-croaking passages of crickets, frogs and other smaller forms of life, then falls as if it is dying to rise once more to a climax in a prolonged scream filling the deep dark bushes not very far behind.

169

Many of the policemen of African and East Indian descent are afraid. They sneak glances over their shoulders.

Abruptly the sound cuts. But in the hearts of many it still lingers.

They plod on.

The man in the lead jerks his right hand up. The men stop.

There, between them and not too far from the new line of forest, a huge tree looms from a gigantic spread of roots which are partly covered by a silhouetted, hedgy tangle of bushes through which a faint glow of fire can be seen. The White police officer, Assistant Commissioner and Crime Chief Maurice Plumb, and a Negro Detective-Sergeant crouch together making a silent survey. Tall grass surrounds the quarry.

'This is it,' the White officer whispers. The Detective-Sergeant pays keen attention to the voice: 'Take half of the men, work your way around and close in from the REAR!' The White officer indicates with a semi-circular movement of his right hand. 'I will continue moving forwards from this point. We'll have him from two sides, sandwiched! We must try to be quiet as we move. He may be asleep or he may well be awake.'

The Detective-Sergeant moves out with his section. Silent bent-backed wraiths fade into the gloomy grass as they move away from the Crime Chief's group which also advances.

In an ensnaring, semi-circular pattern, Plumb's group closes in. The suspect tree looms larger, the glow of the fire brighter. 'So far so good,' Plumb whispers to himself. In his left hand he holds a service revolver at half cock. With his right, he waves his men cautiously on. It is a wide, but tightening dragnet.

On the level, the ground hidden below the dark fuzziness of the tall grass, is soft and, in some places, swampy.

The Crime Chief's group closes in, and each policeman has his own view of the fire. So far, for Plumb, it seems a piece of cake.

Something whip-like rears out of the tall grass close to the face of a Corporal 'OH-GAWD-O-GAWDOGAAAAAAAG!'

The Corporal's silhouetted figure pitches back with the coiled thing trailing back into the ground before him and there is the sound of a body thrashing in the grass. Others, having thrown themselves flat clasp and unclasp their rifles. A few lips mutter prayers, hearts race, fears of sudden death interfere with the mens' normal breathing rhythms. Plumb rises slowly and scurries over to where the man has fallen. Plumb sees a deeper darkness crushed into the grass and switches on the big, hooded torch. At the end of the light-beam he sees a hand. Clawed fingers and thumb surround a clump of uprooted grass. Plumb trains the beam up the arm, over the chest in time to see a thick, shiny-black snake unwinding itself from the neck of Police Corporal Charles Stephens of Hoop Village. The Corporal's eyes protrude as strangulation ends his life. 'BLOODY JESUS CHRIST!' Plumb says below his breath. A shiver crawls up his spine and makes him curl his toes in his boots. 'Bloody Jesus Christ!' The sensation envelops him for a second time. Steadying the beam, he fires accurately into the body of the vicious constrictor halfway out of sight but unable to escape Plumb's tracking torch-light beam. 'I must find the bloody head,' Plumb tells himself and steps after the stretching, slowly convulsing creature. Then he spots the head in the beam of the light. The eyes gleam like evil rubies. Plumb fires, shredding the head. At once there is the sound of a rifle's shot from not far away. The glow of the fire near the base of the tree has disappeared. The Crime Chief does not know whether or not he ought to feel stupid. He just knows that he had to kill the reptile. He takes off his cap, runs his fingers through imaginary hair and puts his cap back on again. Thinking calmly, but fiercely, he hopes the next move he knows he will have to make, will be understood by Gittens who should be closing in from the other side of the tree. He hopes that Gittens will understand and take the initiative. Plumb wishes that he had a loud hailer. He takes a deep breath.

'APATAAAA! SURRENDER APATA!'

No sounds of frogs. No sound of crickets. It is a time for humans.

'GIVE YOURSELF UP APATAAA. THIS IS THE POLICE!'

Three shots follow each other in close succession from the base of the tree, slapping at the night as the echo of Plumb's challenge dies fast.

Plumb reaches into the canvas holster hanging from his belt and takes out a short pistol with a very large bore. It has a revolver's hand grip, a trigger guard with a trigger. He aims it upwards into the sky over the tree and fires.

A dribbling phosphorescence arcs through the night then bursts into a searing brilliance bathing everything below it in an eerie glare.

At the base of the huge tree the policemen see a section of a make-shift bush hut. The flare burns. Something glints metallically from the base of the tree. The descending flare continues to burn.

'FIRE!' orders Plumb.

Detective-Sergeant Gittens knows that something's gone wrong on the Crime Chief's side of things. He has heard Stephens' death scream. He knows that the original plan is blown. Plumb's distant challenge and the shots being fired tell Gittens that he must take advantage of the secrecy which still covers his side of the manoeuvre.

Keeping themselves low in the grass Gittens and his men remain frozen and immobile. The flare, burning brilliantly, descends. They hear once more an orderly fusillade of Plumb's rifles. The flare continues to burn, descending slowly.

Three shots ring out in a one-two-three succession from the fugitive's tree. Heads jerk up to see the magnificent globe of incandescence knocked reeling from the air. Corporal Hutson, a police marksman with Gittens, whispers an obscenity below his breath in admiration of marksmanship. The darkness returns with a seeming show of vengeance. Like the others he makes out Gittens' signal to move.

The Detective-Sergeant edges his men forward using the cover of clumps of foliage. The fugitive's tree is now just a little over six big leaps away. Gittens does a quick reconnaissance as his men wait for another signal to close in.

Six shots crack out from the base of the tree.

Gittens tries to swallow a lump in his throat as he peers into the darkness. He hardly expects to see anyone. Any fool would dig in and keep low. A tear-gas grenade . . . he has no tear-gas grenade. An odour rises from the open front of his tunic and he wonders if it's the smell of fear he's read so much about.

The guns are cracking again from the far side of the tree. Gittens rises from something like the sprinter's start position that he has held in the deep grass and lifts his revolver in his right hand to wave the men through the final distance to accomplish a perfect capture of the gunman who, Gittens imagines, will be too surprised to turn around with all his faculties on the alert. An impulse to rush the fugitive gunman is quenched in Gittens' mind. He feels water trickling below his hairline. 'Take it easy chap!' he tells himself. 'Take it easy. You will get him.'

The firing continues from Plumb's side of the ambush.

Taking a very deep, calming breath Gittens steps off in a crouch simultaneously waving his men forward. Suddenly something rings out sharp and metallic. Detective-Sergeant Kenrick Gittens hears only a fraction of it. One millionth of a second of it. A police bullet fired by a man in Plumb's detachment ricochets from the surface of an aluminium mess pan hung on the trunk of Apata's tree and drills into Gittens' forehead. He drops dead. The policemen behind him throw themselves to the ground. Bullets like supersonic bees now hum through the darkness above the grass in which they lie.

'OH GOD APATA, DOAN SHOOT NO MOE. AH SURRENDER!'

It is a high-pitched voice that wavers, quavers, breaks then simply screams hysterically.

'SHUT UP DeABRU!' shouts Corporal Hutson. The voices draw more fire and the Corporal, now in charge, thinks it would be suicide to lift a head. He waits, thinking of death like all the others, thinking of death and wondering when the bullets will begin burrowing funeral trails through the thin, broken grass about them. 'Move back on your bellies!' Hutson whispers to the man not far from him. The man whispers it to a man not far from him who whispers it to a man not far from him. So they retreat, leaving the dead man.

*   *   *

The Crime Chief and his men fire again ... but there's no answering fire. Plumb is baffled. He thinks he heard an appallingly cowardly screaming from the tree. Or was it beyond the tree? Plumb fears that Gittens' detachment has been shot up. The abrupt stoppage of gunfire from the base of the tree baffles him. Plumb clasps and unclasps the service revolver he holds in his clammy left palm. He raises the flare gun in his right arm. It is reloaded. 'If the bastard's still there,' Plum tells himself, 'I'm going to bloodywell burn him out!' He slips the service revolver into its holster, and with both hands, steadies his aim with the flare gun. He fires into the base of the tree. A light. Tongues of flame. An explosion.

Plumb's section drop to the boggy soil

'OH GAWD. RUN!' a voice cries.

'MOVE ALL OF YOU. FOR BLOODY CHRIST SAKE MOVE!'

'OH RASS!'

The mammoth tree is coming down fast, snapping and splintering, the upper branches hissing through the night air; a dizzy giant falling in flames to the ground.

'RUN RIGBY!'

'AH CYANT MAKE IT SAMMY!'

'OH SKUNT RIGBY! RUN!'

The tree hits the ground, amidst snapping branches, jarring the ground. Then silence.

'ANYONE HURT?'

Silence.

'ANYBODY MISSING FOR JESUS CHRIST?'

Silence.

'RIGBY, SIR!'

'Let's find him!'

Crisscrossings of police torches amidst the branches of the fallen tree and the discovery of a broken body with a shattered spinal column.

Constable Samuel Simpson cries openly.

*　　*　　*

A police truck rumbles along an old dirt road bordered by canals. The driver in the cab feels the presence of the three dead men, beneath the canvas between two rows of silent policemen sitting on benches opposite each other, in the back of the heavy vehicle. Next to the driver sits the Assistant Commissioner of Police and Crime Chief. He watches ahead seemingly blankly. Takes off his cap, runs his fingers over his hairless scalp, puts his cap on again. It is a movement he keeps repeating.

The road is rough but the truck's jolting does not put anyone to sleep. A chorus of dogs howl far ... far away ... but the men in the truck do not hear them. They only hear the throbbing of the diesel engine which has now become a dirge.

CHAPTER 30

One by one, old Adolphus Banze, a veteran woodsman and farmer, takes the bullets from Apata's rifle. He files their sharp points flat then, on each flattened nose, he patiently grooves a deep cross. Within the old man's mind Ronald, his dead son, screams never-endingly because a dum-dum bullet tears a messy hole between his shoulder blades and the light-skinned, Negro Police Corporal, having shot Ronald in his back, still holds the warm .38 Smith and Wesson revolver.

Dating from this tragic incident that took place some decades ago, Adolphus Banze started to hate and still hates policemen; craved an opportunity for revenge and sees the opportunity only now, and in the form of the unconscious fugitive in his house.

One by one, old Adolphus Banze replaces the bullets in Apata's rifle, making sure that should Apata check, the first round will have a sharp tip. As he lays the weapon down there is a smile on his face and he turns and looks at a comatose Michael Rayburn Apata. One of the old man's eyes has a pale bluish veil over the iris and in his seeing eye there is a glint of something far away. His mouth hangs open with a string of saliva in the corner ready to fall to the floor. Just in time he flaps his toothless mouth closed.

'Jerr ... Jerry ... Bevs ... kiss Daadaa ...' Apata mumbles in his sleep. The old man comes closer to the cot on which the fugitive lies. Apata's eyes flutter open and he starts. A face looks down at him. It is not Gerald Tross's but one he does not recognize. His mind reels for balance.

'Apata ...' the face says. 'De man Michael Rayburn Apata, WAIT! NAH GET UP.'

'Who ... Who are you?'

'Me is not a police informah. Me doan want blood money. Me jus' wan ol' man who want help you.'

Apata's breath comes fast. He stares into the leathery face of the old negro Adolphus Banze. "GUN," comes to Apata. He swivels his head, sees it on a low wooden block within his arm's reach, grabs it, checks. It is loaded. He glances at his left wrist: seven thirty. He lays the weapon down and relaxes.

The old man smiles and moves away. To Apata he appears to be around seventy. He is slightly bent.

Apata takes stock of his situation. He is on a sort of couch with a mattress of straw. It is comfortable, even a luxury. Sunlight streams through the only window and makes a shadow pattern on his left arm caused by the overhanging thatch on the roof. Outside he can see palm trees between some bushes. I must have seen a light from this window after stumbling like a wild thing through the undergrowth last night. I must have seen light here and then fainted, Apata thinks. The old man brought me inside. I wonder how he managed that? He must have heard all the firing ...

As he thinks, Apata feels as if he is floating between the floor and the roof.

It is a one-roomed place with walls made of tree bark. On his right a hammock hangs limply slung from two opposite points. Nearby his haversack hangs on a nail in an upright by the door. Its pockets are filled with Queen-head currency notes. Are they still filled? Apata does not care.

He is floating, light headed.

In a corner the old man is making a fire in a clay hearth. Around him is a small assortment of cooking utensils, two dented and flaked cups and four aging tin plates stacked inside each other. Behind him there is a gourd bowl made out of half a calabash. It holds steaming water and a bit of rag that is hanging over the rim and drips water on to the floor which is covered with many rice bags. In the old man's right hand Apata glimpses the blade of a knife.

Slowly he reaches out and takes his rifle. Pain lances through his leg. He squeezes his eyes shut and bares his teeth. When he opens his eyes he sees that the old man is coming his way. The blade in the old man's hand has been heated red hot. Ignoring the gun pointing at his chest he comes forward and lays the knife on the block where the gun was. At the same time he puts the calabash bowl with the rag in it on the floor beside Apata's couch. The old man returns to the fire and puts a water-filled iron skillet on it and blows at the charcoal until it glows red.

'De police bullet gone in yo' foot,' he says. 'It nearly pass through suh it undah de skin. Even dey it can propper pain. Like it touch wan nerve, nah?' He covers the pot. 'But me guh take it out fuh yo' and den me guh put wan magic bush poultice pon am. Small bhai, you guh see wan miracle!'

To Michael Apata it is as though his grandmother and grandfather's spirits have converged into an entity that has possessed this old man. He lays the rifle down gently and begins to trust the old man a little more.

'An' when it come to food son, no problam.' He shakes his head. 'See dah bag in de cornah?' The old man points. Apata looks in the direction indicated. 'Well dat bag full ah ground provishans, PLENTY EDDOE! Dat is de thing yo' need mos'. Eddoe soup. Dat is a good thing when yo' las' plenty blood ... but yo' nah las' suh much. But eddoe soup ah de thing yo' need mos'.'

A lone bird with a sweet song trills outside.

'Nah fret small bhai. ME, ADALPHAS BANZE, guh get yo' strang befoe tomahrah marnin'. STRANG ENOUGH TO GET'WAY.

'Mih hear dem talk how yo' bad, how yo' murdah, how much money yo' rob from de govament pos' office. SUH WHA' IF YO' ROB? Dem White man mo dan rob we foe' parents dem.

'But murdah ...' The old man shakes his head. 'Me know wan murdahrah when me see one, and you nah – '

'SHUT UP!' snaps Apata loudly, grimacing with pain.

The old man turns slowly from the fire. The words have

struck him like a blow. He stares, for the second time, into the deep pit of death at the end of the Winchester's barrel. His lips open and close wordlessly.

'WHERE'S THE RADIO OLD MAN?'

Banze stares at the muzzle of the rifle that points at his chest. He swallows once more. 'It undah de couch Apata,' he croaks.

'BRING IT OUT!' Apata orders.

The old man, frightened and trembling, edges forward to where Apata lies. He stoops under the rifle. The rifle follows him and touches the nape of his neck. He whimpers as he claws under the couch and pulls out the radio.

Apata sighs and lowers the rifle. The old man straightens up. He looks sick and weak.

I'm a fool, Apata says to himself, a big fool! How can I come out of all this? How can I be like I was before. Innocent? Free? Beverley, Gerald, Michelle. I have a daughter. Imagine me having a daughter.

For a moment Apata's expression softens then his look of bewilderment returns. He gazes at the crooked frond of a coconut tree which waves at him through the window. Glenn and last night. He wonders if he shot anybody. I hope, God I hope, I didn't kill nobody, he thinks. I was just firing to gain time. And again Glenn, maimed, grimaces at him. I have to stop fighting against this guilt I'm always feeling, he tells himself. Face it. Face it. I killed him. He must be dead. Jeeze! If I could only close my eyes and blot out everything. If only I could wake up and discover ... what? Parkinson. Chingarus. They were hung. What prompted me into this thing? I cannot win. God knows what happened last night but I'm sure somebody got shot. I was shooting high, I knew I was shooting high. But I started shooting low after something pitched into the grass behind me. Maybe I killed somebody then. There was screaming, plenty of screaming. Apata takes a deep, shaky breath but it does not untie the emotional knot in his stomach. I'm a fool, he tells himself once more.

The old man with the fear drained from him stares at his

young companion who slowly turns his head away. However the old man spots a teardrop which rides down over Apata's cheek bone, trails down Apata's cheek and over his jaw bone. With a shrug of his shoulder Apata wipes the teardrop away. The old man shakes his head.

CHAPTER 31

FRIDAY

Men emerge from a little door within a mammoth metal door in the Georgetown City Prison's fence that towers above the street. Clad in grey caps, grey shirts and grey three-quarter pants they clamber, without fuss, into the tray of the middle-aged Bedford truck. Individuality has been stripped, it seems, from these men casually called criminals. Now they seem to be one living organism but, in reality, they are many private souls with yearnings and passions.

The driver of the truck has not yet emerged. Four warders are with the grey men. They listen to a *Weekday Trumpet* newspaper seller passing on the pavement outside. 'MAD DOG APATA KILL' DETECTIVE SERGEANT GITTENS AN' TWO ODDUH POLICE DEAD. THREE HUNDRED POLICE FOH BIG MAN-HUNT.'

The driver of the truck emerges with a rush from the prison fence topped with spikes and barbed wire. He times his activities against an oncoming car and darts across the street to collect his newspaper. It is only eight pages. A rush-print job. 'Wha'apen Lane?' a prison warder asks impatiently from the tray of the grey truck. But the driver only shakes his head and moves his lips in reading. In the end he says softly, 'Skunt!' Then he looks up to his questioner and says loudly, 'Deh had a shoot out with Apata las' night. And Apata kill Kenrick Gittens!'

The early morning odours of dogs' filth rises rankly from

181

the pavement and street. A hearse from a popular funeral parlour passes with its burden of ex-life shrouded in green.

'Who dead?' another warder up in the truck asks in tones of unbelief.

'Gittens! Ah doan know the other two fellahs,' says the driver as he prepares to throw the folded news up to the first warder who asked for news.

'If what dat papers say is true, then they hardly have police left in Georgetown.'

'What you mean 'if what dat paper say is true'?'

'Man you know how dat *Weekday Trumpet* does lie like ass.'

'But ow man ... even if paper lie, you think it could lie 'bout things like dat?'

'You got a point dere,' concedes the one who was distrustful of the *Trumpet*'s veracity.

'Then, if what it say is true, they hardly have police in this place in truth.'

'What I say is, dat we lucky we's warders cause right now me an' you wouldav been ovuh at Parika preparing to stop bullet if we was police.'

'You think they going to get 'e today?'

'Hear what I tell you, all they going to do today is just watch and plan. I could read dat White man Plumb like a book! Dem people doan give nothing to chance.'

'Apata like he doan give nothing to chance, too.'

'AYE! I think yo' see wheh ah comin' from. Hear, I did followin' this Apata thing since he lash Hoop Village Post Office and I did tell Gweny that dis Apata chap ent no dunce. You hear is how he get away from Hoop Village?'

'Yo' talkin' 'bout how he dress up like a 'oman?'

The other laughs.

'Plumb going to make this thing like a milihtary manoeuvre! He going to keep sentry posted around like what the papers seh, while he plannin' a mastuh stroke and dat mastuh stroke going start tomorrow!'

'Tomorrow?'

'Bet you' battam dollah! Tomorrow.'

'Ent bettin', but Apata, ah sure, plannin' to' fuh he.'

'Well, as the sayin' goes: "Is two thief man does make Gawd laugh".'

'Yo' think them going to catch dis chap easy, though?'

'Yeah man. Plumb is a Sandhurst man, you know. I say! Dat before tomorrow out dem ketch Apata!'

'I thought you name was Peroune, not Isaiah de prophet.'

The truck coughs into life then slowly pulls away from the prison. It passes the mammoth grey Roman Catholic Cathedral of the Immaculate Conception. A large building of concrete. From it an agonized figure of a crucified Christ looks down. One of the men in grey crosses himself. Another grins to see the pious gesture. The hollerings of the Chinaman selling the *Trumpet* fades into the background of the streets. The prisoners make no sound.

CHAPTER 32

FRIDAY

Slowly the big fan turns above the reporting floor of the *Weekday Trumpet*. Cecil Gunraj, a strapping Indian who most of the floor believe is a political genius at twenty-two, silently contemplates the day's headline before him. The sports editor, on the telephone, repeatedly shouts 'LOUD AND CLEAR!' and irritates Gunraj. Every ejaculation of 'Loud and clear' draws a stream of grumbles from the Berbician who is so sensitive at this moment that almost anything may set him snapping. APATA. Gunraj remembers Michael Apata. It was he, Vanier and Apata who sat and waited on the White man Carrington for the interview before entry into King's College. So Apata turned out bad after all! Gunraj sighs. 'They turned you into a monster, boy.' Gunraj takes off his glasses, pinches between his eyes, puts his glasses on once more and once more re-reads the first paragraph of the lead story:

'Mad dog Apata, kill-crazy gunman wanted by the police for murder and a series of other crimes, went berserk last night on the East Bank of Essequibo. He launched a lead storm at a police posse closing in on his little hideout in the centre of the marshy backlands about five miles from the Parika village public road . . .'

Gunraj shakes his head then looks over at the crime reporter now entering the door labelled EDITOR IN CHIEF.

Thirty minutes later Cecil Gunraj sees the crime reporter coming out of the big man's office. 'SPARE ME A MINUTE, SINGH!'

Singh stops and glances in Gunraj's direction. The big man's secretary watches Singh. She notes the way he scratches his right eye brow with his left hand and knows that the chat with Editor-in-Chief Thompson had been somewhat spiritually dampening for the stocky, dishevelled-looking reporter with his badly knotted tie. Humiliation and deep anger with himself is what she clearly senses in the way Singh scratches his brows. Singh takes a deep breath and walks over to Gunraj's desk.

Gunraj pushes himself back from the typewriter before him and looks up with scorn on his face.

'What happen?' asks Singh flatly.

Gunraj points to the newspaper basket. 'You see where I dropped today's paper after I rolled it into a ball?'

Singh snorts. Impatience and resentment well up inside him. 'What you want chap?' says Singh.

'I want to know what inspires you to write tripe.'

'FUCK YOU GUNRAJ!'

Gunraj is up and Singh sprawls on the floor with a busted upper lip. 'Know your place chap!' shouts Gunraj, rubbing the knuckles of his left hand in his right palm. 'Yes ... know you' place. Me ent no dholl and rice coolie!'

'WHAT THE HELL'S TAKING PLACE OUT HERE?' The voice belongs to the Editor-in-Chief. No one answers. The workers gather around. The crime reporter picks himself up. 'Nothing chief,' he mutters, his face distorted. The Editor-in-Chief looks at Gunraj who turns away and sits once more behind his desk. He remembers Vanier. God rest the dead. Vanier and his father both died last year in a crash that involved a pair of commercial aircraft over a region of the Andes. Gunraj sighs and flips on the tape recorder next to the Remington typewriter. The voice of His Excellency The Governor comes through. Gunraj thinks of Apata, of Vanier, of himself. He shakes his head. '"MAD DOG APATA, KILL-CRAZY GUNMAN" indeed.'

CHAPTER 33

FRIDAY

'Beverley!'

'Yes Mommy.'

Then in a broken and defeated tone: 'You see what shame you bring me, girl?'

Mrs Bailey, a woman, but far less than the woman she used to be, gently puts the daily news down and continues to sip the cocoa Beverley has set before her. The newspaper man has just left to shout around the rest of Charlestown.

'And who around here don't know that that child is Michael child, is who don't want to know.' She sighs deeply. 'Ow God ... now you don't only have a real bastard child but the bastard child now have a murderer for a father.' She shakes her head. 'Was best that was Gerald's child. Day after day I wish that child was Gerald child. Too many times I have to say thank God for that young man.' She sighs again. It is as if she hopes to tip a heavy load from her chest. 'Oh God,' she sighs again. 'Shame on top shame...'

Beverley sits huddled at the foot of the iron framed bed on which sleeps the child, Michelle. The lamentations of Mrs Bailey make Beverley tense. She holds her breath but does not realize what she is doing. She wishes her mother would leave and let her be. The woman outside groans as if in pain. Beverley begins to hear her own heart throbbing in her ears. She breathes slowly and evenly as if afraid to do so because if her mother knows that she breathes, she will be told that she has no right to. The baby stirs and whimpers. 'SSSH!'

Beverley whispers. She pats her daugher's back and the infant squirms into a new position. Beverley begins to cry. She leans forward and buries her face in her palms. Tears trickle through her fingers but she does not make a sound lest her mother challenge her right to be upset about anything. A chair scrapes in the kitchen.

'YOU'RE NOT SAYING ANYTHING!' her mother tells her and repeats, 'Jesus me! Shame on top shame!'

Beverley hears the door close and knows that her mother has left to begin her trek to the Stabroek market where she has set up a small haberdashery shop. Mrs Bailey believes that Gerald Tross has done well to have given her the financial backing to that profitable little concern. Only Gerald, however, knows the truth and feels bad about it. He would like them to know that it is Mike's money that performs the miracles. He wants Beverley and her mother to know that Michael is their true benefactor. Many times, of late, Gerald tells himself that he is far from understanding Michael.

'Gerald,' Michael had said after a silence. Gerald felt that Mike had fought to keep his voice firm. 'Jerry, do these things for me but if you think this money's blood money, tell me.'

'What are you going to do now Mike? Mike, they're going to find you. They're going to shoot you down, Mike. MIKE! Mike, people will betray you . . .'

'You won't betray me Gerald. Nothing else matters.'

'My mother would. She's afraid.'

'So what can I do but end what I started and leave a black mark for them to remember me by?'

'But what you going to do Mike?' Gerald had persisted.

'I won't give myself up.' Apata had sighed in the Parikan gloom of night.

'I can't give myself up that's what I mean.' He had stuffed his letters in his jacket. 'I'll read these letters when I'm lonely Jerry.'

'But Mike,' Gerald had pleaded, 'shouldn't I at least let Beverley know?'

Head bent, Michael had stood mute and firm in his silence.

'What will Beverley say Mike?' Gerald had pressed. 'What will her mother say? Her mother will say that I, Gerald, is taking care of them. Not you.'

'Man, Beverley's mother would have nothing to do with that money if she knew it was my money!'

Gerald had nodded.

'Insure Michelle's life for me Jerry. Start her a saving account. Help them all. But secure my daughter's future, first. Please understand, Jerry, I want you to see this as a last will and testament. And don't let them know it's money from me. Promise?'

Reluctantly, Gerald Tross had agreed.

*   *   *

Beverley feels something rising from the pit of her stomach. She feels her lips wanting to move on their own. The child stirs and her eyelids move then open. Beverley picks her up and takes her to the dining table where she sits a while in thought. The newspaper's pages flutter in the breeze from a nearby window. The coffee mug anchors the paper and prevents it from being blown to the floor.

Because of the tears welling up in her eyes Beverley sees the dead men's photographs in a blur. 'Your Daddy,' she mutters, 'ent no murderer baby, your Daddy ent no murderer chile.'

She gets to her feet to take the infant to the bathroom. Michella Apata, though Michelle Bailey on the legal birth certificate, smiles up to her mother, stares up to her mother who breaks down into loud unsuppressed sobbing, 'OH GOD MIKE! YOU COULDN'T REALIZE THAT SOMETHING LIKE THIS WOULD HURT BAD? MORE BAD THAN THE WAY YOU LEFT ME?

'OW GOD MIKE ... NOT BECAUSE MOMMY CHASE YOU, YOU HAD TO DO THIS TO ME MIKE! OH GOD MIKE! O God Mike ... Ow ... ow...'

Another newspaper vendor passes on the street and his calling voice fuels the fire of torment within the heart of the young mother. A three-wheeled truck clatters past leaving silence in its wake. Then Beverley clearly hears laughter coming from a fence, over which two gossiping neighbours talk in hushed tones.

CHAPTER 34

FRIDAY

A few old witches rise from a tangle of small trees. Black sage. The ugly black birds, with their humped beaks, wing their way clumsily to another tangle of bushes. A breeze blows away some of the heat. In the sky a lone chicken hawk is being harassed by a flight of kiskadees shrilling in their own language, or so it sounds, new tactics to each other. The sun glares down.

The Commissioner squints at the feathery dogfight from under shading palms.

Plumb wishes that he had a pair of sunglasses.

The Commissioner stands like a big barrel with a little keg for a head, amidst greenery that threatens to be a wood. He pulls at his great moustache in apparent impatience.

'Won't a local man be drafted in to help us find Apata?' he wants to know.

'I've already laid that on, sir.'

'Good! Then shouldn't we move in today?'

'The local hunter will report this evening sir!'

'But the delay, man. The delay!'

'I can assure you, sir, that Apata won't escape our cordon. I don't believe, in fact, that he will try to break out today.'

'Have it your way, Maurice. I do hope you're right.'

'I know precisely what I have to do, sir.'

Sir Lloyd Alexander Wilkinson tells himself that it is high time to get back to the city. He turns and begins the short trek back to the dirt road.

'I do hope you're right,' he repeats. 'THREE HUNDRED POLICEMEN! I have actually scraped the bottom of the SERVICE AND PROTECTION barrel, Plumb! I have put every ablebodied policeman on manhunt duty! The newsmen are quite correct when they call this the biggest manhunt in the annals of Guiana!'

The Commissioner dabs at the sweat between his chins. 'Magistrates are griping about their orderlies having to be drafted into *our* Apata manhunt. OUR! They do not understand! They do not understand my responsibility! PLUMB, THIS CRIMINAL MUST be found before Her Majesty arrives!

'We do know enough about Apata to be very seriously concerned, Plumb! From what I've read in his dossier he could be a real threat to the safety of our Sovereign Majesty.

'I may be an old man who sees ghosts where there are none. Maybe I am ... but, please, PLEASE, BRING THAT FELLOW IN. In any shape you can manage, hot or cold, though hot, of course, is preferable.'

CHAPTER 35

FRIDAY

The old man shoulders a garden fork. In his waist-belt of heavy black leather, there is a cutlass with a sharp, silvery cutting edge. 'Mih ah guh aback, Apata. Res' til ah come again.

'Yo' like pear? Mih ave a big tree ina de farm. Mih guh bring some fuh yo' to walk wid! If yo' get hungry food deh ina de pot.

'Mih gawn! Nah frighten. Police dem nah guh reach hay today!'

'I could have gone with him, but I'm not free. I wonder what Gerald's doing now and Beverley and my daughter Michelle. I wonder if she's crying.' Michael looks around feeling the silence. 'The old man said that I was safe here, that I must keep resting as much as I can to get back my strength. But I feel strong already.' Apata frowns and tugs lightly at his beard. 'Right now the police are drafting plans to catch me. Right now I know there are sentries posted at good points to stop any movement I make. Plumb, Sandhurst man!'

Apata gets up from the soft lumpiness of the couch. The leg, from which the old man has skilfully extracted the police bullet, is now stiffish though, strangely, not painful. He drags over to the V.H.F. and listens but hears nothing to increase his anxiety.

He goes back to the couch and, lying on his back, tells himself 'SLEEP!' Even though he knows that the time for sleep has long passed. He leans over the edge of the couch and takes up the loaded weapon. He lifts it to his face, takes aim using the telescopic sight and caresses the trigger. The safety catch is on. He puts the rifle down and thinks back, sitting in the posture of Rodin's *Thinker*.

'Who's it?' Mrs Bailey had asked.

'It's me, Michael!'

The door had opened and Michael, because of the way his old guardian had sounded before she appeared, was not surprised to see the sour expression on her face. He had wondered what he had done to be greeted like that but could not find an answer. He smiled anyway and told her hello.

'WHAT YOU WANT?' she asked. Mike grew cold, confused, and angry.

'What have I done to you Mrs Bailey?' he had asked wondering if she had somehow found out that he had made love to her daughter following the death of her husband. But that was impossible, Michael told himself. Part of his anger, and his vision of Beverley as a tattle-tale left him.

'SO YOU WANT TO MARRY BEVERLEY?'

'Could I come in Mrs Bailey?'

'NOT IN THIS HOUSE, YOUNG MAN!'

A vein raised itself in young Apata's forehead and he began hating the woman in front of him.

'I understand how Uncle Joel's death must have hit you, Mrs Bailey, but you have no right to take it out one me,' he told her. 'I don't think I ever gave you rudeness or disrespect when I lived here.'

At that moment he had felt nothing but bewilderment. Something had happened in the time he had been away. Something had been poisoned while he had been away searching for himself in the wilderness. Now he was back to make Beverley a part of himself. Now he was back with over two thousand dollars he had sweated for in the turbulence of the dangerous hinterlands of rivers and creeks. Now he was back to make things better for Beverley, himself and even her mother who now stood before him obviously seething with hatred.

'I would like to see Beverley, Mrs Bailey.'

'What you want to see my daughter for? My daughter don't want to see...'

'MIKE!' shouted Beverley from the bottom of the steps. Neither of them had heard her cross the bridge. Michael turned and saw his woman, all eighteen years of her. He dropped his bag and ran to meet her. Like children, they gripped hands and laughed above the slamming of the door over their heads.

Michael Apata, sitting on the old man's straw-filled mattress, remembers that later they had made love again. And he remembers Mrs Bailey's parting words, 'Beverley stubborn, boy! But Beverley ent going to marry a black skin, ugly thing like you! NEVER! Ah rather kill her before she do that. AS GOD ABOVE ME MICHAEL, AH RATHER DO THAT!'

Michael sits on the old man's couch and remembers that Mrs Bailey had sworn. 'AS GOD ABOVE IS MY JUDGE, BOY, IF YOU COME TO MY HOME AGAIN, AH WILL CALL THE POLICE!'

All that had happened after Michael and Beverley held hands in the yard and laughed for happiness. He told Beverley that he would come back to her that night, and he did. It was then that they had made love for the last time, in the pleased spiritual presence of Mr Joel in his neglected workshop.

Michael reasons that it was on that occasion that little Michelle was conceived. It could not have been any other time. The following day he had departed after having returned, following a night in a Salvation Army rest over, to say goodbye. It was then that he was rejected outright and told what would happen to him if he ever returned. It was then that he knew that a lasting physical union between himself and his woman would be fraught with unhappiness for, as Mrs Bailey had spoken, Beverley had been crying from the welts on her arms and face made by a machine cord some time before he came to say goodbye. At that moment Michael had told himself that he could not have Beverley even though "faint heart never won fair lady".

He gave Beverley all the money he had saved for them because he loved her and could not have her. And that was the reason he had told Gerald that nothing made sense anymore.

Sitting on the old man's couch, Apata remembers that afternoon in the cinema, that time so long ago, when Beverley had said, 'In my family Mike they say whenever a man leave one of the women, regardless of why they leave, he don't come back.' Apata sighs. '"...don't come back",' he whispers gazing to the floor. Deep down in his heart he wants to go back. What does it mean? he wonders. Am I going to die? Apata thinks again of the two criminals on the steamer from Bartica. Chingarus and Parkinson. 'I am Chingarus and Parkinson.' Apata takes a deep breath and clenches his fist so tight that his knuckles become a range of mountains from which run canyons. Then he opens both hands and covers his face. 'Oh Beverley, Beverley,' he whispers, 'am I never going to see you again or touch you again, Beverley, O Beverley.' And he tries to sing the song she liked to sing for him. Halfway through the first line he trails off acknowledging the futility of anything he can do.

By chance he spots the old man's looking glass framed in a thick and heavily designed relief of a laurel wreath. He gets to his feet, moves over to the shelf, and carefully picks up the mirror. Seven years of bad luck for broken mirrors. He looks at himself and smiles to think that Josh Smith always described men with too much facial hair-growth as ugly Arabs. The smile fades from his face as his anxieties launch a new offensive.

'Give myself up? If I do that would I get Beverley? Chingarus and Parkinson. I'll get what they got. So I still wouldn't get to be with Beverley.' He takes a deep breath. 'I don't think they will get a chance to hang me, yet. Glenn.' The name haunts him.

'Beverley's mother is right,' he says. 'I'm no good...

'If the police corners me I'll kill whoever stands between me and ... and ... and what? FREEDOM? What is freedom? Dear Beverley, I don't know if I want to live.'

Apata puts the mirror down and makes his way back to the couch where he lies down then sits up and gets to his feet again. He moves over to the pot, lifts the cover and takes a plate and half fills it. He eats sitting on the floor below the hole in the wall where the old man cooked the meal. He looks out and sees the plantain and banana trees. All is silent. There is only the whispering of the trees. Apata looks again and suddenly freezes with his mouth full.

THERE IS SOMETHING MOVING BETWEEN THE BUSHES NEAR THE PIT LATRINE!

He puts his plate down and drags himself, flat on the floor, back to his rifle. He cradles it, preparing himself for a fight, forcing himself to breathe deeply and calmly. He gets down on his stomach and crawls back to the aperture in the wall. There is a bucket of water to his right. He takes an old kitchen rag and soaks it in case of tear gas. He looks through the telescopic sight and finds the horns of a cow, the gentle eye of a cow filling his view.

Apata breathes out and feels a tremor through his body as he lowers the rifle. He feels weak, closes his eyes and tries to imagine how he will look, dead. Then he remembers that the safety catch of the rifle is still on the way it would have been had he had to defend himself.

CHAPTER 36

FRIDAY

Plumb finds that it is hard to avoid focusing his attention on the red-haired mulatto officer in the office that has been made into a briefing room for the manhunt that will commence on the morrow. Superintendent Clarence Franklin has five percent Negro blood mixed into his racial make up. Generally, however, the locals see him as a nice White man. By police standards Franklin is a good officer and is very well liked by the rank and file.

Clarence Franklin sits and listens to Crime Chief Plumb though in fact he is thinking of his sister Penelope who is confined to a wheel-chair because her legs are badly malformed. At the most crucial times Penelope acts as his conscience and guru. Whenever he feels burnt up about his wife and feels the need to hide in a bottle he talks to Penelope. She was the one who saved him from being classified as "sad alcoholic". He had been heading that way for sure.

He wonders how Penel feels about the manhunt. He wonders how he feels about the manhunt. He finds it strange that he has no firm views. As yet.

The coconut trees outside sigh in the wind. The squeal of metal grinding against metal comes from the train station and workshop linked to the stelling not far away and a car's horn pipes a snatch of "Mary had a little lamb".

Plumb turns his head to the door and says, 'Come in, please, Mr Robinson.'

A civilian enters with a broken single-bore shot-gun. He is the darkest Negro the Crime Chief has ever seen since the start of his sojourn in Guiana.

The civilian looks unsure of whether to say 'Good afternoon, sirs', 'Good afternoon, Chief' or nothing. He decides to remain silent so it is Plumb who speaks first.

'This man is going to be valuable to us. He is a hunter and tracker who knows these parts well. Gentlemen, meet Mr Robinson!' Plumb gestures to the dark-skinned Negro who doesn't know what to do. He stands frozen. Plumb continues: 'A few hours ago he was sworn in as a Corporal and will carry that rank until the manhunt is over!'

'SIR,' interjects an officer from the back row. He stands. 'Question sir.'

'Yes?'

'Why aren't we out there hunting this gunman now?'

'For two reasons Superintendent French! Right now we have forty-eight sentries posted around the manhunt area. The men are hidden and we are hoping that Apata grows restless enough to chance surfacing and tries to escape thinking that there are no policemen around. There is nothing which is as likely to prompt an injudicious move as waiting for something to happen! Especially if the coast seems clear. So this day, when nothing seems to be happening, is part of the manhunt! That is one reason. The other is that in my book, French, unless we are highly organized we shan't even catch a cold. We are not that highly organized yet.'

The officer sits. The Crime Chief turns to the blackboard. Robinson the guest member of the force, still stands. 'Do have a seat, Robinson. Make yourself comfortable,' Plumb tells him, then continues, 'This is where we last saw Apata, last encountered him I mean. These hatched areas are the swamps.' He is pointing at the blackboard. 'So he may have headed in this direction unless he has discovered a new trail all by himself, which is hardly likely.' Plumb points again. 'You will note that this trail heads towards and ends at the river. There are sentries posted at this point, while the police launch, *Elizabeth*, patrols all along here' Plumb's baton follows the course of the river.

'Sah!' interrupts Robinson, still not really confident in a room dominated by khaki and epaulettes. 'Sah, deh dere got another direcshan he could go through an' secrete he self from de police.' Robinson gets timidly to his feet. Plumb looks coldly at the hunter-tracker from Parika. Robinson moves over to the blackboard and points. 'He coulda move through right here, sah!'

Superintendent Franklin is glad to hear Robinson speak. He thinks Plumb sounded too sure of himself speaking of a territory he cannot know much about. The details of the sketched manhunt plan have been provided by members of the Parika Police Station staff.

'But if the gunman get sense,' continues Robinson, a vein visibly throbbing in his left side temple, 'he gon know that police ent know 'bout it and I sure that he done gone through it . . . Dis trail through here.'

Plumb is baffled for the trail Robinson speaks of is not on the blackboard.

'Well gentlemen,' he says, 'Corporal Robinson is proving his value already.'

'Yes sah, please for piece chalk, sah?'

Plumb gives him a stick of white chalk then watches the man's dark hand as it creates, through what is considered swamp, a ragged white diagrammatic trail. Superintendent Franklin wonders whether it is nervousness or an exact representation of the trail that makes the line waver so much.

'Police doan know' bout dis trail, sah! An, if Apata know it, is straight through dere he wouldah go las' night!'

'Shouldn't we call it Robinson's trail!'

Robinson smiles and there's a buzz of good humoured agreement in the room.

'So you think it possible that Apata knows of this trail and could have slipped through it last night, Robinson?'

'Yes sah!'

'Really? How would he have found out!'

'I meet 'e a time sah. But I didn' now 'e was a criminal. Ah few people know Apata well.'

An uneasy silence settles on the room. It is disturbed only by the sound of the wind rattling in the palm fronds outside. A booted foot strikes the leg of a desk making a small explosive sound. The wind also rattles the Venetian blinds. Eventually Plumb says, 'When I first came to this country I was told that a local proverb says, "God helps the thiefman and the watchman as well." Right? He does not take sides.'

This draws some laughter.

'Continue Robinson, please,' says Plumb.

'Dis trail, sah ... is leadin' to 'Dalphas Banze farm.'

'Would this Adolphus Banze help Apata?'

'Yes, sah. 'Dalphus Banze is a helpful man.'

'Is there another way to get to the farm other than by way of the hidden trail?'

'Dalphas Banze farm ent far from de river, sah. If a boat can come through here ... they can get in. The river cut-in to a trench that does lead pas' Dalphas Banze farm.'

'Thank you, Corporal Robinson.'

Robinson retreats to his seat.

Using a sweaty finger Plumb makes a cleaner inlet to the point on the diagram where the farm is supposed to be. Then he circles the farm in red and dots the centre with such vigour that the chalk breaks and falls to the floor.

Robinson the hunter-tracker looks at the shattered fragments of red and Clarence Franklin looks at him.

'Well, gentlemen,' says Crime Chief Plumb, 'that, is that.'

*   *   *

The sound of a truck swinging into the compound comes to the officers. The Crime Chief walks over to the window. He returns a friendly salute to one of the riot squad men, just relieved from the sealed-off manhunt area. They clamber out and drop themselves to the ground. They are evidently glad to be back.

CHAPTER 37

FRIDAY

Superintendent Franklin thinks, 'Tomorrow the biggest manhunt ever seen in this colony will get under way.'

He is looking down on the compound which has become an encampment. The face of Robinson, the dark-skinned Negro who will lead them, steals back into his mind. He combs his fingers through his reddish hair and remembers that his father always said that Judas Iscariot was a demonic spirit who creeps into the souls of men wearing "excusable reasons" as a disguise. 'Remember,' his father had once said, 'Judas still lives and bargains for his thirty pieces of silver.'

Men like hunter-tracker Robinson, he tells himself, always get their due. Then he switches his thoughts to the first encounter with Apata and Gittens, now dead. Franklin knew Gittens well enough to know that he and the dead man could have worked well together.

'WINCHESTAH, EH? DAT IS A BAD GUN!' The word breaks into Franklin's reverie. He listens.

'BETTAH YOU THAN ME STOP BULLIT FROM A GUN LIKE DAT!' And the speaker laughs.

Another voice from the compound adds: 'WELL I DON'T WANT STOP BULLIT FROM NO GUN AT ALL, WINCHESTER OR ELSE! GUN IS GUN!'

Franklin turns away from the window and walks towards his quarters. He hears the slapping of dominoes and the effiminate laughter of Superintendent Goppy. He smells

Brazilian tobacco and also whisky. The letter tempts him but he continues on his way to bed.

Later, lying there, he tells himself that his sister Penelope would be thinking about him, worrying about him and hoping he is not drinking. 'If I get killed,' he ponders, 'I wonder what she'd do? Perhaps she would write poetry about me and grow skinny with grief.'

Franklin smiles up to the ceiling. Two grey lizards, backs arched, are glaring at each other. Away from the pair preparing to do battle another stalks the tip of a protruding nail that looks like a settled moth with white wings because of an old webby deposit over the nail's tip. The little fellow pounces suddenly, then turns away. Franklin smiles and wonders if it is possible for a lizard to feel embarrassment.

He loves his sister and is finding it hard to go to sleep. He gets up and stands once more by a window overlooking the encampment. It is filled with policemen who will, tomorrow, fan out to search the backlands for Apata. Just below him four policemen sit on a stairway that leads to a back door. The stair leads to a pathway to a pit latrine. The four policemen, like himself, are not sleepy. Maybe apprehension of the morrow weighs heavily on their minds. Maybe for them it is, therefore, best to talk of this and that.

Laughter erupts from the quartet and Franklin hears a deep-voiced member as he supports an anecdote. 'I always wanted to beat him! I always wanted to cut his ass! And one night I see him. The son-of-a-bitch was on a bicycle an' I gave him the staff. I lashed him off his transport! LIX? Fellows, like them White men like to say "fellows", he fell. In the end I lifted the bike and dashed it down so that the handles and wheels dem bend up, then I blew my whistle hreeeeeeeeeee ... My story aftuh dat was "Sarge, he throw he bicycle at my person, and I, therefore, had to beat him up to defend myself." And he couldn't say one thing to the contrary because his mouth was so swollen he couldn't deliver himself. "WRITE WAN REPORT!" Sarge tell me, and I gathered pen and paper.'

Superintendent Franklin swallows and wishes he had a drink.

'Chap you's break me up, how you's fit good english in you' laugh story dem,' says one of the group.

'But duh's how you's have to deal with "bad Johns". Ah will tell ya'all of me and one dey's call Bogart.'

'BOGEY FROM CONGA BASIN?'

'Aye man ... that's de bugger. One night I went on beat with a crow bar 'cause ah know ah woulda see Bogart. Unlucky fuh he, he was coming from a late show, so I tail 'e until he reach a dark area. Then I confront he an' ah throw the iron bar straight to 'e chest. Well he had two choices. Was either he catch it an' get arrest for walking with a housebreaking implement, or take the full force o' de crow bar in 'e chest. Well, if ya'll know Bogart, ya'll would know he ent no strengthuh. So Bogey catch it. MAN, was police story, fingerprint and four months in 'e rass.'

Penelope Franklin always tells her brother that most policemen are evil because they get snared by the very evil they try to combat. Franklin remembers her saying, 'We can kick the criminal and torture him because of course we never trust him. Soon we tell ourselves that no one's worth trusting since this thing you fight, this evil, is within everyone. Before you know it, Clarence, you become a criminal in your own behaviour by constantly illtreating criminals. Eventually, too, you become a criminal in your attitude and view of life and you end up being ensnared by the very force you try to fight.'

'I guess,' Clarence had replied, 'it is like Brer Rabbit and the tar baby. Seeing the tar baby in his path Brer Rabbit flies in a rage and decides to kick and punch the object of his hatred to get it out of his way and he gets trapped by his own actions.'

She had been pleased because he had understood her and had illustrated her point so well.

From below the open window the laughter from the quartet on the stair's lower treads grows less and more of what is said is pulled through yawns. Soon men are muttering of rest. 'Well,' Franklin hears clearly, 'I think I is going to rest Gawd material until tomorrow.'

'When Apata,' butts in another voice, 'might rest it permanently for you.'

Getting to their feet, the last bit of good natured laughter flowers then dies under more yawns.

*   *   *

Silence.
Silence falls over the encampment. The clock at the head of the corridor ticktocks ticktocks, ticktocks, ticktocks tic-toc-tic-toc-tic-toc-tic-toc . . .

CHAPTER 38

FRIDAY

The old man has just come in. Outside, the owl hoots
spookily from across the swamps. Because of the draughts,
the flame from the bottle lamp casts wavering shadows. In
the old man's hands is a stout walking stick that Michael
may have to use to move. He lays it on the floor beside
Apata's couch. Apata turns and faces him.

'How are things, old man?'

'Mih bring some fruits fuh you.'

'Are there policemen out there?'

'Yes Apata. Me see wan police boat ah walk up and down
de rivah.' He leans his fork behind the door then goes over
and rests his cutlass next to the hearth.

'Actually, me nah see none policeman ina de bushes dem.
But dem deh.' He shakes his head. 'Dem deh.'

Apata sits up and the old man sees the gun.

'Me very knowledgeable in soljah an' police mattahs. Suh
me could tell yo' wha' ah happen right now.'

Apata lays the weapon across his thighs and looks at the
old man whose lips tremble as words pass them.

'Dem set up something like wan cardan round de whole
area dat dem think yo' is in. Suh all, ALL round dem gat
plenty plenty policeman hidin'. An' dem nah ah move. Dem
jus' a watch. SUH IF YO MEK A MOVE! DEM KETCH
YO LIKE IGUANA!' He places avocado after avocado in a
flaked bowl on the floor. 'Ah wan White man, me shore, who
ah arganize dis thing. An since 'e nah know dem back parts

dese, he nah guh move wild. He ga get people who know how de walkings guh . . .'

Apata sighs. 'Crime Chief Plumb,' he whispers. The old man giggles.

'An' me guh tell yo' something.' He nods his head. 'He guh mek 'e move tomorrah an' dat is de time when you guh mek you move.'

'How would I know when he makes his move, old man?'

'Nah bother, mih boy . . . yo' guh know.' The old man smiles.

To Apata it is nothing to be humoured about. The old man's expression changes. In the flickering light from the lamp his face clouds over. He says disparagingly, 'Mih pass through Mase'n farm. De man things dem ah dead. De damn things ah 'e farm ah cry out fuh attenshan!' He sucks his teeth.

'People are afraid I kill them. That is why they neglect their farms.'

'Dem nah gat sense!'

Apata remembers the letters Gerald wrote to him. He places a palm above his heart and feels the wad of letters under the bush jacket. In an inner pocket of Archibald Glenn's jacket.

The old man moves to the kitchen corner. Apata's gaze follows him. The old man squats before the large pot which he opens and proceeds to fill a bowl with food.

He eats.

Through a filled mouth he begins to speak, 'De Queen comin' me boy. Dah ah guh be big to-do ina Georgetown.' The old man smiles a mouthful smile and thinks of his serge suit embalmed by napthalene balls in the chest below his hammock. Again the owl hoots across the swamps. The old man silently farts and hopes for limited pollution.

'Pa! . . .'

With his one good eye the old man looks at Apata.

'Why do you live alone?'

Adophus Banze puts down his bowl. There's still food in it. He gazes at the floor, shakes his head and rises up slowly. He moves to the shelf on the wall behind the doorway. On the shelf there is a goblet made out of fired clay. Reaching behind it he lifts out a browning photograph. The frame is thick and intricately ornate. He hands it to Apata. Apata takes the old photograph and looks at it intently. There's someone in a coffin. There are flowers bunched from the neck of the dead down to the waist.

The face!

Apata raises his head and looks at the old man. The old man looks at Apata. Apata looks at the photograph. In the background there are people. Their faces are too vague to make out but there is a White man in the middle of the crowd. To Apata he feels like a good White Man. His hand rests on the shoulder of the Black man closest to the coffin. The Black man's head is bent. He is looking at the man in the box.

The owl hoots again from outside and sounds as if it is much closer.

'De chap in de caffin is Ranal. Mih boy Ranal. Wan police murdah Ranal ten years ago.

'He was de only pic'ney me evah mek. Something happen to me back.' The old man shakes his head. 'Ah couldn'ah mek no mo' pic'ney. But police murdah Ranal ... a-an' he nah did wrang.'

The old man shakes his head and stretches his hand out to Apata who gives back the photograph.

'E nah bin wrang.' He looks at the photograph. 'Yo' see al dat flowers ah 'e ches'? Eh?'

Apata nods.

'Well de man ah de funeral parlour had fuh full up de hole de bullit mek ah Ranal ches'. Wan police bullit. He shoot Ranal through 'e back wit' wit' a kinda bullit dat 'e flatten ah de point. Dem flowers dem ah camaflahge.'

'What happened to the police who shot your son through his back?'

The old man bends his head, hugs his knees, shakes his head, 'Nothing Apata.' Then he's silent.

'And what you did, old man?'

'Nothing, Apata, nothing.'

He rises to his feet and takes off his khaki shirt and remains in his vest with his trousers rolled up just above his knees. He takes off the trousers now and remains in a pair of striped under-shorts and string vest. He moves to his hammock, climbs in, and reclines. The hammock, distorted by his body, casts a grotesque shadow. The old man thinks of his son. Then falls asleep.

The owl, too, seems to have gone to sleep.

A praying mantis moves slowly, stalking something by the bottle lamp. The dull thud of a coconut as it hits the ground punctuates the insect noises outside.

Apata dreams that he is well ahead of the others. He's moving, moving. The riverbanks, pulsatingly colourful, flash by in sunny blurs shimmering through port and starboard walls of backwash crystallized by the rays of the Easter sun.

*   *   *

As Apata sleeps the large ugly printing press over a shallow concrete pit smeared with the oily blackness of ink, prints, folds and drops into piles the news for tomorrow: SATURDAY. The Editor-in-Chief of the *Weekday Trumpet*, who seldom visits this clanging monster, picks up one of the printed sheets for a first scan. The engineer watches the White man and wonders what it is that causes Thompson to be in the building at this ungodly hour.

The ink is still wet: "NO NEED FOR ANXIETY!" the headline, in bold type, declares, "MICHAEL APATA WILL BE CAUGHT WITHIN THREE DAYS."

CHAPTER 39

SATURDAY

Someone looking down from a high vantage point would see a helmeted stream of figures in black, wending their way in single file behind a very pink man close behind a very dark man.

Crime Chief Maurice Plumb and a detachment of policemen, led by hunter-tracker Robinson and his two buck dogs, trek along the single trail into heavily jungled Parika backlands. The sun, not too long having broken past the shortest trees, spills its rays and through the foliage still wet with dew, uncountable patches of new light flicker. The bushes are silent and vapours rise from things that grow. The steady brushing of men against leaves and outgrowths into the path they tread is a constant sound. A bird, far away, begins a ceaseless, hypnotic melody. A few heads turn in its direction, then come back to the unfolding path.

The mammoth search party is split into three groups each involving over eighty, well-armed policemen.

Plumb's detachment *Naamsec One*, is part of the first shift that is broken into four detachments. Three others comb the jungle from different points.

Ahead of *Naamsec One*, the hunter-tracker Robinson wears a helmet. His little dogs scamper forward sniffing at the ground before him. Slung around his left shoulder is his single bore shotgun. In his right hand is a sharp cutlass which he uses now and again to lop off branches that overhang the path, branches that may brush the White man's face. Secretly it is one of Robinson's self-appointed concerns.

Plumb and his section move through the old trail that leads them to the place of their first encounter with Michael Apata and the continuous hissing of their passage has become just another background sound.

*   *   *

Superintendent Clarence Franklin stands by the helmsman in the forward part of the police patrol launch, *Justice C.*, registered to carry fifty policemen inclusive of her small crew. The boat is very fast and is driven by a pair of powerful in-board engines. She cleaves her way through the brown water of the Essequibo. Gazing at the foam-crested, coffee-coloured backwash carved by the high speed bow of the launch, Franklin forgets Apata for a moment.

On a pair of long padded seats, running along the port and starboard of the launch, there sit twenty policemen. Ten on each side to balance the boat. Each man has a gun. Save one man, all the rest carry .303 rifles. A Sergeant of the riot squad holds the muzzle of a Thompson machine gun pointing to the sky above where, through cirrus clouds, the sun slants and glints on the unsteady water below.

*   *   *

The trail opens once more to that event-filled space in which the great tree was felled by an explosion. Plumb treads through the light tall grass and remembers the death scream of Corporal Charles Stephens, the crushed body of Constable Victor Rigby and the surprised look on the face of Detective Sergeant Kenrick Gittens' corpse. A creepy-crawly sensation tingles around Plumb's scalp and his head feels as though it is growing larger by the minute. Plumb treads after Robinson and a stream of men fall in behind. Plumb has come to equate death with grass. Green has become the colour of death though he has, until now, always associated black with death.

They file through the grass and soon they will reach a region that is lightly forested.

Plumb treads after Robinson with the stream of men behind him. Each of those who follow wears an expression which either truly reflects his feelings or a false face. They show, one might say, a kaleidoscope of emotional colours.

*　　*　　*

'BOAT COMING, SIR!'

Superintendent Franklin makes out the V-shaped bow wave of an approaching speed boat. He lifts his binoculars and looks. 'SERGEANT MENTORE!' he calls.

The Sergeant with the submachine gun comes forward and takes up a position from which he can cover the approaching boat.

The Superintendent points to a loud hailer which the helmsman hands to him. The boat skims towards them with the water slapping her hull. Franklin notes that the boat is being driven by a woman. She sits behind a low wind-shield with her blond hair streaming out behind her.

'STOP! I REPEAT, STOP! THIS IS THE POLICE!!'

With the powerful outboard engines reduced to a growl, the boat slows then stops, bobbing on the river with the engines in neutral. The police launch circles the little blue boat with its White occupant. No one is crouched behind the seats. *Justice C* circles closer. Once they are alongside the policemen see the irritation on the White woman's face though her expression is partly concealed behind large blue, cat-eyed sunglasses. Her full breasts rise and fall slowly. She is wearing a green bikini.

Franklin looks down at her and likes what he sees.

'What's under there please?' Franklin asks politely, pointing.

'PICNIC BASKET! SUITCASE!'

Both her hands grip the steering wheel so that the veins on the back of them stand out.

'LIFT IT!' he says tersely, 'IF YOU PLEASE, MADAM.'

She twists around. Drags the covers off. Superintendent Franklin bites in his bottom lip, then smiles. There is no other place in the little boat to hide.

The boat has twin outboard engines. Both black. Something about them suggests strength and arrogance. Franklin notes the name of the boat: *Hiawatha's Song*.

'My apologies, Madam, for interrupting your journey. We are searching for Michael Apata. All river-craft have to be searched!'

'DO I LOOK LIKE A NIGGER SYMPATHIZER!'

American! Franklin tells himself. 'No madam, but you do look like someone against whom a criminal might hold a gun in order to sneak past unsuspecting BLACK policemen! Thank you for your co-operation.'

Before long *Hiawatha's Song* rounds a distant bend where the misty bushes seem to grow across the river.

*   *   *

Robinson raises his left hand. Plumb does the same, and the sign is silently passed down the ranks. The manhunters stop.

Robinson picks up a broad leaf with old blood stains. 'BLOOD, SAH,' he tells the Crime Chief who kneels beside him with bared clenched teeth. Because of the heat two of the top buttons of his tunic are undone. Robinson points to a slightly disturbed patch of ground. 'Apata res' hay, sah, like 'e did bleeding and he use dem leaves by dat brick dere to sap it up.' The little dogs sniff about the clump of dried leaves stuck together. Plumb nods and hopes that the bullet has caught Apata some place vital. It would reduce the length and danger of the search.

The little dogs are now pulling at their leads. Plumb sees the trail continuing on ahead but notes that the dogs are sniffing off to the left side. He remembers Robinson's secret trail.

'Let me have your cutlass Robinson . . .'

Plumb slashes at some bushes off the side of the path and a new trail is revealed. He is pleased with himself. If one knew nothing about it one could miss it.

212

The new trail is overgrown by very tall grass.

Plumb pitches forward and in an effort to save his face brings his gun arm up. His hand strikes the ground and his revolver goes off.

Flat on his stomach he mutters, 'Jesus Christ!', then, slowly, he gets up, untangling his left foot from a snare made with plaited blades of grass that forms an arch from the ground like a polo neck.

The policemen who, at the sound of the shot, had flattened themselves into the sides of the trail and those who are on the ground, climb to their feet without concern for the leaves and grass clinging to their uniforms and exposed parts of their bodies. Sergeant Hutson passes his thumb over a pair of cuts below his right eye. They were made by the razor-sharp edges of the grass.

Plumb's face is pale. His revolver hangs limply in his left hand. His officer's cap lies on the buttocks of Robinson, the hunter-tracker. Robinson the hunter-tracker lies dead. The corpse is sprawled on its belly. There is little left of the head. A corporal turns his head away wanting to vomit. A constable, who promised himself to be brave, trembles and the little dogs sniff and run around the corpse that used to be their master.

'There's been an accident,' Plumb begins apologetically his eyes never leaving the body. Without looking he points with his revolver back to the grass trap. A policeman moves away from his superior's line of fire.

'Tripped,' says Plumb. 'My revolver went off. A bad accident. Damn.'

Sergeant Hutson, uses the dead man's cutlass, and cuts a fresh leaf from a banana tree and covers the part of the body where the head used to be.

* * *

With the engines throttled back, the police launch growls slowly into Robinson's inlet which would not accommodate two such vessels side by side. The passage in from the river is overhung at irregular intervals by trees and tangled bushes that reach out from the grassy banks.

Because the river is low, the current runs against the boat. With the engines murmuring, it noses its way upstream. The sound of her engines rebounds from those parts of the bank that fall sheer from the grassy plateau to the smooth milky-brown shore which gradually slants down to the water.

Robinson. Franklin thinks of the man, Robinson. He has picked up the report of the early fatality:

> "ROBINSON KILLED IN AN ACCIDENT. BODY BEING BROUGHT OUT. REQUEST TRANSPORT FOR SAME AT POINT OF ENTRY INTO MAN-HUNT AREA. OVER."

After the altercation with the rude American woman a degree of relaxation has seeped into Franklin's team. There have been a few jokes made and rewarded with laughter. But the report that has first crackled through has changed all that as a drop of lime would curdle a spoonful of fresh cow's milk.

The launch rides in against the stream but many within her are apprehensive. Adam's apples rise and fall. Lips are pursed and licked. Throats grow dry and are cleared on the sly. Eyes stare. A flight of black birds bursts from a thicket. A policeman jumps out of his skin but no one laughs. Maybe after the hunt is over it would be remembered and there will be laughter.

The water runs against the bow of the launch on which Superintendent Franklin stands. He sees, on a stretch of tangled bramble bushes on the right bank, a passage that leads off from a low rickety landing. At the head of the passage there is a pole, topped with a cow's skull bleached white, stuck in the brown soil. Franklin points to it. The helmsman nods.

*　　*　　*

214

The dogs aren't interested in going forward anymore, it seems. They potter and linger. They hold their heads low. Plumb feels idiotic. He lets them go after restraining himself from kicking them. To hell with the bloody dogs, he tells himself. He is beginning to feel more and more incompetent as the seconds slip by. The dogs scamper back the way they have come.

Plumb lifts the peak of his officer's cap and wipes perspiration from below his cap line.

On the left and right lie swamps. The mud smells foul. A few disgusting flies persistently alight on his now red face.

He presses on.

The trail opens into a grove of gigantic trees. He remembers Constable Rigby.

Plumb's right hand comes up in a signal, "STOP!" The other arm signals, "SPREAD OUT! PREPARE FOR AN ENCOUNTER!"

There's a house in a clearing beyond a cluster of trees. In his ears the sounds made by his men mix with the beat of his own heart. Plumb takes off his cap, slides his palm over his damp cranium, puts his cap back on and then signals to the police marksman, Sergeant Hutson. Hutson knows what he is supposed to do.

Darting to a tall tree with close-meshed, dark-leaved foliage, he climbs quickly and his Mark 4 rifle, complete with telescopic sight, dangles from his shoulder as he ascends.

Plumb checks the position of his men and is satisfied. 'I hope everything goes well,' he tells himself. He signals. The policemen begin closing in cautiously. Plumb thinks of Stephens and the snake.

The house is encircled. There is a window opened.

Plumb chooses a moment and scurries over a few yards of low-growing grass. He gains the vantage point of a palm tree. He takes an easy, deep, lung-filling breath, whilst clasping and unclasping the service revolver in his left hand.

'THIS IS THE POLICE!' he shouts. 'WE HAVE THE BUILDING SURROUNDED.'

The old man tumbles in alarm from his hammock even though he knew the police were coming. The sound of the White man's voice shakes loose something in his failing determination.

'SURRENDER APATA! YOU HAVE THREE MINUTES TO SHOW YOURSELF UNARMED!'

Plumb and the others watch and wait, their guns at ready. ONE ...

The only movement, so far, comes from a loose coconut branch hanging and swaying from a nearby tree. The branch is dead. The policemen slip on their gas masks. So does Plumb.

TWO.

On Plumb's wrist the watch ticks very loudly.

'DOAN SHOOT! OW MIH LAWD, OFFISAH SAH, DOAN SHOOT!'

'IDENTIFY YOURSELF!' orders Plumb.

'AH-A-DELPHAS BANZE, SAH!'

'SHOW YOURSELF.'

Sergeant Hutson, in a sniping position, sees a white cloth rising to the frame of the open window. There is a hand below it. Hutson grinds his teeth.

Plumb wonders if it is a trick.

The frightened face of an old Negro eases into view.

'LEAVE THE HOUSE AND COME FORWARD IF YOU ARE ALONE!'

Hutson's sniper's sight imprisons the old man the moment he appears at the doorway, as it had imprisoned his signal of surrender, as it now imprisons his head. The cross sights would likewise imprison anyone hoping to use the old man as a shield.

Plumb's revolver is at full cock.

The old man stumbles forward, alone. He brings with him the smell of human filth. He keeps coming until the White officer appears like a ghost from behind a palm tree. The old man's good eye pops momentarily. Gas masked, to the old man, the Crime Chief looks like a demon. Plumb takes off the mask.

'TURN AROUND!'

The old man obeys and Plumb wrinkles his nostrils. Touching the nape of his neck Plumb propels him at pistol point back to the house.

He pushes the old man through the doorway. One of the rice bags that covers the floor trips Banze and he falls heavily, feeling a crippling shock of pain dart through his body that is already weakened with fear.

'GET UP BANZE!'

'Owlawdgawdoffisahsah jus'nowjusnow ... O-O-O-GAWDSAH! Jus'now ...'

What the bloody hell's he trying to tell me, Plumb asks himself? A fire smoulders in a corner. Plumb moves away from the old man on the floor. He leans out the window. 'CONSTABLE!' he shouts.

'SAWH!' answers a policeman. Lennox Kirton.

Kirton's face is square and he looks like a stereotyped American gangster. In the form of a taunt, he was once asked, why he had absented himself from all of God's tenderness classes before he was ushered into this dimension.

Kirton moves his bulk in obedience towards the door. His strides are long.

His friends say that when it comes to shoes Kirton goes down to the shoe-maker in America Street to have special over-sized ones made. There's always a joke about the size of Kirton's feet and his feet tell something of his height. Kirton is a door bender. He has to bend on entering any door of average height. Word has it that he got into the Force because of his height and not because he had any sort of intelligence.

Before he left the Eve Leary barracks yesterday, he had bragged: 'BET AN' SURE! ONE AH ME BULLIT DEM GAFFA LADGE AH BAD MAN APATA BACKSIDE!' There was much laughter from Kirton after he had said it.

But now Kirton is serious. Whenever a White man calls Kirton he is serious. Bending, he enters the home of Adolphus Banze, and sees him grovelling on the floor.

'CONSTABLE. I WANT THIS MAN ON HIS FEET. I DON'T UNDERSTAND WHAT HE'S TRYING TO TELL ME.'

The suffering man turns, and the good eye falls upon Kirton's face. Fear of the White man is replaced by fear of the Black man.

'Ow! Mih tellin' de offisah dat ah gon get up jus' now. Mih ah feel terrahble pay-pain all ovah all ovah mih bahdy when mih go' fuh move. Suh pick mih up offisah pick mih up, son. OH GAWD AH BEGGIN' YO' SON PICK MIH UP.'

'GET UP! DE OFFISAH WAN' TALK TO YOU'!' barks Kirton.

Christ! These people are brutal! Plumb tells himself. But he does not think of intervening. He knows that this is no time to be soft. He wants to get a lead from the old man. He is sure that Apata was here.

'YO' HEAR WHA' MIH AH TELL YO'?'

'Why not pick him ... ?'

'GET UP! DE CRIME CHIEF WAN' TALK TO' Kirton's heavy-booted right foot lashes out, 'YOU...'

'CONSTABLE ...' Plumb interjects too late.

Baby-like, the old man whimpers as his body arches in a very apparent spasm of pain. Constable Lennox Kirton has kicked Banze in the area of his left kidney.

Plumb generally feels indifferent to colonized peoples but now he hates one ... Kirton. He hates Kirton this moment with a contempt he reserves for snakes and bloated tropical toads.

Looking at the Crime Chief, there's bewilderment on Kirton's face. He doesn't seem to understand. He thinks that what he just did would have the approval of the White officer. But the tone of Plumb's reprimand lingers in the air and there's a look on the face of the White man that weakens Kirton's knees.

'BLOODY JESUS CHRIST, CONSTABLE!' shouts Plumb, 'He's one of your own! ISN'T HE?'

Kirton doesn't answer.

'ISN'T HE? ANSWER ME!'

'Yes sir,' mumbles Kirton with eyes focused to the floor.
'GET THE HELL OUT OF MY BLOODY SIGHT FOR CHRIST SAKE!'

Constable Lennox Kirton turns and moves off, bumping his head on the top of the doorway. Inadvertently, he fingers a dent in his helmet as he leaves, feeling like the shortest man in the Force.

With an effort the White man lifts the old Black man on to the same mattress that Apata slept on hours back. The skin is broken where the over-sized military boot connected. Even though Adolphus Banze is dark the swelling on his back is darker yet. Plumb looks at the blackman's eyes. There's a veil over the iris of one and out of the good one a tear trickles to fall on Plumb's hand. Plumb wipes it away. He knows that time is being wasted but decides to do something for the man lest he allow himself to drop into the category of brutes like Kirton and many other such natives who exist. Plumb calls for the first aid kit.

CHAPTER 40

SATURDAY

BACKSWING OF THE PENDULUM:
The old man sat up. The hammock swayed, and the creakings of the ropes made Apata stir to full wakefulness. He had been restless as he slept because apprehension of the new day had burrowed up from his subconscious and had plagued his dreams. His dreams had made him restless enough for the creakings of the hammock's ropes to have stirred him to full consciousness.

The old man's eye was upon him.

'Small bhai,' he said gravely, 'de police comin'.'

Apata's eyes screamed.

'How do you know old man?' he asked in a whisper.

The old man climbed out of his swinging bed. 'Mih people jus' tell me son. An' mih people doan lie ar guide mih wrang.'

Apata felt his arms, as they supported him in a sitting position, trembling.

'Dem jus' start. Dem far from 'round here. Nah get confuse Michael. Nah get frighten.'

RADIO! Apata dug under the cot and dragged out the V.H.F. set, clamped the earphones over his head and listened. Radio silence. The old man saw furrows erupt on Apata's forehead. Apata's heart-beats thumped wildly in his temples. His head felt as though it was non-existent.

Breathing hard he tried to clear the dizziness that was rising from the pit of his stomach.

The old man eyed him in the light that still flickered from the bottle lamp. Outside the darkness was thinning out into dawn.

Apata sighed, trying to calm himself and he sought within himself for something rational to say to cover his terror of the day's expectations. Glancing to the lamp he spoke: 'The oil lasted?'

'Mih nevah sleep through de night wid darknis'. Mih does always get up middle ah de night an' put mo' oil.' The old man remembered that when he had, Apata's sleeping face had been grim and, as he watched him, Apata had muttered a name.

The shadows wavered about them and the old man saw the sinking of the young man into himself. Banze's mouth shaped as if he would say something. His lips opened then they closed. It was as though the old man had changed his mind. Then his lips parted again and his mouth hung open, until a strand of saliva stretched itself and dripped onto the floor. He was thinking.

'Well . . .' he said at last and ambled to his kitchen corner where the fire-place was. He rolled up the canvas that covered the open section on the wall there.

Outside an orange glow was evident beyond the trees, beyond the patterned silhouettes of trunks, boughs and leaves against the dawn. The old man started a fire before rising from his hunched position. He moved over to his food corner and took a hand of green plantains from off a bunch. He fried them with dried fish. And as the old man made breakfast, Apata paced about the cot he had slept on. He seemed restless.

The old man was now making a thick porridge with the flour from finely ground plantain strips that were dried in the sun.

'Old man? Paa?'

He heard the tremor in Apata's voice and smiled patronizingly at him.

221

'I can move good, you know ... I can move well.'

Sadness lowered itself deeper still into the old man's heart.

'Use de stick, son or yo' go' strain de foot.'

An emotional lump rose in Apata's chest. He swallowed in order to send it back, but it would not sink. It was as if the emotional lump came higher with each intake of breath. The smell of the breakfast assailed his nostrils and he told himself that he would not be able to eat. Worry filled him. A deep and mournful sound surrounded the little one-roomed house. To Apata, the sound was familiar but he was having difficulty in placing it. It came again and he heard it with foreboding. Uncertainty showed in his eyes. The old man saw it as he had earlier.

'Dat is Brownie, mih cow.'

'YES, OH YES! I saw her yesterday.' Apata took a deep breath.

'Mikey?'

'Yes ... Paa.'

'Yo' frighten?'

Apata laughed silently. 'I don't know.'

'Nah frighten, man! Si' down. Nah frighten. Si' down an' say de twenty-third psalm over an' over in yo' mind!'

Apata sat, then his lips began moving.

*   *   *

Outside, tender golden sunlight mingled with a mistiness that slowly blew away. Apata checked his time. It was six forty-five. The dew-wet leaves and fronds gleamed freshly and the morning felt as innocent as Eden probably had been before Eve beguiled Adam.

The old man silently repacked Apata's haversack whilst Apata ate slowly.

'Doan lef' nothing fuh manners, small bhai.'

The old man ambled outside and returned shortly with a veteran of a water bottle. 'Yo' guh carry dis bottle wid milk 'roun' yo' waist.' Moving to a ledge above the window the old man took down a battered mess pan that Apata might use for cooking. Apata remembered the one that he had hung on the tree under which he rested before he heard a blood curdling scream in the night. He paused in his eating. The old man noticed.

'Force it down if yo' have to, small bhai. Mih know wha' ah happen ah you' stomik but yo' gaffa eat!' Then the old man sneezed.

'Paa ... tell me ...'

'What' son?'

'Tell me, and don't be afraid ... Do you think I'm guilty?'

'When yo' young, small bhai yo' nevah does guilty. Yo' does nevah guilty when yo' young.' He folded a thick, old blanket in a roll that Apata could easily carry and, as if that was all there was to his answer, he straightened from the rolled and tied blanket and packed haversack.

'Yo' believe yo' can move good wit dis?' he said, referring to the haversack.

'It doesn't look heavy.'

'Naa. It not heavy. Strap dis blanket 'round yo' ches' like wan bandahleer. Ah pack every lil' thing yo' go' need fuh stay alive if yo' get las'. But yo nah go' get las' if yo fallah de trail mih draw fuh yo'. Yo nah go' butt up wid no policeman alang wheh mih draw. But still yo' gaffa walk wid yo eye skin an' yo han' ah de gun triggah!'

Apata felt the left side top pocket of Glenn's bush jacket then lifted the haversack to his back. Bending his knees he tested the weight. The old man had assured him that the haversack wasn't heavy. He was right. It was only now that Apata realized, too, that the old man was also right about his miracle bush poultice. He had tested his weight by bending his knees and had forgotten the wound. He muttered what his Granny Jane always muttered, 'Wonders never cease but daily increase.'

Apata thought of the radio. It was designed to be carried on the back and reasoned that it could stop a police bullet but a haversack of light food couldn't. He slipped the haversack off and rested it back to the floor.

'WHA'APPEN? You'in goin no mo'?'

Apata grinned. It was his first light-hearted expression that morning.

'Yes, I'm still going, but I'm going to put the haversack in front of me and the radio on my back. It's better there.'

'Dat true.'

Like an after-thought, the old man moved to his clothes chest and dug out a little flat plastic bottle, whitish, with a little black cap. The label on it read: I-N-S-E-C-T R-E-P-E-L-L-E-N-T.

'Ah get dis when ah used to wo'k ah de Yankee Naval Base.'

'I heard my father used to work there too,' mumbled Apata. A new tenseness was beginning to creep over him now.

'Dat gon keep de pests away from you. A-an' in case yo' get shoot Michael, jus' remembah how to use de miracle bush an' de tobacca leafs dem. Yo check yo ammunishans dem?'

Apata nodded. He found it difficult to speak because of the lump elevating from below his sternum.

The old man, looking beaten now, placed an old felt hat, the rim flopping with age, onto Apata's head. Apata picked up the powerful rifle with its telescopic sight and then the walking stick.

He stepped into the old man's arms. The old man hugged him and dampened Glenn's bush jacket with tears; and Apata found himself gulping in order to stem his, but failed. Then he pulled himself together. He eased the old man away from him but Banze clung to an arm.

'Gawd be wid you son.'

'Take care Paa.'

'Gawd guh wid you son.'

'See you old man.'

'Gawd be wid you son.'

Apata smiled.

'Gawd walk wid you son.'

'Thanks old man.'

'Tek care.'

Apata walked away.

CHAPTER 41

SATURDAY

'What is wrong with this man?'

'Ow sah . . .' begins the old man in a cracked, pained tone. 'Ow sah . . . ah wan ah alyuh police kick me ah mih back sah . . . owwww sah . . .'

'CONSTABLE KIRTON KICKED HIM, SIR.'

Superintendent Franklin swears silently.

'Ah wan big strappin' Black wan sah . . . ow Gawd sah . . . Gawd go' sin am sah . . .'

Franklin stares at Sergeant Hutson but can tell that the man on the couch below him has begun to cry for it sounds through clearly in his voice: 'Ow sah . . . some ah we own people really cruel to awe own people in front'a baccra man, sah . . .'

'WHO DID THIS, HUTSON?'

'I told you sir, Constable Kirton, eight eight six two, sir!'

'Kirton?'

'Kirton, sir.'

Superintendent Franklin bends to the old man and, with the gentleness of a good nurse, lays his right palm on the old man's forehead as if feeling for a temperature. 'What was done to help this man Sergeant?'

'Ow sah . . . ow sah . . .'

'SUPERINTENDENT?'

Franklin sighs. 'What was done to offset this man's suffering Sergeant?' he repeats tiredly and his tone suggests rising anger.

'Crime Chief Plumb did the best for him with the first aid kit, sir!'

Franklin shakes his head and grunts. 'Turn on your side a bit, old man ... yes, like that. Good. Now let us see...' Gently he touches the small of the old man's back. He winces. Franklin beckons Hutson over.

'See that Sergeant?'

'Yes, sir.'

There is time, the Superintendent tells himself. 'Superintendent Franklin!' Plumb had said, 'will patrol up to this point and move into ... let's call it Robinson's inlet ... then work his way in and drop off at this point and trek in to the farmhouse. Like this, Apata can be sandwiched. That is if he is found in the farmhouse. If not, Superintendent Franklin's group will establish a sort of outpost at that point until the shift's over. Also, at the farmhouse, Franklin's detachment will be on the alert for anything. At a minute's notice, he must be able to take to the river. ANY QUESTIONS?'

That was the way the Crime Chief had put it in the final briefing, yesterday. Franklin dabs the bruised skin with a bit of cotton wool. Hot water! Franklin tells himself. Since I was just a kid, hot water was the household balm for swellings.

'Do you think he's injured badly Sergeant?'

'I don't know, sir!'

'Ow sah ... police shoot me bhai Ranal ah 'e back. Ow ... Ranal an' 'e bin-nah fight, yes ... but Ranal na had gun sah. Police prappah bad sah. But you good an' kind sah. Tell dem de small bhai nat guilty sah.'

'Which small boy, old man?'

'Apata sah. Apata good like me own son. Apata nah murdah de White man. Apata seh 'e jus' shoot de white man ah 'e knee cap an' lef' 'e a fahres'. Apata nah murdah 'e.'

'Nobody said that he killed the White American, old man. After we catch him, we'll know.'

The old man shakes his head. 'De only time police go' ketch Apata, sah, ah when 'e body fall.'

'What do you mean?'

'Eh-eh! Me nah hear yo' offisah.'

'Now, this is going to pain. Al'right?'

'A'right sah.'

'You said that the only time we're going to catch Apata is when his body falls. What do you mean?' Franklin kneads the swelling in the old man's back.

'OW GAWD SAH!'

'I'm very sorry about that ...'

Franklin keeps the conversation going. He hopes that the old man's mind may be shifted from the expectation of pain. 'Tell me about Ronald, your son.'

'Ranal had fire ah 'e head, sah. Sah, Ranal, sah, wouldah nevah shit 'eself up like 'e father when 'e hear baccra man v'ice call from outside, sah. But all de same sah, all de shame guh go 'way ... cause mih guh dead, sah.' The old man shakes his head feebly. Water runs out of his seeing eye. 'Sah?' he now says enquiringly.

'Yes, old man?'

'Mih hope Michael nah kill you sah.'

'There, old man.' Superintendent Clarence Franklin stands up from the couch. 'You're going to rest, now. Right?'

To Hutson, who appears at the door, he says: 'I don't think it's too bad...'

'I don't know, sir.'

To the old man Franklin says, 'Old man, no one will give you any problems.'

The old man whimpers an answer of gratitude.

*   *   *

The Crime Chief looks at his watch uncertainly. A sixth sense tells him that the old man lied. So, instead of having taken the trail indicated by Adolphus Banze, he has taken another. But now Plumb wonders if he was wrong about the old man. Plumb's compass is his intuition. Over and over he hears the locals say that turning back means bad luck. He decides to press on, though, not because of any local supersitition. Turning back now, he thinks, will indicate to the men behind that he lacks self-confidence and is a bungling White officer who tripped and caused the death of a man, a bungling officer who fired a flare into the base of a tree and caused the death of a man. 'The widow maker!' Plumb's conscience tells him, 'The widow maker!'

Plumb waves his men on with his gun hand.

From a high vantage point one would see a string of figures trailing behind a figure in light brown. They are trailing through the light forest that makes up part of the Parika backlands.

* * *

A hidden police sentry feels fatigue enveloping his body. A detachment of manhunters has just passed and he plans to tell the others of the strain of sentry duty. Being on the eleven to seven shift he will be relieved in half an hour's time. He pulls his sleeve back over his watch and takes a new grip of his rifle with his right hand. He resumes his watch along the trail. His eyelids are heavy and he remembers a friend who always sleeps in the late cinema shows and who talks, time after time, of using matchsticks to keep his eyes propped open. The police sentry smiles, yawns and wonders whether he looks like a World War II Japanese soldier with bushes stuck in his helmet as he crouches there behind a tight clump of brush just off the trail. He yawns and thinks, 'SARGE? Sarge! The trees ... the trees are moving!' Bataan? Back to Bataan? He yawns and a bird, far away, breaks into a kind of forlorn song that drags sweetly. The police sentry listens and listens, thinking of his birds at home. Slowly his thoughts of his collection of caged birds cease to be thoughts and become dreams.

Apata comes out of hiding and sneaks past the posted sentry. He moves stealthily along a path covered by Plumb's detachment earlier. Suddenly he breaks off from the trail and crouches under a little tree with a cutlass-wounded bough. Bending lower still, he crawls under a bush at the base of the tree. Burrowing on he emerges to a view of an inlet that runs out to the river. A great tangle of bushes growing from the embankment slants steeply down to the water. He's about ten yards from it. From where he crouches, on all fours, he can see that the bushes bend over to the inlet's face and he knows that, under a dense overhang, he will find a boat. It will be well camouflaged and he will be able to lie in it and wait out the brightest part of the day.

*　　*　　*

'CRIME CHIEF'S ONTO SOMETHING, SIR!'

'Duty calls, Wendy,' the Deputy-Commissioner of Police tells his wife. He returns the telephone to its cradle and, gripping his walking stick, he pushes himself to his feet.

He enters the radio room which is the location of the blackboard with the labelled, chalk-drawn manhunt plan, a radio, and a Corporal, a technician, sitting behind the desk on which the radio rests.

'ALERT SECTION THREE. APATA MAY BE IN YOUR AREA. BE ON THE LOOKOUT. I REPEAT, BE ON THE ALERT. HE'S MOVING FROM THE FARMHOUSE POSITION ALONG TRAIL "E" SPREAD OUT IN YOUR SECTION.'

Biting nervously on the stem of his unlit pipe, the Dep-Com. glances at the blackboard. Section three, he thinks, trail "E". Then he realizes that trail "E" according to the plan runs no more than a hundred yards from an outlet to the river. I wonder, thinks Taylor the Deputy-Commissioner of Police, if Plumb has thought of the possible amount of hours lead Apata may have had on them. He frowns then says, 'Let me speak to Plumb, Corporal.'

He takes the unlit pipe from his lips.

*　　*　　*

The engines of *Justice C* are running at speed as she cleaves the water close to the banks of the river. From the launch Superintendent Franklin and his men wave now and then to members of shore-line patrols. Franklin nods to the helmsman who, on this signal, locks for the centre of the river.

Superintendent Wellington, in charge of the shore-line patrols, flashes a great smile at Franklin riding in the bow of the launch. Franklin does not see the smile, only a pink hand raised in a mock salute from behind a clump of green. From the centre of the river the members of the shore-line patrols cease to be individuals. They are merely puppets lazily beating the bushes.

According to Dep-Com. Robert Taylor, Apata could possibly have headed towards an inlet. Has he? Franklin wonders. If he has taken to the river the shore-line patrols under Wellington should have spotted him. Would they? Would a man try to make an escape by boat in broad daylight? Taylor may have a good point in believing that Apata may have taken to the waterways in order to escape the sentries, wait until dark then slip out to the river and make a break for it. PATROL THE INLET! Taylor has ordered.

Franklin feels that Taylor may well be very right.

He lurches heavily as the launch comes round in a sweeping turn and heads towards another inlet which is overhung with a growth of bamboo trees.

'Take it easy, Fraser,' he says to the helmsman.

'Yes sir!'

Franklin steps aft, down from the wheel house, to where the men sit tensely.

'WHAT WE'LL ALL BE DOING IS LOOKING FOR SIGNS OF ANY BOATS HAVING BEEN PUSHED OFF THE MUD. BOOT PRINTS. WE'LL PROGRESS UP THE INLET AS FAR AS POSSIBLE! Every man must be ready to shoot to kill if necessary! And necessary it may be to save your own, or a friend's life! APATA IS A CRACK SHOT!'

The overhanging bamboos scrape and brush whisperingly on the wheelhouse of the launch as she penetrates into the new inlet. Far ahead, a big tree overhangs at an acute angle from one of the banks and heavy parasite vines, like heavy cables, hang low to the water's surface that is dark brown and reflects sections of the bank's vegetation and the sky.

'Sergeant Mentore!'

'SIR.'

'Take a position behind the wheel house.'

'HUTSON.'

'SAWH.'

'I need a pair of men with cutlasses on the bow, to clear the path when necessary.'

'SAWH.'

*　　*　　*

Apata, lying within the little dugout canoe under the dense overhanging shelter, hears the sound of the police launch coming into the inlet. The engines' grating grows louder and louder and creates a feeling that affects his bowels. He grips his rifle tightly with sweaty palms. What's going on? he wonders. Did the old man talk? That is not possible. But what is going on? The boat's engines stop and there is the sound of a gun-shot, a rifle shot.

What does it mean?

THE ENGINE SOUNDS PICK UP ONCE MORE. And get closer and closer. The sound is all around him. Apata dries his hands and takes a new hold of the rifle. He caresses the trigger with the sounds of the engines almost on top of him. He sees the boat. Sweat runs down his face and he tastes its saltiness. His eyes are narrowed and a grim thought possesses him surprising him and scaring him. He will drop the White man with the red head first. Then he will take the broad-faced Riot Squad man who holds a Thompson machine gun. To Apata that man is the most important. Certainly, he decides, he will take quite a few with him.

A cold ache seizes his mind and all those he loves slip through his imagination.

Wavelets from the passing police launch rock Apata gently and leave him wondering if he's indeed a "killer" for he would have shot as many of the men in the launch as would have been necessary to drive them away.

Anyway, he will have to move out from where he is at the moment. Before the launch, he had seen a shore-line patrol that could have found him if it had been thorough.

As the hum of *Justice C*'s engines die away down the inlet, Apata turns onto his stomach. He listens for voices. There are none.

He must move now.

*   *   *

The corial he is paddling is small, Apata tells himself, but that is to my advantage. I'm not doing badly even at a snail's pace. If I make a mile in two hours it will still be good going. Then I'll beach at night fall, think a bit and push off for real. I shall do all my travelling at night, all of my travelling at nights. I'll have to be careful with those foot patrols in the daytime, seeing that they concentrate on the shorelines. He hears the humming of the police boat's engines again. Must stop and keep still in the shelter of that grassy overhang coming up. Lie low once more until the boat passes.

When is something seen but not seen? What explains that phenomenon? A layman might blame it on absentmindedness. A naturalist, or a person knowledgeable in military matters would say camouflage.

And Apata is seen but not seen as he makes good time in a dugout canoe that looks like a clump of riverside bushes when it is moored to any part of the river banks.

Franklin looks through a pair of binoculars. He sweeps the distance before them. The light is dying rapidly. He checks out the left then right banks which are rapidly growing more indistinct in the dusk. He lowers his binoculars.

*   *   *

The *Elizabeth*, called out by the Crime Chief, follows in the wake of *Justice C*. An officer, unaccustomed to river work, is in charge. He feels the need to relieve himself. He taps his helmsman, an Indian with a quick wit, on the shoulder, 'Nature calls, Narine,' the Coloured officer says.

'Nature, sah?'

The officer suspects that Narine understands, yet, he rephrases his statement, 'Narine, I want to shit!'

'Yes, sir!'

'Put me off on that patch of beach near that old palm tree coming up on the left.'

The launch is brought round in a sweeping curve to head for the shore.

*   *   *

Apata watches the approach of yet another police launch and then he realizes that it is one that has passed him before. He peers through the sight and is strangely calm inside. Over-confident?

The launch comes closer. It is clear that it is coming in to land men. Apata waits, unmoving. He no longer needs to spy through the sight on the rifle. With his bare eyes he sees *Elizabeth* gliding past his hiding place. It noses into an open space less than fifty yards from where Apata bobs below the bank of the river.

Apata tells himself that he will be able to kill them all if need be. Again he surprises himself with this stream of murderous thoughts.

A Coloured officer steps gingerly from the boat to the shore. He disappears behind a thick growth of bushes a little way from where the launch waits with engines running. The policemen who are left on board seem to be amused about something. Apata guesses what they are laughing about.

The Sunday Trumpet

Sunday, August 7th   *6 cents*   *1959*

GUNMAN OUTFOXES POLICE
Hunter-Tracker Robinson Killed!

Yesterday, in the wake of an accident that resulted in the death of a hunter-tracker employed by the police to assist in tracking down fugitive Michael Apata, the day-shift search parties, which had been covering the

manhunt area and sections of the river, returned in low
spirits to their Parika post. It was clear that Apata had
outfoxed them.

The Farmer and the Gunman.

'Three days ago I was going aback at my farm and
suddenly a Negro man with a lot of hair on his face like
the man Castro, jump out from behind a bush and
pointed a gun at my stomach. Then he told me, "HAND
OVER YOUR FOOD. OR I KILL YOU." I was really
frightened, so I gave him the saucepan with my hassa
curry and rice. Then he told me that he was the man
Apata and if I told anybody that I had seen him he would
find me and cut my tongue out. "WALK ON YOUR
FEET AND NOT YOUR MOUTH!" That is what he
said to me. He even told me that if I didn't listen, my
wife and daughter would suffer because he would rape
them and kill them.'

*　　*　　*

Lela Gobin is just half way through the column.
'Harrydada, Mish!' she calls as she looks at photographs
of her husband and the reporter who wrote the story.
'LOOK YO' NAME AND PITCHA INA TODAY
TRUMPET AH TELL LIE!'
'Yo' expec' me fuh tell de reportah dat de blackman nah
binnah threaten mih fuh truth? Eh? DAH WAN BLACK-
MAN! Me nah like Kaapaar! De fastah dem police kill 'e
black rass de bettah fuh awe!'

*　　*　　*

234

The Daily Clarion

Monday, August 8th   *6 cents*   *1959*

POLICE ACCIDENTALLY KILL MURDERER RAMISH GOBIN

Yesterday a police marksman shot and killed a suspicious character who was trying to escape from a police patrol launch by slipping out of the river into an inlet that would have been impossible for the police launch, *Elizabeth* to have gotten into. The police patrol was combing the river for signs of fugitive Michael Apata who, the Crime Chief believes, has definitely taken to the river in a bid to make a break for Bartica. The man in the boat was mistaken for Apata He was wearing a hat.

When the craft containing the dead man was pulled alongside the police boat it was then discovered that he was Ramish Gobin, an Indian farmer.

Before the day was out, the headless body of another Indian farmer was found. His name was Rai Gobin the brother of the man, Ramish Gobin, who was accidentally shot by the police river patrol. The brothers Rai and Ramish were twins.

According to the police Rai Gobin was gruesomely murdered. Lab tests on the body of the man shot by the police proved that blood from under his nails and the blood of the man found decapitated were identical. Following investigations, it was discovered that Ramish Gobin had had a life-long grudge against his twin brother whom, Ramish believed had a farm which rightfully belonged to the latter. Footprints in the sand near the murdered man's riverside farmhouse, matched with the footprints of the dead Ramish Gobin whose right foot lacks a big toe. The murder weapon was found in an Esso drum in the murdered man's yard. On the evidence the police conclusion, a police statement said, is indisputable.

CHAPTER 42

MONDAY

'Is fate take a hand, yesterday, you know sir,' says the helmsman, conversationally, referring to the report in the newspaper. 'Was the same chap who say, in yesterday papers, that Apata meet he and threaten he. I think that if he had get away with that murder, Apata would'ava been getting the blame today.'

Superintendent Franklin nods and says, 'You could be right.'

He turns and, through a window in the wheelhouse, he peers out at the men under his charge. They are gazing at the river bank. In the stern, Sergeant Mentore sits easily with his Thompson machine gun.

"WHOOP! WHOOP!" sounds *Elizabeth* going the other way closer in to the opposite bank. *Justice C* returns the friendly signal.

*   *   *

The Commissioner of Police sits in his cream-walled office. He is wondering if Apata carries, along with the stolen Winchester weapon, a police .303 rifle. The report on his desk says that Detective Sergeant Kenrick Gittens was killed by a bullet from a police rifle, a .303.

There is precise rapping on his door.

'Come in Andrea.'

'The Robinson widow to see you Commissioner.'

236

'Yes, I'm expecting her. Send her in, will you please.'

Andrea leaves the room. The Commissioner gets to his feet and remains standing. He turns away as the wife of the ex-hunter and tracker comes, with unsure steps, into his office her whole house could fit into.

Turning back to her he says gravely, 'Good morning Mrs Robinson. Would you please take a seat.' He comes out from behind his desk and speaks sympathetically and apologetically to her for some time, then after about fifteen minutes, he calls in an accountant who pays the widow a large sum of money.

Mrs Robinson leaves, still unhappy, but sure of a financially stable future for herself and children.

The Daily Trumpet

Tuesday, August 9th   *6 cents   1959*

APATA TWO GUN KID

Gittens Killed By Bullet From Police .303 Rifle.

The post mortem of the late detective Kenrick Gittens has revealed that he was killed by a bullet from a .303 rifle similar to those that are used by the police. This evidence suggests that the police may have to accept the evidence of a World War II veteran, who lives on the West Coast, that he saw a man who fits the fugitive's description carrying a firearm resembling a .303 police rifle. His report was not treated seriously, at that time. Now it may be possible that Michael Apata carries two rifles.

Let's Count Down For Her Majesty

The date for the arrival of the Queen has been announced, and preparations for a glorious welcome are well under way . . .

CHAPTER 43

TUESDAY

The new morning sun glistens like a popular calypso on the mind of a calypso lover. The dock workers, below a boat hauled in to be cleaned of barnacles, joke among themselves. Says one: 'APATA GOT DEM RASS IN PICKLE.'

Says another: 'Me meet de man Apata you know!'

'Aw! Guh suh! Which Apata you meet? Mus' be Apata picture in de newspapers.'

'I ENT JOKING. I MEET APATA WHEN I USED TO WORK AT VERGENOEGEN.'

'An' when yo' wake up what happen?'

The leading doubter raises his voice and hails over to another group of workmen: 'HEY BOYS! JEETRAM SAY HE MEET MICHAEL APATA.'

'HEY JEET! WHY YOU DOAN OPEN A DISPEN-SARY WIT' DEM PILLS YOU'S WANT WE SWAL-LOW?'

Jeetram ignores them, shrugs off their doubts and resumes scraping barnacles off the stern plate in front of him.

*   *   *

Bascom sits doodling with carpenter's chalk on a sheet of brown paper and eventually comes up with a way to mount a bren gun onto the police launch. He would not mount it on the wheelhouse, as indicated on the working drawing left by the Crime Chief but on an iron rail on the boat's forecastle.

He tells himself that the Crime Chief did not think his plan through. If he had followed it the machine gun and the search light, which is also on the wheelhouse would have got in each other's way. He moves to the metal-work shop where his men are. He explains to them what has to be done and they follow his instructions which they find easy to understand.

They make a mount for the gun out of metal piping. The weapon, without its magazine, lies hard and cold on a work bench guarded by a grim looking constable.

Two hours later the gun is fitted onto the police patrol boat. And tomorrow morning guns will be fitted on all the patrol launches. Aboard the *Sir Richard* the machine gun is set to be used by a gunner in a prone position. Bascom asks the Constable to get down and test the feel of it. He climbs into the vessel, walks to the forecastle, lies on his stomach, grips the gun, swivels it around and then nods.

'You believe it going to work good, starboy?'

'Yeah man!' says the Constable getting up.

'Ah mean, when it firing you think it going work good?'

The Constable shakes the gun as if trying to wrench it loose from the mount. 'Yeah man, it going work good.'

And metal-worker Bascom feels the thrill of accomplishment. A little later Crime Chief Plumb returns. He walks over to the workshop and reappears with Bascom who tries to match strides with him. Bascom, however, is too short and ends up looking ridiculous but the watching dock workers do not laugh. They have noticed the object in the White man's hand. The word *magazine* goes around like a rumour and tools are put down.

Plumb nimbly alights on the bow of *Sir Richard* and takes the gunner's prone position. He knows that his instructions to the metal master were rather scanty and is not upset because the man has relocated the gun on the forecastle. Plumb has always acknowledged the existence of natural genius. Also he feels that the man Bascom has guts, the guts to back his own initiative.

He notes that the way the gun is mounted the roll of the

boat will not upset the gunner. He tries the swivel on which the weapon is mounted and marvels at the metal-worker's ingenuity. He inspects the welding work with sensitive fingertips and finds it neat. THEN HE JAMS THE LOADED MAGAZINE INTO POSITION and the machine gun becomes alive and lethal.

Plumb looks around, seemingly unaware of the audience on the dock. He looks to his left and sees weathered rotting piles that mark where an old section of the wharf used to be. He bends his head, braces the stock of the weapon into the crock of his shoulder and squeezes the trigger. Bits and pieces fly off the wharf in response to a stream of bullets while the noise shatters the awe filled silence. Plumb takes his finger off the trigger while wood splinters still fall to the choppy river's surface.

'RANT!' hisses a worker.

'SKUNT! DUH'S FIRE POWER!'

'Duh's the first time I see and hear one a' them things fire real-real, yo know.'

'Shit boy. White people, eh?'

'DEM FUCKIN' PEOPLE GREAT!'

'"DEM FUCKIN' PEOPLE GREAT" MY SKUNT! AL'YO DOES OVER-RATE DEM PEOPLE. YA'LL KNOW HE'S WHO?'

Silence.

'HE IS FUCKIN ASSISTANT COMMISSIONER OF POLICE AND CRIME CHIEF OF DIS COUNTRY! Yes. Maurice Plumb. Duh's de man. The man in charge of the manhunt that runnin' FOUR days now. Good. He rass White. SO HOW COME THEY CYANT CATCH MICHAEL YET? Doan worry wit' all that poppy show he givin' we dere. He cyant knock Apata with duh. And I bet ya'all something...'The talker is grinning. Plumb lets loose another burst of gun fire.

'AH BET YA'ALL ANYTHING.'

'What yo' bettin' man? Come straight!'

'That if he push he luck too far ... Michael Apata kill he.'

'What stupidnis you talkin' Calduh?'

240

'Brogan, I bettin' you ten dollars Michael going kill he skunt.'

'Bet gone fuh pay day, right?'

'Right.'

*   *   *

Plumb climbs back on to the dock. The men drift back to continue their work. The echo of gunfire has died from the air but lingers still in the minds of many who, over rum, would tell friends about it ... who as old men in rocking chairs, would tell their grandchildren of the gun test.

A seagull swoops low squawking strangely but no one appears to notice it. The steamer from Wak-en-Naam is coming in early with not many people on board.

'Well done Bascom,' says Plumb. 'Good man.'

But the handshake, Bascom expects, doesn't come. Plumb walks away to the waiting police vehicle. The moment he slams the door it roars away.

Says Calder, 'Ya'll all see he going dere? Apata got he rass head in a mass!'

The men at the Parika docks admire the way Calder directs his words. Many dock workers tell themselves that if Calder had gotten a break in book education he would have been a British Guiana scholar.

Brogan thinks now of the bet he has made with Calder. 'Tell me something Calder man,' Brogan says. 'You believe Apata kill de white man? The American?'

'Nobody ent know but the police make it look like de boy do it fuh sure, even though they jus' speculatin'!'

'Wha' 'bout Gittens?' asks an Indian worker.

Calder laughs derisively.

'Ya'all see duh rass in today's papers? Eh? How Apata got two gun and some war veteran tell them that he see Apata with a police-ish looking rifle and is only now they realize that the veteran did right an' all dat KUNT? Hear man, all dat is LIE. Leh we reason it out then. First, dis VETERAN. WHO HE? WHAT HE NAME? WHEH HE LIVE? WHICH VILLAGE?'

241

The greater percentage of the workers, gathered around, begin to nod their heads.

'NEWSPAPERS!' continues Calder. 'SEH WORLD WAR TWO VETERAN WHO LIVES ON THE WEST COAST.' Calder cuts his fulminating and laughs good naturedly. A few of the men around him laugh too as they wait for him to complete his statement.

'MAN?' he continues. 'WEST COAST IS A DAMN BIG PLACE! And duh's what making the lie so hard to prove! Leh me tell ya'all what really happen dat night man. POLICE SHOOT POLICE IN POLICE CROSS-FIRE and dat is easy to understand 'cause we have plenty JACKASS in we police force!'

The laughter dies quickly for Calder's face is recomposed to speak again: 'But it sad though.'

*　　*　　*

The compound of the Old Man's residence is built like a piece of England. It is a pity Sir Lloyd Alexander Wilkinson cannot speculate on aesthetics at this moment. This is the fourth day of the so far abortive manhunt. The Commissioner of Police reaches the door and rings the bell. The butler appears and bids him enter. The butler is a Black man filled with good etiquette, a very good student of English mannerisms. 'His excellency the Governor is expecting you, sir! Follow me, please sir?'

The Commissioner of Police follows the back of the butler until the back stops and turns before a great door. The butler throws it open and moves aside. Ushered in, the Black servant closes the door after the servant of Her Majesty.

CHAPTER 44

TUESDAY

Apata prays against the glare of the lightning as thunder
breaks from the skies. He feels cold and uncomfortable but
he never ceases his rythmical paddling. Lightning flashes
again illuminating the river, making everything as light as
day. In that brief instant Apata notices another police boat.
He slows and turns into the bank. There he grips a clump of
bushes and prepares to wait out the probing of another
searchlight. The going's difficult. The going is slow, too slow
for safety. The brilliant beam passes over him and the boat
hums by. Apata tells himself that he will move on but then he
hears the sound of engines again. He grabs the clump of
bushes once more to wait out the passing of another boat.
This one hums close and suddenly the engines are cut. Apata
grips the bushes fiercely and wonders if this is it. The beam
from the launch's searchlight drags closer and closer. It
lingers on a bush a few yards from where Apata is tucked
behind the greenery. Apata discovers a prayer on his lips as
he clasps and unclasps his gun. The beam begins to scan
towards him and then it lifts over him and the engines roar
into life. Now all Apata feels is the steady downpour of rain.
There is no shelter and water cascades down his face and
body. At the same time the engines of the police boat,
heading away, pick up to a higher pitch.

*   *   *

'Shocking weather,' the officer in charge of the launch grumbles as he turns up the collar of his jacket. He is lucky to be in command of a launch with a canopy. Every time the lightning flashes his eyes scan the water in each brief but powerful illumination. At the briefing they were warned to expect that the fugitive might well try to evade them by using bad weather to his advantage. All the searching boats are now equipped with spot-lights that are manually operated. On the morrow they will be issued and fitted with machine guns.

The officer yawns. Half an hour more and then I can head back to port, he tells himself and, out of the corner of an eye, sees his helmsman nodding and barks at him to wake him up and finds the man's alarmed response amusing.

After half an hour the *Rita Elm* heads back to port in Parika. They pass the *Elizabeth* going out on patrol with a man huddled in the bows behind a search-lamp. The figure wears a helmet and a thick rubber poncho. Water-proofed and as comfortable as a duck.

CHAPTER 45

WEDNESDAY

Apata camps deep in from the shoreline where the police launches and foot patrols are concentrating. Last night he made little progress and with the aid of the telescopic sight had seen the searchlights of three boats sweeping his escape route. He chews his food and finds it difficult to breathe because mucus is blocking his nose. Because there could be police about he decides not to risk blowing his nostrils free.

Deep in a thorny thicket Michael peels the old man's blanket from his shoulders and thanks the old chap from the depths of his heart. The night has been terribly cold. He lifts his head and peers with burning eyes through the netted tangle of the thick foliage under which he is folded like a burrowing animal. The sunlight sparkles through the canopy above him like a billion bits of diamond. He rubs his palms together, then unwraps the rifle from an end of the old blanket. He rubs the rifle as if it is a companion also in need of warmth. Apata tells himself that he ought to venture out instead of sitting tight and waiting for someone to discover him and shoot him down like a crab dog in the brush. But then again, he tells himself, that he should not venture out, at least not yet. He thinks of the old man's boat well hidden under an eroded river bank. It is a long way from his present hiding place. He wanted to be sure that if they found his canoe they would not find him nearby. Also he made sure that they should not trace him easily to this thorny thicket in the middle of a swamp. From the position of the hidden boat he has left boot prints designed to lead the hunters in the wrong direction. Apata knows they would work but fears that he may lose the boat. Then, suddenly, he realizes that he should have stripped it of its camouflage. 'JESUS!' Apata swears then curses to himself on realizing that the boat, with the bushes seemingly growing from it, would easily be identified with him, hence making them most meticulous in their search. 'I'm a fool,' he says to himself and feels miserably hot with the sun, the moisture and the heat of himself. He decides that he has to get out. But now the rain is falling again. 'Jesus Christ!' Never has he ever been so miserable as he is now. He bends his head as the clouds darken and tells himself that he must think. Think! It is the only thing, he feels, he can do. Think! He wipes his mouth with the back of his hands and feels the roughness of his face. 'Shave off all this fucking hair off my face.' He pauses. 'Why am I cursing?' He fumbles under the blanket and brings out an avocado pear that is soft and rotten. He bites into it and chews it skin and all even though he knows he shouldn't. He spits out the purple-black skin. 'Am I turning into an animal? JESUS ... what have I done? Chewed a pear? *Bitten into an unpeeled pear and chewed it?*' He smiles into the damp blanket that is folded in a huge knot below his sternum. He begins to feel a pain in his neck. 'A pain in the neck.' Apata smiles. 'A pain in their neck,' he tells himself as the thunder rolls above him. Absentmindedly Apata clears a piece of the ground before him and uncovers a strange insect. It is something like a beetle but horned and hairy-legged and to him ugly and repulsive. Most people are afraid of snakes, but not he. Since he left the old man's place he has seen lots of snakes. No bother. But insects. With his heel he grinds the repulsive thing into the soft ground, grinds it into a white-black squashiness. Then he wrinkles his nostrils even though there is no smell. All that stinks is he, grown too sweaty and the rotten smell of damp earth and decaying leaves.

Apata clears a part of the ground before him and, with a twig, carefully draws a map of Guiana. Then he sketches in Parika and the islands, Leguan and Wak-en-Naam. He digs the Essequibo. Water falls from his brows into the river he has drawn. 'They know I was born in Bartica so they will conclude that I will try to make a break for home. They're right. They'll seal off my escape route and in the canoe I will be a dead duck. They'll find it. So I have to make a break-through whatever they put up to stop me.' He shakes his head. 'Make a breakthrough with what?' He sighs. 'I want to die in Bartica.'

Apata doodles aimlessly on the ground and destroys his river. Whilst he scribbles in the earth he thinks his river looks like a grave. Absentmindedly he fills it in. 'What must I do? What can I do?'

He hears a shout, followed by a gun shot. He freezes though the sounds come from a direction that does not surprise him. Footsteps. Bootsteps. Two policemen trot past. Apata shudders and fits the telescopic sight onto the rifle. Another pair of men rush past and Apata knows that they have found the little canoe. He prays that his deception with the boot prints works. So long as they keep slipping by where he sits, sweating. It works. He thinks it is working. He must, he tells himself, get out before things change. He knows that there are clever men out there and he knows that deception is not forever. He has to get out! He hears a howling sound from the river. He recognizes it. He hears it again. He knows the sound well. The song of the patrol launches, their mournfully hooting sirens. He must get out of the thicket! He hears the voices of men, voices that come and go. He must get out or risk being found. They are not all stupid out there. There are bush men amongst them, country men like himself. Black bucks!

The voices fade into the distance and he tells himself again that his deception is working. Now is the time to move. He humps the radio onto his back. The haversack, what of it? Apata decides to leave it where it is. He hides as much money as he can about his person and suddenly he thinks of Beverley. Beverley. Just like that Apata's whole being screams for Beverley and his hands inadvertently push down on his aching groin. He sighs despondently.

The rain ceases. The sun peeps out and Apata moves through the back of the thicket that faces inland where there are more swamps, palms and great clumps of bushes.

*   *   *

Twelve o'clock. The sun stands high and streams through clouds empty of rain. Apata, with bushes and leaves stuck about his body, crouches and checks his surroundings. He is on the look out for more sentries. With his rifle he crawls and freezes, crawls and freezes, crawls and freezes until he attains the top of a grassy mound from which a flat expanse of green stretches before him. The wet grass glistens now that the sun shines. The rifle is wrapped in the leaves of the wild eddoe plant, for Michael has read too many books and has seen too many films where, due to light glinting off a metallic part of someone's weapon, they were betrayed. The damp under his stomach grows warm and Michael smells the earth and the crushed plants below him that exude a fragrance which smells like the perfume that was sprinkled on his dead grandmother. He sweeps the distance before him through his telescopic sight. He sees undulating ground covered with shrubs and trees. 'HEY!' whispers Apata his sight fixed onto a grove of coconut trees, 'There's something going on over there.' Without the attachment on his rifle he can only see a clump of palm trees. Lifting it again to his eyes he sees a naked White woman running playfully from behind the trunk of a tree. She is followed by a White man who is also naked. They disappear.

*   *   *

Watching the arming of the police boats Calder tells himself that the hunt is getting bigger than he expected it would. There is a lot of police activity on the docks. Calder has counted ten patrol boats and he has heard that the police have rented quite a few small boats for the big river hunt tonight. It is not the bet that he has made which weighs on

248

him. It is the enormity of what Apata has gotten himself into, that grieves him. 'IS ONE MAN THEY PLANNING TO GET WITH ALL THAT?' he asks himself and roots and cheers for their quarry. To Calder, Apata is a double image of himself. And, as far as Calder is concerned, Apata has done something that many Black men would do, given the guts, given the motivation, given the anger. Calder settles himself onto a great greenheart pile that will eventually sink deep into the mud below him and become part of the new stelling. He wonders how the whole thing started. Behind him he hears the spitting of the welding torches in the metal shop and on the docks where the police patrol launches are being fitted out for OPERATION DRAG NET.

*   *   *

'WHAT THE HELL?'

'Get up slowly with your hands on top your heads. Both of you!'

'John! It's Apata the crimi...'

'Shut up, or I'll blow your head off.'

The White man raises his torso with his hands on his head as if he's doing a gymnastic exercise. Apata reads the surprise on his face and smells their rankness.

'Get up, Sally,' the man says calmly.

'Like thi-this?' she asks pleadingly, her eyes darting from Apata's face to the hole pointing at them: the barrel of the high-powered rifle.

'Yes. FOR CHRIST SAKES GET UP!'

'Americans,' Apata tells himself. They are both up bending their heads below the tent canvas over their heads, Apata throws a coil of green nylon rope, which he has picked up just outside the open flap, against the woman's naked breasts.

'TIE HIS ARMS BEHIND HIS BACK. DO IT WELL IF YOU VALUE YOUR LIFE.'

She scrambles for the rope as it falls to her feet and begins, hurriedly, to tie her lover's hands as ordered whilst her lover bends forward.

249

'TAKE YOUR TIME! AND TURN SIDEWAYS SO THAT I CAN SEE THAT YOU'RE NOT COCKING THAT KNOT.' They both turn. 'PULL THAT KNOT TIGHTER ... TIGHTER!' Good! Now tie his feet!' After she has done her work Apata ties her up and leaves them lying together. The woman stares at him fearfully. She's on her back. Her firm breasts heave with anxiety on her whitish pink chest. The man's eyes are hard and there's alarm in them as they dart from his woman's breasts to Apata's criminal face.

'Put your mind at ease, sir,' Apata smiles. 'I'm not a rapist. Nor am I an impulsive murderer. I couldn't and didn't kill Glenn. It is the same with you. I can't kill for killing's sake. I haven't even gagged you because that would be cruel. All I have are *needs!*' The rifle still covers them.

'What needs?' the man asks.

Apata laughs without knowing why. It is not the man's question seemed funny. Maybe it is just being with people again, being together with human beings.

'Canned foods, milk chocolate, anything to kill this weakness that creeps within me.' He takes a deep breath and continues longingly, 'To see my face, to have a shave. You see I have a feeling that I won't come out of this thing alive. It ... it is something my grandfather ... my grandfather ...' He trails off as though spent and picks up a red blanket from the floor of the tent and flops it over the couple's shame. The woman closes her eyes with relief from the tension. The man blinks in surprise. Then he frowns.

In a moment the sun will disappear, ushering in the night.

'There's food in that blue box. Everything you've asked for and in the little box next to it there is a shaving set.'

With his gun still pointed at them Apata reaches for the larger box. Only then does it dawn on him that there's no need to cover them with the rifle. He lowers it and opens the food box. He glances around the tent that is slowly growing dim and sees a kind of satchel. He takes it up and fills it with the things he needs. After that he bites into a family sized bar of Cadbury's chocolate and then astonishes the woman by lying on the floor of the tent and gazing at the green canvas roofing above his face. It is a moment of relaxation, of return to something like normal circumstances.

Soon he turns and realizes that the tent flap is open and the night is coming quickly. He gets to his feet, closes the flap and asks for a light. He is told where there is a battery-powered lamp which he switches on. Next he opens the little box and finds a shaving set and a mirror. He looks at himself and realizes that he looks a real savage. No wonder, he thinks, I scared the woman. He takes some water and shaves his face. Clean shaven he looks, to himself, someone he remembers. He tries out a smile. It works. I can still smile, he muses. It's good when you can still smile. He swivels his head before the hand mirror. In the mirror he notices a green bush jacket hanging on the wall of the tent. Indicating it, he says, 'I'll take that.'

'All right with me, Mike.'

'You know my name.'

'Everybody knows your name, Joe.'

But the White woman's eyes are closed. Probably she's praying that it turns out to be just a dream.

'You couldn't have come up here on foot. Where's your boat?'

'There are two boats in an inlet not far from here. One of the boats is white. The other is blue. Take the blue one.'

'WHY YOU ROTTEN . . . !'

'SSSSH!!'

'WHY SHOULDN'T HE HAVE YOURS?'

'CHRIST! CAN'T YOU THINK? Blue will be hard to see against the green if he's hoping to make a break for it tonight. But white would give him away. He would be asking for it.'

'Alright! You don't have to shout at me!'

*   *   *

The Crime Chief stands peering ahead at the water lit by the glaring beams of the powerful searchlights on the bows of three boats moving abreast. In ten minutes, or less, they will rendezvous with the rest of the launches and smaller boats that will make up *Operation Drag Net*.

*   *   *

Hiawatha's Song skims over the dark-skinned river. Apata tells himself that he's going to make it past all the blockades, make it past any police launch before they know what's happening. They won't be expecting him in a boat with a pair of powerful engines. He has already done something like one mile. The going is good. There's a turn coming as the bushes tell him as they loom closer and closer like an uneven wall. Apata is enjoying the ride. His body is rested and fed. The White man and the woman, the Americans, were nice to him in their own way. He had untied the woman, allowing her privacy to dress, and she had cooked for them all. As a meal it was not bad for White cooking.

He guns the throttle and begins to take the turn. Coming out of it he sees a great many lights on the river. Four big lights with their beams criss-crossing half a mile, or a little less, ahead of him. He spins the wheel to the left. The boat veers on the water and heads towards the bank. Apata makes out the flicker of a torch on the shore where he had instinctively intended to hide. He spins the wheel to the right and the boat tilts on to its starboard side and heads away from the left bank only to see that there are more little lights ahead. Thinking quickly, as the distance between himself and the big lights, five in all now, reduces, Apata swears and feels behind him for his rifle. He props it atop the low windscreen of *Hiawatha's Song*. Suddenly, brilliant things soar into the night. FLARES! Apata sees the police boats clearly now as they see him approaching erratically. Five patrol boats are bearing down on him. Apata feels himself trapped, with no hiding place, in a vast and open yard nakedly illuminated by a thousand searchlights. No hiding places ... only lots of spaces in which to run. Apata wrenches the wheel left, then right, then left, then right. The boat dances on the water like a wild trapped thing. He hears loudspeakers bellowing across the glittering water. There's a police patrol boat about fifty yards to his right. He turns the wheel left and veers away from its glare while he fires at it. The light shatters and someone curses across the water. He decides to chance the left bank once more but a police launch peels off from the formation and blocks his way. Apata thinks desperately and glances over his shoulder. There's another boat turning in to take him from the rear. He fires the Winchester blindly ahead and shatters another searchlight. Why aren't they shooting? WHY? Apata spins the wheel to the right, hard to starboard. The snarling boat lifts and turns as if on an axis. Applying full throttle Apata breaks for the right bank and stays on a straight course. Another flare bursts this time behind him and he sees his own shadow on the gleaming forecastle of the sleek racer. He holds a straight course, regardless of the little lights ahead. Now he hears the sound of machine gun fire. He spins the wheel right, leaning himself heavily with the banking boat which creates a mountainous wash that upsets the little boats manned by startled policemen who believed the power boat was bent on ramming them. 'This is it!' Apata tells himself as he hears a chorus of voices, behind him, crying out for help.

He hits a turbulent wave and *Hiawatha's Song* bounces, touches down and skids off, humming deeply. A shower of bullets stitch the water on Apata's right. Something stings his left shoulder. Something else slams into the V.H.F. set on the little seat behind Apata. The right side of the windscreen shatters. Holding himself low Apata makes enough distance to get beyond the range of the gunners in the police launches. So he runs and the sound of the growling police launch engines pick up sharply behind him. Chase. He glances around and sees a light pulling away from the other lights. Trying to gain on him? Can't catch him. Apata runs before them all and even the lights ahead of the other lights fade into the background. Something whispers over his head. Something, he is sure, whispered past the back of his neck. Apata glances at the shoreline to his right and sees light winking: rifle fire. He pulls away from the banks of the river and takes to the main channel. The Bartica regatta comes back to Michael. 'I'm a two-time winner,' Michael Apata tells himself. 'I'm a two-time winner. Nothing can catch me. They can't catch me.' He feels again the burning in his left shoulder. Pulling up his knees, he holds the wheel between them to keep the boat on course. With his right hand he feels his left shoulder and discovers blood, not to his surprise. The boat hums and the bushes flash by in a dim blur. Why weren't they firing at first when I was shooting? WHERE AM I HEADING? Back ... BACK TO WHERE? The boat hums and the bushes flash by in a dim blur.

*   *   *

The police launch, *Justice C*, spearheads the others patrolling in section Q. Franklin feels sick at heart having found out that it was officially planned to lay the blame on Apata for Gittens' death. The World War II veteran who had reported the sighting of a man resembling Apata with a .303 police weapon was fabricated by his superiors. Having found this out Penelope's strictures about the police plague his soul.

Now a report that has just come in says Apata is heading their way. Superintendent Franklin knows that if he were to order all engines stopped and all lights doused, Apata would run into them and they would easily catch him. But Superintendent Franklin, haunted by the evil of what he has found out, issues no orders. His boats plough on aroaring and agleaming.

*   *   *

Apata slows with a burbling of engines, then stops. As the boat bobs in an eerie silence, he checks the radio. Dead! If the bullet had hit him, he too might have been dead. His left shoulder is getting stiff. He sparks the engines to life and soon they take on a constant humming as Apata moves steadily down river. Suddenly a thought strikes him. They

254

weren't shooting because they were unsure whether he had a hostage on board. They assumed that the boat had been stolen and perhaps they thought he had forced the owner on board with him to see him through, to get him past them. 'Hell, that is what I should have done. I should have used one of them as a bargaining piece, passport. SHIT! Well, as grandfather always said: "Boat gone a falls, cyant turn back!"' The boat hums steadily and the bushes flash by in a dim blur.

Apata sees the gleaming, probing fingers of light tipped like a spatula. He is almost three miles away when he spots Franklin's patrol and decides against being made minced beef in a police-burger. He cuts the engines. The boat bobs and Apata thinks. He feels his blood trickling down inside his sleeve. He takes a paddle that was wedged behind the boat's pilot seat and uses it to make silently to the river bank to his right. Then he stops and tells himself that that would be a wrong move. He puts down the paddle and lifts the radio on to the driver's seat having decided to swim ashore. The distance between the network of light and himself has gotten less. What stopped him landing from the boat? Intuition. There would be police waiting for him. So Apata decides to swim silently to the beach but first he has to make some preparations.

He locks the steering wheel for a straight run and starts the engines, leaving them in neutral. The next step is to take off one of the engine cowlings and place the satchel and his ammunition in it. When he lowers himself into the water the cowling floats in front of him. He comes around to the pilot's seat and puts the engines in gear and opens the throttles. Then he pushes himself away as the boat roars off blindly on its own. Apata cannot hear the reports but he sees flashes from the shoreline and daringly heads in that direction. The flickering of torches begin moving away along the bank as if trying to keep track of the boat which runs true towards Superintendent Franklin and his half of *Drag Net*.

Apata swims quietly ashore with his rifle, held in front of him, supported on the engine cover. In the shallows he waits and listens but hears no voices so he climbs up on to firm ground and waits. He knows the shoreline will be teeming with policemen. He hears voices and soon a patrol comes by and from what they say it is clear that their shift has just wrapped up.

'Suh wheh we ah head now?' a voice asks.

'Farmhouse outpos',' comes the curt reply.

'Trus' Millin to ask a stupit' question.'

And Apata feels the old pain in his leg. He feels the pain and tells himself that he has to find the old man. The cold earth and the exposure to the elements must have undone the repair the old man did to his leg. Also his shoulder is still feeling numb but not painful enough to render his arm a liability. Crouching, Apata weighs the gun in both hands, then lifts it and sights along the barrel into the backs of the receding policemen going down the trail. After a moment he follows them. 'The old man,' Apata tells himself, 'I must see the old man.' As a chill creeps through his body. 'I must see the old man.'

CHAPTER 46

THURSDAY

Michael Rayburn Apata sits, hidden, high up in a large cassia tree that bears a hard-shelled pod fruit called "stinkin'-toe". The tall tree overlooks trees of lesser heights and, through a triangular gap in the overhanging foliage of the lesser trees, Apata sees the yard of the old man and can examine it in close up through his telescopic sight. He notes that the policemen are spread out and active around the yard. They seem to be searching for something. The activity slows as they find what they are looking for. Quite a crowd of them gather around a tangle of bushes in the area of the old man's latrine. The White officers are fanning their faces with their hats. A constable in black takes off his helmet and Apata can see the man shake his head slowly and sadly. Apata knows, at once, what they were looking for and what they have found.

*   *   *

The sun begins to sink on the other side of the sky. Soon it will be three o' clock. The sun burns down on Apata as he watches the policemen dig rhythmically. They dig and throw up the earth. They dig and dispose of the earth to the right ... dig and dispose of the earth to left. Dig ... earth to the right. Dig and earth to the left. Dig ... and tears roll down Michael's cheeks, over his jaw and into the stubble of hair around his heavy lips. He stares glassy eyed and weeps because the old farmer, who helped him with food, care and shelter, has died. He loved that old man who had grown inside him to become his own grandfather. He cared with all his heart for the old man who believed that youth could never be guilty. Apata weeps high in the cassia tree and feels that it is pointless to go on. There is no purpose in anything any more ... in life, in continuing to live. And the old man's hatred for the police takes hold of Apata and becomes a terrible demonic obsession.

CHAPTER 47

THURSDAY

On the roof of an old pit latrine, behind which the old man was found, a little brown bird hops. In the silence, his toes scratch at the rusted zinc sheets. Behind the latrine a patch of yellow grass, in the shape of a man-sized foetus, marks the spot where the body, beginning to decompose, was found.

'Let us observe a minute's silence for the dead,' says Plumb, remembering Robinson, remembering Gittens, remembering Rigby and remembering, now, the old man, less than six feet away below where he, Franklin and the rest of the squad of Constables stand.

Franklin looks down on the raw mound of dirt that marks the grave of Adolphus Banze. He ignores the lingering stink from behind the latrine and wonders if anybody else can hear his heart beating.

An old frond that has lost all its chlorophyll hangs limply from a short coconut tree nearby.

A bird twitters from afar and above, very high above, a carrion crow flies in lazy circles.

A tiny fraction of a second after Crime Chief Plumb starts to go slowly to his knees the airless day is penetrated by the sound of a rifle shot. Plumb has a bloody hole torn in his head just above his right ear. His body jerks twice then lies still.

Franklin and the rest stand frozen, blank, uncomprehending.

Constable Kirton screams, clutches his abdomen. The echo of another rifle shot ripples through them all.

'TAKE COVER! TAKE COVER! TAKE COVER! TAKE COVER! TAKE COVER!' Franklin shouts, almost screaming. He dives behind an old galvanized drum painted in red next to the pit latrine. Two Constables take to their heels and Apata blindly turns his attention to them. Two shots. One Constable falls with a shattered leg. The other arches his back as a bullet strikes him between the shoulder blades severing his spinal column. He is dead before his face hits the ground.

Superintendent Franklin is afraid like he never has been before and feeling sure Apata is using dum-dum bullets, his fear is nourished. He makes a great effort to get control of himself. 'It's up to me now! It's up to me now!' He does not say the words, only thinks them. Aloud he asks, 'WHO HAS THE RADIO? THE WALKIE-TALKIE?'

'It's on the Crime Chief, sir!' comes a shaky reply.

'Jesus Christ,' Franklin whispers to himself. 'I have to get that thing!' and wonders if Apata will hit him. 'Got to get that thing!' He takes a very deep breath and looks around. Where can he be? Franklin wonders. Where can he be? 'ANYBODY WHO SEES WHERE THOSE SHOTS ARE COMING FROM, SHOUT! TAKE A LOOK AT THE TALLER TREES! HE MAY BE RANGING ON US WITH A TELE-SCOPIC SIGHT! STAY IN COVER! DO NOT SHOW YOURSELVES! I'M GOING TO TRY TO GET THE RADIO OFF THE CRIME CHIEF'S BODY! HUTSON!'

'SIR?'

'IF I'M KILLED ... TAKE OVER.' Franklin tenses himself ... counts from one in his mind, and on *three*, launches himself from behind the drum. Something whips the cap off his head, a clump of dirt kicks up by his left foot and he drops behind Plumb's body. Cover. The echoes of two rifle shots ripple through the nearby bog forests.

'I THINK I SEE SOMETHING OVER THERE SIR!' shouts Sergeant Hutson.

'WHERE MAN? WHERE?'

'IN THAT BIG TREE NEXT TO THAT STINKIN' TOE TREE!'

'ALL RIGHT HUTSON AND ANYONE ELSE WHO CAN GET A BEAD ON THAT TREE, GIVE ME COVERING FIRE.'

The policemen begin to fire into the tall tree so close to the cassia tree and Franklin dashes back to safety. 'CEASE FIRE!' commands Franklin. In the ensuing silence there comes the sound of barking dogs. 'HUTSON.' The Sergeant dives to join the Superintendent. In his hand is his rifle with telescopic sight. 'What did you see, Hutson?'

'A man, sir. I saw him move.'

'Your rifle ...'

Through the telescopic sight Franklin examines the foliage of the suspect tree. 'GIVE ME YOUR HELMET!' Franklin tells Hutson then Franklin lifts it above the drum they are using for cover. The helmet is poised on the muzzle of the sniping rifle. It draws no fire.

'Maybe we got him sir.'

'We cannot be sure of that from here.' Franklin lifts the walkie-talkie to his face.

*   *   *

'FRANKLIN TO PARIKA. FRANKLIN TO PARIKA.'

'Come in Franklin ...'

'FRANKLIN TO PARIKA!'

'Sir!' the radio man shouts for the Deputy-Commissioner.

'FRANKLIN TO PARIKA. WE'RE UNDER FIRE BY APATA. REPEAT, WE'RE UNDER FIRE. THE CRIME CHIEF IS DEAD. TWO OTHERS ARE DEAD – OVER AND OUT!'

'HULLO FRANKLIN. HULLO FRANKLIN. TAYLOR CALLING FRANKLIN. COME IN FRANKLIN!'

There is no response. Only static. Deputy Commissioner of Police Robert Taylor looks at the microphone in his hand and says, 'Plumb's gone!' His tone is incredulous.

*   *   *

261

'Damn!' Franklin swears having lost contact with Taylor. He looks at the tree that strives to be as tall as the cassia tree. He considers the fact that for some time there has been no rifle fire and decides to chance approaching the base. 'Hutson!' he says.

'Sir?'

'We'll try getting below that tree ... work our way under cover until we're there. What do you say Hutson?'

'Yes sir,' Hutson answers quietly.

They branch out using whatever sensible cover there is between the old man's compound and the trees. Hutson is the first to reach the immediate area of the trees and cringes inside on realizing the glaring mistake he has made. At the base of the cassia tree and not the other in which he believes he had seen the movement of a man, he sees a pair of discarded top boots.

'I made a mistake, sir,' he says to Franklin now lying prone next to him.

'You're only human, man,' Franklin murmurs. The sound of police dogs comes to them. 'I think he's slipped us again.' The Superintendent rises and gingerly approaches the roots of the cassia tree. 'Blood,' he says looking down. 'Let's get back to the radio. We need dogs.'

*　　*　　*

The Dep-Com. picks up Franklin once more as Franklin calls in the dog handlers. Soon his thoughts drift from the intermittent voices transmitting and receiving. He thinks of Maurice Plumb. The late Maurice Plumb.

'Maurice dead. Jesus,' Taylor whispers as he remembers all the words of the Commissioner of Police.

'Crime Chief Plumb was killed just minutes ago Alex!' he had said and, after what seemed a very long time of silence on the telephone line between them, the Commissioner had replied, 'Oh my God,' in a whispering, broken tone. Then after another spell of silence the Commissioner had said, 'Who's in charge now?'

'Superintendent Clarence Franklin, sir,' Taylor had said, suddenly formal. 'But Apata is on the run with the Superintendent closing in, according to the latest report, sir.'

'Yes. Give Franklin all the help he needs ... and Bobby?'

'Yes, sir?'

'I don't think we need a prisoner.'

'I understand, sir.' The Commissioner had then hung up.

*　　*　　*

From where they stand blood trails and footprints lead off into the vast swamps ahead of them. The dogs sniff and whimper in seeming frustration.

'Taken to the swamps,' says Franklin.

The dog handler nods. 'The dogs think so, sir.'

The Superintendent lifts the walkie-talkie to his lips once more. He talks to Taylor and waits to see how fast the Deputy-Commissioner will react. The response is almost immediate. The manhunt is now his.

Franklin tells Taylor that Apata is out in the swamps which spread out from where he stands. Their quarry is now barefooted and must be severely wounded. After Superintendent Franklin signs off he thinks that with a cordon of police tightening around the swamp, Apata has truly become a "public enemy" who must be hunted down ruthlessly. And now Franklin thinks of Penelope, his sister, and hopes for her forgiveness. Franklin tells himself that he may have to kill or give the order to kill and thus gamble with his soul's salvation.

Franklin hears the aircraft before he sees it. The aircraft passes overhead and drops lower over the vast swamp into which Apata has fled. The plane turns tightly and starts a series of low level passes over the distant trees then it banks around and starts to make tighter circles over parts of the area. The engine cuts, the plane glides and sails like a silent yellow bird, in a graceful descent until the engine barks again into life and the aircraft lifts once more and flies off into the dying light of the sunset. As Franklin watches it disappear instructions for the evening shift of staff are being received. Sergeant Hutson approaches the Superintendent and shows him a pair of spent shells and a sodden envelope addressed to Michael Apata at an interior station.

'This, I mean these, were picked up below the tree, sir.'

Franklin takes the articles. He stuffs the spent bullet casings in a pocket. The letter he continues to hold, feeling uneasy.

CHAPTER 48

THURSDAY

The trucks rumble into the brilliantly lit encampment. It is seven o'clock in the evening. A tangle of humanity stands about the gates of the Parika police station compound.

'WHO DEAD?' someone shouts impatiently from the crowd. No one seems to know as yet. It is only known that there have been deaths.

'Lawd!' a voice laced with lamenting supplicates, 'Dis ting gettin' from bad to worse!'

The bodies covered with canvas are unloaded from a truck with the police emblem. The locals outside the fence are silent now as they push forward to see and gape.

After the dead have been lowered to the ground the damp and muddied policemen of the ill-fated section descend from the transport that was also a hearse. The tall White officer with reddish hair, the locals note, has mud on his face and his tunic is torn across the left breast. He has also lost his cap.

Franklin dismisses his men to their private nightmares, then starts off with a deep sigh for the Deputy Commissioner's office.

Soon the word ripples through the curious onlookers. 'THREE DEAD!'

'WHO DEAD? PLUMB? In all Gawd's truth? CRIME CHIEF PLUMB?'

'Yes. Plumb, de White offisah.'

'WHA'? AIRPLANE AH SEARCH FUH APATA TO'?'

'Like you deaf Crab? You didn' remembah hearin' a airplane flyin' ovuh roun' half pas' five or six?'

'RASS BHAI! APATA IN 'E RIKATIKS!'

'Ah wonduh who is de other two who dead?'

'Ah think one name Kirton, and the other name Jaisingh!'

'Rass ... Apata in 'e rikatiks ...'

*   *   *

Alone in his room, that he shares with another officer now on the evening shift, Franklin reads the waterlogged letter. The photograph of a baby girl dries under the heat of a table lamp.

Dear lost brother Mike,

Let me be the first to congratulate you on being a Daddy. This is telling you, that you've given Beverley a beautiful baby girl. Her name is Michelle. Yours truly is the Godfather. Chap, the baby is a sweet mixture of yourself and Beverley. The enclosed photograph will tell you that I'm right. Take a look at the picture. What do you think?

Everybody missing you badly Mike. Hear man, for some reason, life without you to gaff with is really stale and pointless. Missing you then Mike is painful to me, well just imagine what Beverley is going through then. Christ man Mike! Why don't you come back and take your woman? But to think of it, you may be right. Beverley like she likes to be around that miserable woman who's cruel to her.

Before you left Mike, you said that nothing was important to you any more. But Mike, must you allow Beverley's mother's rejection of you to affect you like that. So much that you're hiding up in the interior? Mike, please man, don't allow your heart to destroy you. I know you've had some hard times, but life sometimes goes like that. Mike, I'm sorry if this letter proves that I don't understand you. I won't care if really I don't since the only things I want you to bear in mind are the following: that you're my spiritual brother and closest friend. Two: that you have a

266

beautiful baby girl to love and live for and, three: Beverley loves you.

Why don't you come back? Daddy always asks for you. He says that any time you come down, you could stay here in Parika. He even went as far as say that he wouldn't mind if you came here and lived with us.

Really think of the things I've said Mike, think of us in your daily plying along rivers and think more of Beverley, the mother of your daughter who loves you only, despite the pressure she's up against from that mother of hers. Take care.

> *Gerald ... Your brother.*

The Deputy-Commissioner reports to the Commissioner in Georgetown City. The Commissioner reports to the Old Boy and the Old Boy, filled with the date of the Royal Visit, stands at a great window with heavy drapes overlooking his garden and thinks that his headaches are too many. Not far away a lone frog, from a little pond, croaks on into the night.

*   *   *

The Weekday Trumpet

Friday, August 12.   6 Cents.   1959.

CRIME CHIEF PLUMB AND TWO OTHER MEN KILLED.

Gunman Still At Large

In the continuing hunt for Apata, Police Constables Lennox Kirton and Robin Jaisingh were shot and killed shortly after the death of Crime Chief and Assistant-Commissioner of Police, Maurice Plumb. A police statement late last night said: "Crime Chief Plumb and his detachment were burying old farmer Adolphus Banze, who had been found dead behind his latrine, when a shot rang out and felled the Crime Chief. Another shot followed, and Constable Kirton was also killed. As the men scattered to find cover, two men panicked and ran. They were brought down by the fugitive's fire. Jaisingh was killed by a shot in his back. His spine was shattered. The other, Constable Bovell, was shot in the leg. Superintendent Clarence Franklin, took immediate control of the section and was fired upon in his bid to retrieve the police transmitter-receiver left on the Crime Chief's body. Apata was concealed in the upper branches of a tree that overlooked Banze's farmhouse. Several volleys were discharged into the tree at the base of which blood smears and empty shells from the fugitive's rifle were later found. Police dogs, brought into the hunt, were soon hot on the fugitive's trail. Boots that belong to Apata were found at the approaches to a vast swamp. There was also blood where the boots were found. It was clear, yesterday, that Apata had taken to the swamp which was scouted by a spotter aircraft but visibility was poor because nightfall was approaching. The patrol returned to Operations Head Quarters last night with their dead." Today marks a full week since the manhunt for fugitive Michael Rayburn Apata started.

Light Aircraft To Do More Spotter Work Today.

Mr Euris DaSilva, city businessman and owner of a light aircraft, will do more spotter work for the Police Force today. Mr DaSilva has personally volunteered his services to help speed up the capture of fugitive Apata.

CHAPTER 49

FRIDAY

Glancing over to make sure that the policeman with the submachine gun is seated and belted securely, DaSilva releases the wheel brakes. The plane lurches forward and picks up speed. The engine vibrations shudder through the frames of men and machine. DaSilva eases the column gently forward, and the aircraft lifts its tail wheel and gathers speed for take off. The engine hums evenly. The wild-pea bushes leap by in a light green smear. Flying speed is attained. DaSilva eases the column gently back. The policeman next to him feels a momentary sensation of lift. They are airborne.

After flying straight and level for a while DaSilva puts the aircraft into a climbing bank. Having attained a thousand feet he points the aircraft, sprayed in brilliant yellow, to the West.

Square fields drift by below. Some ploughed, some having different shades of green. Now and then the aircraft drops briefly before rising again. 'IN THREE MINUTES!' DaSilva shouts to the Police Sergeant next to him, 'WE'LL BE OVER THE SWAMP' The policeman nods and peers down intently. The aircraft hums on. The policeman stops looking at the passing countryside and moves his gaze to the array of instruments before him. Then he looks away to a patch of passing cloud before he resumes watching the landscape and the cloud shadows sweeping over the land below. 'BRACE YOURSELF,' warns Da Silva. 'WE'RE

GOING IN.' The policeman tightens his stomach muscles. The aircraft banks and drops towards the wide Parika backlands. 'FOUR EYES ARE BETTER THAN TWO,' says DaSilva. 'KEEP A GOOD LOOK OUT.'

Above the hum of the engine the radio behind the pilot's seat crackles. The Sergeant turns in his seat and fits the earphones on his head. The engine hums. The tops of trees flash by under them.

'OHQ TO SPARROW. OHQ TO SPARROW ...'

'SPARROW RECEIVING. GO AHEAD OHQ.'

'CONCENTRATE ON SECTOR QE AND QF OF SWAMP LAND AREAS. REPEAT. CONCENTRATE ON SECTORS QE AND QF OF SWAMP LAND AREAS. OVER.'

'SIR! Something look like blood on this leaf!'

'LET'S KEEP MOVING.'

Waist deep, Superintendent Franklin holds his revolver above his head as he and his detachment feel their way through the swamp. All pray for the end of the ordeal.

'SIR.'

Franklin turns.

'An envelope, sir.' The Constable waves a soggy rectangle and pushes the muddy water before him as he wades to the Superintendent. Franklin wipes the envelope on his tunic and makes out the same handwriting that was on the one Hutson found under the cassia tree. He reads the name and an old address of the man they would catch today. Franklin folds the letter and tucks it into his tunic.

'THAT WAY!' he says and points. The big wading continues and he hears the sound of an approaching aircraft The wings glint in the sun as the machine banks and begins to circle the area ahead of Franklin and his men.

The radio carried by a Corporal crackles:

'SPARROW TO ALL PARTIES IN SECTOR QF. SPARROW TO ALL PARTIES IN SECTOR QF. WE'VE SPOTTED A MAN MAKING FOR THE TREES. COCONUT TREES. COCONUT TREES NEAR AN

INLET. WE'RE FLYING DOWN LOWER. CANNOT MAKE OUT IF THE MAN IS APATA. OVER.'

'WE KEEP HEADING THAT WAY!' Franklin points and shouts though they can see nothing but undulating swamps and clumps of bushes before them.

DaSilva climbs away from the tiny figure down below. Could it be a woodman? he asks himself. He banks and dives. The policeman is startled to see earth rushing up while the man on the ground begins to run in an erratic pattern. DaSilva pulls out of the dive and does a steep turn around the running figure. The policeman stares and prepares to transmit. 'IT'S HIM!' DaSilva shouts above the sound of the engine. 'I'M COMING TO BUZZ HIM.' Full of macho bravado DaSilva bares his gold capped teeth. 'I'M GOING TO ATTACK HIM HEAD ON! HE'D BETTER DUCK!'

Apata stops and acts like a trapped thing with no place to run. DaSilva grins. The policeman grips the microphone and stares. Apata suddenly drops to one knee and aims his rifle at the aircraft hurtling towards him and fires several shots in rapid succession.

Superintendent Franklin and his men hear the aircraft then see it rising out from the foliage of the coconut grove. The engine is sputtering, firing unevenly. At about a thousand feet it levels off, the nose dips. The engine only picks up at intervals. Finally, there is silence. The aircraft is coming down.

'WE'RE HIT IN THE ENGINE! WE'RE GOING TO CRASH LAND! CALL BASE.'

But the policeman doesn't respond. His lips tremble and his eyes glare wildly at DaSilva. Then they slowly shift and fix to the ground coming up at them. His palms are flat against the window at his side and his palms are splayed in a terror that is deep and terrible.

'JEEZE MAN. I'M GOING TO GET US DOWN SAFE! THIS HAS HAPPENED BEFORE! SEND A MESSAGE! TELL THEM IT'S APATA DOWN THERE!'

'HEY LOOK!'

The policemen on the ground see the aircraft's powerless descent.

'SOMETHING WRONG WITH IT.'

'SPARROW TO-TO ALL PARTIES. WE'RE HIT BY APATA!'

'OHQ TO ALL PARTIES. APATA MUST BE KILLED. SHOOT ON SIGHT. REPEAT, SHOOT ON SIGHT. OHQ TO SPARROW. COME IN SPARROW! COME IN SPARROW!'

'CALM YOURSELF MAN!' shouts DaSilva, 'CALM YOUR FUCKING SELF. YOU'RE A POLICEMAN ... PULL YOURSELF TOGETHER. I'LL GET US DOWN SAFE. OH, HOLY MARY!'

DaSilva takes the aircraft down in an easy glide. They are nearer the river.

DaSilva eases the column forward a bit more to overcome the drag caused by the motionless airscrew. Except for the whistle of the wind, silence reigns in the cockpit where DaSilva is concentrating on what he has to do while the policeman sits staring with stony, dilated eyes peering through his splayed fingers that are like a lizard's paws against a window pane.

The aircraft heads towards an open field across the river.

The green hurtles silently up from across the river.

'No,' gasps the petrified policeman and the green ground across the river comes up steadily.

'NO-O-O-O-O!' screams the policeman and jerks the control column back from DaSilva's hands. The Piper Cub rears up, as if to climb, stalls and falls like a yellow brick into the river.

'Oh Gawd ...' groans a policeman who sees the crash and Apata is forgotten for a moment. A party of his comrades stand immobile on the left bank of the river and watch more and more bubbles gurgle up from the spot where a yellow wingtip shows above the water fifty yards from the shore.

'Sir ... like the plane crash!'

272

'Yes,' says Franklin. 'From the sound there is no doubt about that.'

Gunfire breaks out from the coconut grove less than half a mile away. They have just left the swamp. 'CLOSE IN! THIS IS IT!'

There is more firing and Franklin wonders how many have died.

'THE GOING HERE IS FIRMER! DON'T BUNCH UP. SPREAD OUT AND START MOVING. REMEMBER WE'RE IN THE OPEN. THINK AND MOVE CAREFULLY.'

'WELLINGTON TO FRANKLIN! WELLINGTON TO FRANKLIN! FROM OUR POSITION AN INLET SEPARATES US. APATA'S ON YOUR SIDE OF IT. OVER.'

'CAN YOU SEE HIM? OVER.'

'NO, BUT HE'S IN ONE OF THOSE BLOODY PALMS AND HE'S FIRING AT US.'

'HAVE YOU ANY CASUALTIES? OVER.'

'TWO WOUNDED. OVER.'

'KEEP HIM PINNED DOWN. KEEP EVERYONE OUT OF SIGHT AND KEEP HIM PINNED DOWN AND DISTRACTED. OVER.'

Franklin moves in closer with his detachment as the sound of rifles cracks through the air. The grove of trees lies less than three hundred yards away now. 'Your rifle! Hutson!' Hutson hands it over and Franklin peers through the telescopic sight. He stops abruptly. 'I see him!' he says softly.

Franklin shakes his head. 'His back is to us! I want to give him a chance to surrender. I-I would like to do that.' Then he raises his voice and calls to his men, 'SHOOT ONLY ON MY ORDERS!'

He waves the men forward and the firing continues. It is sporadic.

'Now,' says Franklin. 'Quietly, we'll move until we come to that big semi-circular bush. Then we will lie down and take up positions from which we can cover him. Pass that on.'

'Yes sir!' Hutson does as he is told.

Random shots snap from the air less than two hundred yards away. The bush with the semi-circular shape is much closer. The men hurry across the few short yards and drop into position. The grove of coconut trees can be clearly seen and between the flittering branches of the palms comes the sound of a rifle.

Franklin, flat on his stomach, crawls over to a little shrub. He wants a view of the fugitive. Hutson moves behind Franklin. 'See him, sir?'

'Yes, yes, I think so.' Then firmly: 'Yes! There he is! The tall central tree with the trunk shaped partly like the letter S!'

Hutson works a round into the breech of his rifle and sights.

'Clear?' asks Franklin. Firing breaks out once more.

'Yes sir.'

'You want to take him? After we challenge him?'

'If you want to, sir. It's alright.'

Franklin thinks of Penelope. If he allows the Sergeant to kill Apata, he would feel as though he levered the sin of killing on to a fellow man.

'Let's spin a coin,' suggests Franklin. 'Tails for me.'

And whilst men hug the ground and think of death, two others watch the brief fall of a nickle onto a patch of earth over which a black ant crawls.

Hutson smiles and hands the rifle over.

Beyond the crossed wires in the telescopic sight Apata can be clearly seen. He crouches in the heart of the coconut tree. The branches wave above and below him. In his hands the high-powered rifle is held ready for firing, levelled on a truss of dry coconuts. Franklin can see that the policemen on the other side of the inlet are holding all Apata's attention. He is now firing back with economy. Seemingly two rounds to every six from the police.

'You don't have him clear, sir?' asks the Sergeant wondering why Franklin has not fired.

'APATA-A-A-A. SURRENDER. YOU HAVE NO WAY OUT. YOU ARE TRAPPED.'

The police rifle-fire ceases and the ensuing silence stands alone.

'APATA. YOU HAVE NO WAY OUT. SURRENDER. WE CAN SEE YOU CLEARLY. DROP YOUR RIFLE AND SURRENDER TO THE POLICE.'

The fugitive turns unhurriedly bringing himself and his rifle round to face Franklin. Franklin tells himself, 'If he lifts that barrel I'll fire! If he points that rifle, I'll shoot!'

But the fugitive with the barrel of the high powered weapon lowered, just stares back challengingly.

The police pinning down Apata on the other side of the inlet hear the calls being made to him to surrender. 'Come on Franklin,' grumbles Superintendent Wellington, the officer in charge. 'Shoot the Black bugger out the tree will you?'

There is silence. Wellington swallows then tells his small detachment, 'I'm going to try to get a better position from that rise. When I dash for it give me covering fire.'

The rise he speaks of is a mound of hard-packed dirt that was topped, just half an hour ago, with light green grass. Now the grass is smeared with the darkening blood of a Corporal who was wounded in his neck and lives because he was lucky or, as he thinks, because he had been silently feeling his rosary. There are also the blood stains of a Sergeant who was hit in the shoulder and a leg. Now Superintendent Wellington decides to prove what a brave Englishman he is. If, that is, he makes it alive.

He raises his gun as a signal and then sprints to his objective under a volley of gunfire. Crouched behind the rise he sits tight and waits. No fire is returned from the tree. 'Now!' Wellington tells himself and raises his head to peer over the top of the mound. He lifts his head above the mound and sees that the fugitive has his back to him. Apata wears a bush jacket that is dirty but not old. There is a lump under the left sleeve above the elbow which suggests a bandage.

'APATA-A-A-A!' comes Franklin's challenge again.

'GIVE YOURSELF UP! DROP YOUR GUN IN THE WATER OR WE'LL BE FORCED TO FIRE. WE CAN SEE YOU CLEARLY!'

'Please Jesus!' Wellington prays behind the mound, 'Please don't let him drop it.' He kisses the breech of his rifle then brings it to bear and aligns his sights on Apata's back. Gently he begins to apply pressure on the trigger but, as he does so, all the condemnation he has heard of shooting a man in the back spins through his mind.

Franklin is confused and uncomfortable. What the hell should he do? How can anyone shoot a man who just sits and glares at him with his rifle held low and unthreatening.

Superintendent Franklin takes his right hand off the rifle butt.

'Allow me sir,' says Hutson.

Franklin hands the gun over.

The weapon snuggles onto Sergeant Hutson's cheek and the magnified image of the fugitive remains still. Hutson aims at Michael Rayburn Apata's left breast. 'The manhunt ends now!' Hutson tells himself. 'The manhunt ends ...' HE SQUEEZES THE TRIGGER.

Apata twists and his head crashes against the firm spine of one of the palm fronds. His hands reach out and claw unresisting air. He falls gracelessly, headlong. His rifle spins away and strikes the tree trunk. There is the sound of a splash as Apata's body strikes the waters of the inlet and men run forward expecting to see it come to the surface.

Bloody wavelets ripple outwards towards the banks. The police in close ranks crane to see what happens. A batch of blood-stained envelopes comes to the surface and mingles with a few dry leaves and a few currency notes. On the broad leaf of a wild lily a droplet of spilled water gleams like a jewel, a ruby. The rifle sticks in the mud below the root of the coconut tree from which Apata has been shot.

*   *   *

The two officers face each other from across the inlet into which two policemen, stripped down to their underwear, have slipped. They wade out and, at the centre, they dive together towards the bottom.

'WE GOT HIM AT LAST, EH?' says Superintendent Wellington.

Franklin looks at him, suddenly sure now, that Hutson was right.

'I told you, sir,' whispers the Sergeant, 'that someone else fired around the same time I fired.'

Franklin nods, then looks coldly at Wellington. 'WE GOT HIM AT LAST,' agrees Franklin, 'BUT I DON'T THINK YOU SHOULD HAVE DONE THAT.'

'You mean, shoot a man in the back?' Uncomfortable in the open rebuke from a fellow officer, Wellington laughs a little.

Franklin, shaking his head pitiously, turns his attention back to the inlet.

An elderly Police Constable is crying but no one takes any notice of him.

Franklin pulls at the lobe of his ear and continues to gaze at the water that is being disturbed by the divers who may be grappling with a body. Perhaps the inlet is very deep at that point.

A man surfaces, exhales, snorts, then says, 'Nothing sir.'

'What do you mean, man?'

The other policeman surfaces and declares, 'No dead body down there, Superintendent!'

Franklin says to Hutson who stands by his side, 'Are you sure you hit hm?'

'Yes sir. Here.' Hutson points to the left side of his chest.

'I hit him, too!' Superintendent Wellington volunteers without being asked. 'Right between his shoulder blades. THE MAN'S DEAD, FRANKLIN.'

As if to himself Franklin says, 'Where's the body, then?'

'Try again?' says Wellington. 'Use more divers this time!'

'Let me have the radio,' says Franklin, wiping perspiration from his brows with the back of a hand.

Body or no body, for him, it is finished.

EPILOGUE

Twelve police divers, experienced in such matters, failed to find Apata. Promptly a police launch was called with ropes and grappling hooks. The inlet was dragged, so were the areas of the river close to the mouth of the inlet. However, no corpse was found on the eventful day when Michael Apata fell into the waters of the inlet.

As might be expected, there was much argument and speculation. Some supported a theory that the fugitive swam underwater and escaped. Then there were a few who fervently believed that he was taken to a new life by supernatural beings. They based their theory on the way he was found as a baby when his parents died on their way down to Bartica. Yes, there was much speculation and argument. There was one thing, however, that many who took part in the manhunt, and were present when the body fell, agreed upon. It was that Apata was killed. There was the testimony of Sergeant Hutson's marksmanship and the six sealed letters that were fished from the inlet's surface. Each had the same kind of bullet hole through its purple tinted stamp printed with an Amerindian shooting fish with a bow and arrow. Undoubtedly, the envelopes had been together inside Apata's bush jacket.

And the second day passed into the third day.

The sun rose from below the horizons ...
climbed,
pinnacled,
descended ...
and died ...

into darkness ...

Six times.

Eventually the seventh day dawned, stayed her time, then went and the Commissioner of Police terminated the search. The newspapers all carried an imaginative story that suggested that the body of Michael Rayburn Apata was found on the seventh day after his fatal end and that, due to its acute state of decomposition, it was buried in an unmarked grave somewhere in the backlands where the manhunt for the living body, which brought death to eleven men, had taken place.

*   *   *

Satisfied that the Black criminal was no more, the colony settled down to anticipate the arrival of Her Gracious Majesty the Queen. When she did arrive she toured Georgetown City in an open-topped glossy-black limousine. And there was festive dancing in the streets.

THE AFRICAN AND CARIBBEAN WRITERS SERIES

The book you have been reading is part of Heinemann's long established series of African and Caribbean fiction. Details of some of the other titles available are given below, but for further information write to:
Heinemann Educational Books, 22 Bedford Square, London WC1B 3HH.

CHINUA ACHEBE
Arrow of God

A brilliantly told story of the pressures of life in the early days of white settlement. First winner of the New Statesman Jock Campbell Award.

HAROLD BASCOM
Apata

A young talented Guyanese finds the colour of his skin an insuperable barrier and is forced into a humiliating life of crime.

T. OBINKARAM ECHEWA
The Crippled Dancer

A novel of feud and intrigue set in Nigeria, by the winner of the English Speaking Union Literature Prize.

BERYL GILROY
Frangipani House

Set in Guyana, this is the story of an old woman sent to a rest home where she struggles to retain her dignity. Prize winner in the GLC Black Literature competition.

NGŨGĨ WA THIONG'O
A Grain of Wheat

'With Mr Ngũgĩ, history is living tissue. He writes with poise from deep reserves, and the book adds cubits to his already considerable stature.'

The Guardian

GARTH ST OMER
The Lights on the Hill

'One of the most genuinely daring works of fiction to come my way for a very long time.'

The Listener

CHINUA ACHEBE
Things Fall Apart

Already a classic of modern writing, *Things Fall Apart* has sold well over 2,000,000 copies. 'A simple but excellent novel . . . He handles the macabre with telling restraint and the pathetic without any sense of false embarrassment.'

The Observer

ELECHI AMADI
Estrangement

A portrait of the aftermath of the Biafran War by one of Nigeria's leading novelists and author of *The Great Ponds*.

ZEE EDGELL
Beka Lamb

A delightful portrait of Belize, a tiny country in Central America dominated by the Catholic Church, poverty, and a matriarchal society. Winner of the Fawcett Society Book Prize.